NIGHT OWLS AND SUMMER SKIES

NIGHT OWLS AND SUMMER SKIES

REBECCA SULLIVAN

wattpad books W

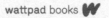

wattpad books

Published in Canada by Wattpad Books, a division of Wattpad Corp.
36 Wellington Street E., Toronto, ON M5E 1C7

www.wattpad.com

First Wattpad Books edition: May 2020
ISBN 978-1-98936-525-0 (Softcover original)
ISBN 978-1-98936-528-1 (eBook edition)

Library and Archives Canada Cataloguing in Publication information is available
upon request.

Printed and bound in Canada.

1 3 5 7 9 10 8 6 4 2

Cover design by Jenn Kitagawa
Cover images © Jenn Kitagawa
Interior images © Artspace on Shutterstock
Typesetting by Sarah Salomon

To my tea suppliers.

To the girls who like girls.

To the people who support me on Wattpad.

ONE

My dad held his hands at the bottom of the large steering wheel. It drove me nuts because when he'd tried to teach me how to drive (and failed miserably) he'd yammered on about keeping my hands on the ten and two positions. But that was the past, and it wasn't me who had been driving for an hour straight. I couldn't complain about my sore and stiff leg muscles, at least not out loud—not unless I was willing to listen to him rightfully grumble in return.

A couple of days before this trip, he sat me down and said that no matter what, by the end of June we had to make the trip up from Boston to Maine to visit Mom. Now, seeing the beach along York Harbor and the happy families emerging from their campers and making their ways to the rocky beach made me regret my choice to come. Once upon a time we were them, spending hot days together swimming in the sea and eating ice cream. We didn't need to take this route to get to York Heights, but it was as if Dad sensed I needed a few minutes to absorb that we were back. The salty breeze caressed my face from the open window and memories of us as a family washed over me.

The coast couldn't go on forever, and the van found its way to York Heights, passing by my old elementary school and onto the road that led to my mother's house. Tall trees stood on both sides, offering the long row of houses a sense of privacy. I'd gotten so used to the city—the high-rise buildings, the masses of people, the wide sidewalks—that I had forgotten that we used to live so uncomfortably close to nature.

In a way, I missed the coast of York Beach—this little village in Maine and how it always felt like summer. Not that I remembered much. When I tried to picture my old classmates' faces, they were just blurry images and one semidecent image of my childhood best friend, Jessie. On the day we left this town to move to Boston her freckled six-year-old face had tears running down its cheeks, and her hands were wound in her curly brown hair. When we came back briefly for eight months when I was fifteen, it helped that she'd sent pictures in the mail. Jessie and I didn't connect that much—so much for the lifelong friends you're supposed to make at age six—and I made few friends. No one particularly memorable.

Dad pulled up beside the four-foot high, grey stone wall that separated the road from my mother's house. Once he turned off the engine, the noise of the tools clattering around in the back of the vehicle stopped. With all the traveling he did for work, it always came as a surprise that none of his carpentry equipment or projects smashed into smithereens. He'd had this blue work van for years, and it always shone, tended to with care, as he did with all aspects of his life, namely me. We didn't do anything, not so much as move to get out of the van. We couldn't believe this was how our day was going.

"Okay, I'm willing to compromise," I said, breaking the silence.

"Emma, we are at your mother's doorstep. I think it's a *little* late to compromise. You'll have the summer to catch up with Jessie. It'll be fun."

"Dad, we weren't all that close to begin with. I sat with her at lunch sometimes, that's about it."

"You've been writing back and forth since you left. You're probably closer than you think."

"Writing someone and being friends with someone are completely different things," I insisted.

"You used to be close. Don't you remember?"

"When we were *six*, not so much when we were fifteen." I dismissed him. "I'm willing to spend two weeks of summer with Mom."

"Emma," he said, and then sighed.

"Two weeks is a significant amount of time." Prodding his leg with my shoe made him turn in his seat to look at me. His face held reluctance, and I knew he didn't want to drop me off here. "Two weeks with you? That's like blinking. Two weeks with her? Just the idea of blinking hurts. That's constant arguing, possibly crying—angry tears, of course—slamming doors, endless swearing . . ."

"Since when do you slam doors?"

"I don't," I said pointedly.

His expression was torn, and he mumbled to himself, "This was the arrangement, Em. If we don't go with it . . ."

"I turn eighteen near the end of summer. I'll legally be an adult. She can't request access to me."

"Think of it this way—one more summer and then you're an adult. Neither your mom nor I can tell you what to do. But I sure as hell don't want you vanishing into thin air when that happens. You hear?"

"This isn't a compromise in the least," I complained.

"It's all I've got," he said. "Are you being testy because you're leaving someone *important* behind?"

"Nope." Choking on my own laughter, I continued. "Did you

know that depression can and will deter people from interacting with you? Not even bullies. The lack of reaction freaks them out. Besides, being homeschooled for the year didn't give me a chance to meet someone. Or reunite with anyone, really."

Dad gaining custody and moving me in with him and out of York when I was nearly sixteen was the right decision in the end. He took action and got me a personal tutor at home while I worked on my mental health. I spent my senior year, my final school year, at home.

He snorted, turning away to rub his jaw. "You react to plenty nowadays. Don't roll your eyes. You can rejoin civilization next year, if you want," he offered. "You don't have to put off college for a year."

"It's not that I'm not ready—I honestly don't know what I want to do with my life."

"You are ready," Dad said. "You can put up enough effort to joke about it. You're managing it much better now. You'll call if you . . . can't? I'll always be here for you."

"Yup, Dad. I will."

"So, no girlfriends?"

"No girlfriends," I confirmed.

After we got out of the van, he helped me with my luggage. In with my belongings were all sorts of his equipment: a toolbox with hammers, screwdrivers, and nails; a saw with its rusted handle; and a bunch of black-and-yellow chisels, a constant reminder that carpentry was a form of art. Then there was his latest project: a bed's wooden structure. The smell and the dust made me feel warm inside—it was familiar, homey; it was him. I missed him already, even the ugly purple work sweater he insisted on wearing that morning even though it was practically summer.

In front of me was the house that wiped the joy out of my life in one full swoop. It was where I spent the first six years of my life, and random spouts of vacations whenever my mom was available, but the memory of the last time I tried to live here was a shadow I couldn't escape. The house had always been painstakingly quiet. During the day while I was at school, my mother spent her time out, and she was also out during the night doing who knew what. According to the planner on the fridge, she went to her book club, wine tastings, any number of social outings she never spoke to me about. The one time I put a parent-teacher meeting on her planner, she scribbled over it and missed the meeting.

My dad lugged my suitcase onto the doorstep, and he was as reluctant as I was to ring the doorbell. With a grunt, he turned to his side and jabbed his shoulder into the bell. When nothing happened, he knocked against it again, and this time it rang.

"Next summer, you can lay on the couch and do nothing. You can volunteer somewhere, though. I know back home Elizabeth down at the wheelchair association always needs a helping hand. Getting out there, getting real life experience, and helping people. Sounds a little tempting, doesn't it?"

"It doesn't sound like the worst idea," I admitted.

"But the rest of your time? Fair game."

"Mom doesn't know that lying around's my favorite pastime."

"There will be a dent in her couch. One week in and she'll figure it out." We shared a grin.

The door flew open. I had just enough time to grab the handle of my bag before Mom ushered me inside. The door slammed shut behind us. The last time I'd see my dad for two months ended abruptly as she dragged me down the hallway without a word.

The house had changed so much since the last time I'd been here. New paint, barely used furniture, a fresh pinecone smell, and any pictures that might've included my dad and me were either in storage or thrown out. There were only pictures of my mom partying with friends, and of the pets she had throughout the years. The rejection clung to me like a cloak that ran all the way down my back and stretched on for miles and miles. My mom sat me on the couch in the sitting room.

"Emma, honey,"—she flopped onto the opposite couch—"as you can see, I'm a little frazzled. We're going on a cruise for the summer. Exciting, right? Don't unpack."

"A cruise?"

"Yes, we're leaving once our ride gets here."

"Ri-i-i-ght," I dragged out. "How long is this cruise for?"

"Two weeks," she answered. "Then we'll likely go to another vacation spot for the rest of summer. Spain, maybe? Rome sounds nice, too, right? Maybe we'll go to both."

"I guess so."

She buzzed around gathering toiletries and phone chargers and either dumped them into one of the many suitcases spread across the floor or into her purse, perched on the coffee table. The television blasted the weather report, so it wasn't too awkward. The lack of conversation wasn't a big deal because we never made eye contact. In fact, the paucity of interaction made it easier for my brain to pretend there was no one else in the room.

When a car out front honked, my mom and I lugged our stuff outside. The driver was kind enough to help us push it all into the trunk. I spaced out as they chatted with each other, and climbed into the backseat. Mom climbed into the passenger seat instead of into the back with me. What the hell?

"I've heard a lot about you, Emma," the driver said. "You're going to have a fun summer. Fresh air, a hell of a lot of sun—"

"I suppose Mom gets your services a bunch?" Practicing small talk could be preparation for being out on the open water on a giant floating hotel where I'd be stuck in a tiny room with my mother. "Sure. Maybe once the shock wears off, I'll be able to process it better."

"Services . . ." he mumbled.

"Speaking of surprises, Mom, you should have told me when I called you last week about this cruise. Do I need my passport?" The bag on my lap grew heavier. "Have I packed the right stuff? Do we have time to go shopping? Hell, where are we going? It's a lovely surprise, but it would've been nice to be prepared."

"I have your passport in my purse," she said.

"Has it not expired yet?" I asked. "I'm almost sure it expired in March?"

"It's not expired, Emma. Relax, I have everything we need."

Her calm tone didn't soothe my rigid muscles. "Where does the boat cruise to? Where are we boarding? Where are we going?"

"I have the itinerary here, one second." She took her time fetching the pamphlet from her purse. "Here we go. We're departing from Boston, don't huff at me, Emma . . ." She deserved it—I could have waited at home for her to pick me up to take me on this grand surprise. ". . . that's leaving at four. It's eleven, isn't it? We have plenty of time."

"You're the planner, you tell me," I said. "Where are we going, though? On the cruise?"

"The Caribbean—St. Thomas, Virgin Islands; St. John's, Antigua and Barbuda; Bridgetown, Barbados; Castries, St. Lucia; Basseterre, Saint Kitts and Nevis; and Tortola in the Virgin Islands again," she read from the list. "There will be a few days at sea, that'll be fun, right?"

The anxious pit in my stomach slowly dissipated, and my head filled with circus music and flashing images of long days exploring different islands with sandy beaches while eating exotic fruit at beautiful resorts.

"I've heard nothing from you in a while." Mom ignored the driver and twisted in her seat to face me. "Any news? Boyfriends I should know about?"

"Still gay, Mom. I suppose the correct term would be lesbian, but gay kind of sits better with me."

"Emma, please. Not in front of our company."

"He drives people places—I'm sure he's heard a lot worse than girls loving girls."

The driver stared at the road and the atmosphere in the car grew uncomfortable. I couldn't blame him—being stuck with arguing customers sucked. My mom flicked on the radio and stuck in a random disk. Apparently, listening to Christmas music in June was better than talking about my sexuality.

There had to be something positive about the situation. For one, being on a cruise ship meant constant activities, exploration, and space. The amount of time in a confined space where my mother and I would scream and shout at each other would be minimal. Especially on the days we explored, when hopefully we would be too tired to talk when we returned from whatever adventure awaited. With those thoughts circulating in my mind, sleep soon took over.

✦

The car came to an abrupt stop, jolting me out of my quick, fifteen-minute slumber—definitely not long enough to have reached any port back in Boston. I felt impatient because I'd already spent enough time in a car that morning, hours that hadn't been necessary, and I wasn't prepared for this redundant trip. Gathering the bags around me, I exited the backseat. The car had pulled into the big, wide, grassy parking lot of Camp Mapplewood, the most heinous place on earth. Half asleep and only cluing into where we were now, I didn't want to believe it.

Maybe it took my mom tilting my chin up so that I saw the sign to get the message. That all-too-familiar sense of foreboding came back with a vengeance. The best way to avoid disappointment was not to expect anything from anyone. Yet my mother had sent my brain into a frenzy of excitement at the prospect of traveling and then snatched it away all too soon. My expectations were dropped into the dirt and stomped on until they were buried deep.

"I'm not going on the cruise, am I? You meant you are," I stated quietly.

"Well . . ." She patted her bag inside the trunk and shut it. "Not exactly, honey."

The driver got out of the car and leaned against one of the doors and said, "I'm not your mom's go-to driver, Emma."

He scooped up Mom's hand, and the light reflected off their rings perfectly. It was fortunate that I could blame my misty eyes on the glare of the silver. Before I could pull it back, my voice made a strangled, *hurumpfff*-like sound. The driver's offended expression didn't make me feel guilty in the least. He was a complete and utter stranger. It was uncomfortable that a person so important in my mom's life knew about me, but I didn't know about him. They were *married*. They'd had a *wedding*. I'd never gotten an invite. No matter how much it hurt that she didn't think to invite me, let alone tell me about one of the most important days of her life, it pained me more that it didn't come as a shock. The blow of my parents' divorce hadn't come from her either; it had come solely from Dad. Most news did.

This wasn't only a cruise. It was a *honeymoon*. Another kick, another stomp, and the final light went out. The twists kept piling on, and with them, my chest heaved in an effort to breathe. My new step-father's face, the rings, the suffocating, towering trees—everything burned into my brain until all I saw was red.

"Let me get this straight," I said, teeth gritted. "You're going on a cruise with your driver. Your husband. You're abandoning me here? At Camp Mapplewood? When you *only* get me from July to August."

"Honey . . ."

"Stop ignoring me—the point. You're leaving me at *camp*. Which is the place responsible for my PTSD?"

Beyond the sign was an entirely different planet. Everything about it terrified me, from the whistle of the wind under the moonlight to the raindrops that pelted against leaves or the top of the fabric of a tent. Even the roofs of the cabins beneath the stars gave me hives. The list continued as an endless line of things that contributed to this dark feeling in the pit of my stomach. Maybe it was the constant tension in my neck as I prepared for attack. Perhaps it was the creepy crawlies scurrying in the dark.

"I thought you would've grown out of this difficult phase by now," my mother said. This statement caused a sharp pang in the middle of my chest. Another shot fired. She tossed her husband, whose *name* I still did not know, a look, like the stranger knew me at all. "Your father has always wrapped you up too tightly. He took you out of school. He took you away from York. He never encouraged you to broaden your horizons, Emma."

"He concentrated on more important stuff like me getting help and showing concern for my mental health?"

"This is an opportunity for you to finally make some friends, to see Jessie again. Since her, you haven't made an effort to engage with people. I want that for you, without your dad interfering and coddling you."

"It was needed, Mom. I was a zombie when I lived here."

"You seem fine to me."

"Yes, now, after *Dad* got me help." Silence. Speaking of help, where were my anti-anxiety meds? I rummaged through my bag and found the bottle. Good. Even if I planned on continuing to use the techniques my therapist gave me, it was nice to know they were there for short-term relief if I needed it. I admitted, "We're pen pals, me and Jessie."

"That's good that you kept in contact, but face-to-face interaction is so much better. Trust me. This will be good for you," Mom promised. "Ethan, help Emma carry the bags."

"Sure," Ethan said.

My teeth ground together and I trembled as we ventured into the grounds of the camp and stood in line for the sign-up table outside of the main building not too far away from the cars. Lots of kids were being dropped off by their parents, mine were no exception;

from the outside it looked so normal, but it was anything but.

I knew I had to call my dad and grabbed my phone out of my pocket. He planned to stay with his brother up in the country to work with him. The phone reception up there was terrible, so I had to call now, before he reached my uncle's house in the next few hours. I was about to dial when Mom snatched my phone out of my hands.

"Hey," I protested.

"You'll end up thanking me for this," Mom promised. "Someday, you will."

"You can't force Dad to give you access to me for the summer, not utilize that visitation, and then restrict my communication with him."

"I haven't the slightest notion where your dramatic nature came from, Emma," Mom said, powering off the phone. She kept it clasped in her hand as we moved up the line. "I've taken the phone from you because camping regulations dictate there are to be no cell phones on the premises."

"Dramatic? Mom, I'm not the one who got married on a whim to Ethan here and didn't tell her daughter. That was you. I want to speak to Dad. He'll listen to me."

"We didn't want it to be a big deal, Emma. I'm sorry. I didn't think you would want to hear that sort of news."

"You found a guy who makes you happy, I am happy for you. But don't you see why I'm mad? It's one thing to not let me tag along on the cruise, which I wouldn't have been hurt by if you'd let me stay with Dad, but I'm at Camp freaking Mapplewood."

"I am paying a huge sum of money for you to be here, Emma. It's an opportunity."

"I never asked you to," I exclaimed.

"And who knows? Maybe you'll find yourself a boyfriend."

"A what? The fifteen-minute car drive didn't suddenly make me straight, Mom."

She made a face and hushed me as we stepped to the top of the line. My mother handed my phone over to the camp's director, Mr. Black, who had been in charge of the place the last time I'd been here. Mr. Black placed the phone in a tray full of the other campers' various technologies. In return I was given a registration document and that day's schedule. After I successfully signed in, I dropped my luggage with everyone else's inside the hallway of the main building. I watched as my only way to freedom was carried away and out of sight—the only way to get out of this mess left with Mr. Black.

Mom brought me in for a hug and the warmth and care that lingered from Dad that morning vanished into thin air. No trace of my father's reassurance stayed behind to keep me company.

"This *will* be good for you," Mom said. "I swear it."

"There's no changing your mind, is there?"

"I'm afraid not. You be good, okay? Smile, honey, it's the start of an adventure!" Those were her final words before she slid back into the car and took off with Ethan—the guy who wasn't only the getaway driver.

Two

The edge of York sat next to the sea, but Camp Mapplewood was too far inland to feel the freshness of the salty air. The oddly earthy and damp smell of the woodland couldn't wash the bitter taste in my mouth away. The entire camp was trapped in a circular band of trees, none of which stood out or looked any different from the next. The extent of trees and general greenery that I could deal with was beside my mother's house—her little garden and shrubs. That's what I had mentally planned for: open spaces and beaches, not an assault of evergreens.

Ever since successfully managing my depression with my dad, I wasn't trapped by it as much. It had been nearly a year since I'd felt the swell, and in the moment when I was handed the clothes that weren't on my back, the moment it hit that I'd be stuck here against my will, the black clouds resurfaced, and it sucked. The shouting, the yelling, the harsh whispers between my parents in the night clawed at my brain.

Now surrounded by roughly fifty other teenagers, I was trapped at camp the same way I had been trapped in that unhappy home.

We were gathered like pigs for the slaughter, helpless to prevent the inevitable summer-long stay. Even though my mother had dropped me off at the campsite one hour ago, a certain amount of rage still coursed through my veins. A number of awkward kids stood around holding their middles and crossing their arms, but then there were a few like myself—those of us on high alert, desperate to be anywhere else—slapping the air, hoping to end the buzzing of blackflies. It couldn't only be me; there had to be others.

Mr. Black chose who went into which cabin. He put the campers into a distinctive category with a group of people that they'd pair up with for the rest of the summer—forced family-like conditions that resulted in some people making the best friends they'd ever have, and people like me feeling lonely and alienated for eight weeks. Even if we had the choice of who we could bunk with, it wasn't like I was close to anyone there.

As I waited to be called, I shuffled to the notice board to reintroduce myself to the camp layout. It had been years since I'd been here. On the map of the camping grounds, we were by the entrance, where the main building sat to the left, Mr. Black's office, the infirmary, and the canteen inside. Farther up was the arts and crafts building, the recreational hall, and finally the six counselor cabins. To the right were the campers' cabins. Farther up to the right was the court that could be used for activities like volleyball and general exercise, and next to it, a rock-climbing wall. There was a path dead in the center of the camp that led to several dirt trails through the woodland that all led to a giant lake. Like most things about this camp, I'd blocked the layout from my mind, and as a result, the only familiarity was the sensation of dread and heaviness in my legs.

Resting against the bulletin board, before I zoned out I made eye contact with someone familiar. Jessie. She shoved by campers who blocked her way and came to lean against the board with me. Her face had lost its baby chub and her freckles had multiplied, covering not only her cheeks but her entire face. Her hair was darker now, dyed a plum-brown color.

"Emma!" Jessie hugged me briefly. "I'm so happy to see you, but what the hell are you doing at this camp? I know you come back to York for summers but never to camp? Never again? Not after the first year you came here."

"Short story really—my mom told me we were going on a cruise. She eloped with a guy called Ethan, planned a honeymoon, and failed to mention until an hour ago that I'd be here instead of joining them. So . . . it's nice to see you, too, Jessie."

"You realize you're at a camp, right? A summer camp?"

"I'm *too* aware," I replied, suppressing a shudder because the cabins behind the board, while homey in a cute way, were positioned directly beside the woods. The bark on the trunks was meant to act as a protective layer for the trees, but to the touch it was rough, scaly, and gross. Then there were the branches with their sharp edges covered by glossy leaves, pretending they were safe and hunky-dory. No, those trees couldn't trick me into a sense of security and safety. "I'm trying not to think about it."

"I'm happy you're here because now I don't have to send a letter about everything that happens," Jessie said.

"It was a little overwhelming to get an entire summer's worth of letters in one go," I admitted.

"I have yours with me. All of them." Jessie swung her backpack around to her stomach and unzipped it. "It gets boring at night, so I bring these with me every summer."

"I'm slightly flattered?"

"You should be."

I never read anything she wrote more than once, not because what she wrote didn't interest me—it did, of course it did, I cared about her life. The letters were more personal than an exchange of text messages, more personal than a phone call even, but I felt no need to relive the past. I wanted to move forward in life. My friend stood in front of me, in the flesh, and I had nothing to say. That was the lovely thing about writing letters—there was no pressure to say something right off the bat.

Jessie didn't have the same anxiety and asked, "When did you last go here anyway? Around twelve, right? If only they implemented the age limit back then, huh? Who knew fifteen- to eighteen-year-olds like to camp? And is it still a thing? Your fear of camping?"

"If you'd asked me yesterday, I would have said no, maybe not so much, but now that I'm here . . ."

"At least there are cabins to hide out in."

"Cabins beside the woods. Woods that contain a variety of scary creatures, Jess. And trees. Trees are the absolute worst."

"You never told me what really happened, though. It's time to spill the beans, the suspense is killing me," Jessie said. "Your mom knows, right, and she still dropped you off here?"

"That sums her up. She either doesn't care or doesn't believe me." I kicked some gravel. "I climbed a tree and got stuck for the night. Stupid, I know. It wasn't some big, bad traumatic event, but the woods are something that I'd rather avoid, you know?"

"Maybe if you focus on the positives instead of the negatives, this summer won't be as bad as you think it will be. Project what you want to happen! What do you like about the place?"

I surveyed the area while thinking about how to explain how much of this place caused a severe contempt to rise in my system.

Ever since Mr. Black and his wife moved to town and set up Camp Mapplewood back when I was ten years old, the kids and their parents at my old school never stopped talking about it. My old classmates raved about their time at camp during the summer, and couldn't wait to go back the next year. Mom had always wanted me to go back, wanting me to socialize and to get a little sun on my skin. After the first year that I went, I was no longer eligible to go because they raised the ages of those allowed to attend to fifteen to eighteen. When I finally did come of age, Dad had moved me to Boston with him.

"Like? That's a hard question. Hate on the other hand? The people, for sure," I offered. "And to add insult to injury, they took my phone away."

"Everyone's phones have been taken away," she said. "It's so we're not distracted from talking to each other in person or something. Mr. Black said it a bunch of times last year. It makes sense."

"I'm beginning to understand why you have my letters."

"I need something to put me to sleep," she teased.

✦

Mr. Black was a poster for a middle-aged dad. He had collar-length hair and stood a couple of inches above six feet, with a well-toned medium frame. He flipped through his chart and started calling out names. As he called our names, he gave us one camp hoodie and five camp uniforms, which included orange T-shirts, with cute little pockets on the top right of the chest, and black shorts.

"Emma Lane, Abby Thompson, Lauren Peterson, Gwen Black, Jessie Anderson, Kendra Marshall, Mike Hanley, Mason Erikson, and Bennie Crowley, you're in cabins thirteen, fourteen, and fifteen, and a counselor will be assigned to your activities as a group, known as the Beavers."

"Beavers?" My scoff was loud.

"Can you let it go, it's not as bad as it sounds," Jessie whispered.

"We're not even ferocious bears that bite or jellyfish that sting. What does a beaver do? Slaps the water with its tail and chews on some wood? Ohhh, I'm terrified."

Hearing me speak, Mr. Black said, "I'm afraid those names have already been taken. You can find the full list of groups on the bulletin board later if you want to check those out and apply for a transfer. But keep in mind, beavers are the second largest rodent in the world. They adapt to new environments quickly and defend their territory quite aggressively. You're quite the predator."

"Emma," Jessie said, "we're at the top of the rodent food chain. That's something ferocious."

"Second best to a capybara," Mr. Black said.

"I'm not even going to ask what that is, but I can assure you, an investigation is in order," I said.

"I'll set aside time to discuss the creature with you," Mr. Black promised, handing over our cabin keys to Jessie. "You can head back to your cabins and settle in. The introduction assembly starts in half an hour in the recreation building. And lunch is late today, two o'clock—starting tomorrow it'll be at noon. You'll all get an official time schedule when you are appointed a counselor after lunch. You won't be lucky and land my wife, Julie—she's one of our camp cooks. Two other favorites of mine are my kids, Walter and Vivian." He whisper-shouted, "Don't tell the other counselors, though." In a normal tone he continued, "All the information you need to have a successful summer is in your registration packet."

Jessie dragged me over to join our group, and we headed for the main building to grab some of our luggage before heading to our assigned cabins to set up.

I purposefully dragged my feet. "Calm down."

"One of the cabins is supposed to have a big hole in the floor," she stressed, tugging harder. "We don't want that one. Especially with your fears of creatures and whatnot, you don't want to end up in the one where they can actually get *into* the cabin."

"I don't think I'm the only one with that particular apprehension. Don't they do inspections? They used to."

"They have the counselors do random inspections at least once a week."

"Maybe the hole has been filled?"

"Still, not a risk I'm willing to take."

After grabbing only my backpack from the hallway in the main building, I zoned out during the walk to our cabins, and my roommates were decided for me. Jessie was pulled into a small group with two other girls: one short and graceful with spiky black hair, and the other, who laughed excitedly. Their names were Kendra and Gwen, I guessed, but I didn't know who was who.

Now with the girls in my own cabin, their faces seemed familiar, but I had blocked out so much. The taller girl, Abby, was someone quiet, and Lauren was someone at the top of the social food chain. Well, as far as the fifteen-year-old version of her could get.

Sidestepping, I checked under the single bed, their stares boring into my back—no gaping hole. Clearly the camp was on top of their maintenance.

"Aren't you going to take that single bed?" Abby asked, taking the lower bunk bed as I put my backpack on the top bunk.

"Not unless I want to shiver to death," I said.

"Being closer to the ground is warmer," she said.

"No, heat rises. Plus, creepy crawlies are more likely to attack you than me all the way up here."

Plus, the single bed sat beneath the window, with a clear view of the forest. At night the light in the cabin would attract moths, and suddenly I could hear the fluttering and could see them butting against the window vividly, waiting for the opportunity to sneak inside and fly up my clothes. From the bunk bed, I could *choose* to look down to see that horrid sight or not. I changed into one of our assigned orange camp shirts and slipped on a pair of the shorts.

Lauren surged toward the single bed and groaned. Shoulders rigid, I was prepared for a fight for the top bunk—after all, if I was maybe in for nearly a two-month stay, it was sure as hell was going to be a comfortable one. Instead, she slumped onto the bed, roughly shoving her luggage to the end.

"Wait . . . you went to camp before, right? Shared a cabin with Jessie?" she said as I was about to attempt to escape the musty, moldy cabin.

"Lauren, right?" Saying her name out loud? *Something didn't feel right.*

"You remember my name?"

"I just said it, didn't I?"

Lauren stood still, as though in deep thought. "Jessie probably talks about me." She gestured toward the other girl, quietly sitting on the bed. "And this is Abby, in case you forgot."

"Nice to see you again, Emma," Abby said.

"You too," I said. "Now that the reintroductions are over, I'll see you all later . . ."

Lauren called after me, "There's an assembly . . ."

I couldn't have cared less about the assembly. I was on a mission.

✦

When you're a kid and you remember places—buildings, structures—they seem big, but when you come back to them, they're regular sized. The opposite was true of Camp Mapplewood. The forest sprawled out from every angle, huge, looming, and ominous. Beyond the campers' residences, there were the counselors' cabins, the lucky ones who weren't forced to share. The arts building was a greenhouse with tables and shelves overflowing with supplies, from what I could recall. Curiosity drove me to peer inside. It wasn't brand new anymore, that was for sure. Paintbrushes were jammed in jars, the projects of old campers clung to the walls, and they even had a mural on the ground of handprints. The Blacks had added a garden plot to the grounds a couple of feet away from me, adding the reds, yellows, and purples of vegetables to the ever-same background of the green and brown trees.

My surveillance had a mission—the toolshed beside the arts and crafts cabin, where the counselors had carried the plastic boxes full of technology. It was one thing to be forced to sleep in an unknown location for nearly two months, but taking my phone was another thing altogether. Even if I didn't have anyone to talk to outside of the camp other than my dad, it was the principle of the matter.

It was broad daylight, the least expected time for someone to break into the locked shed. My strides were long, yet casual enough not to draw attention. I plucked a bobby pin out of my hair and got to work on the padlock, cautiously looking around every once in a while.

A slight breeze brushed a cold wave over my warm skin. The day so far had been calm, the weather betraying my emotions. As soon as the door was unlocked, the shed offered a totally different atmosphere from outside—for one, there was no window, the dust-filled space creepy and prisonlike. My foot edged the door open, revealing a surprisingly fresh scent of roses that caused my senses to go haywire, the base of my neck burning hot. Stepping inside, my instincts screamed that this probably wasn't a smart idea, considering I could immediately feel a pair of eyes on me.

"Maybe you should have waited until it was dark for this oh-so-surprising break-in," a velvety voice said. "It happens every year. Aren't you going to turn around?"

"With my arms where you can see them?" I said.

"No. I've changed my mind. Go on, retrieve your phone. I'm curious as to what's so important that you'd risk getting kicked out camp."

My eyes finally adjusted to the dark. "I can get kicked out?"

"The idea sounds appealing to you?" she said.

I walked farther into the shed, my fingers brushing against boxes in my search. "You should go fetch your superior. Write a detailed report. I'll get this and my bags while I'm at it."

"No," she responded dryly. "I don't think I will."

I whipped open the box labeled *L*. There were too many phones of the same make as mine, meaning I had to go through them one by one to see if any of the home screens matched.

The girl stood inside by the door. It was too dark to really see her. Her body language was relaxed. She was in complete control of the situation, and for some reason unknown to me, it was infuriating.

"May I ask, why the hell aren't you reporting me?" I questioned.

There was a low chuckle. "Because you want me to."

"That is . . ."

"Counterproductive?"

"Evil. You sound young enough," I noted, refraining from cracking a few phones. "Young enough to be a camper. You could be here to get your phone back too."

"Or I'm doing my job."

"What job is that?" I found my phone and held it up to my face. "Camp counselor, are you? Bit young to be management."

I shone the flashlight of the phone in her direction but her back was to me, as she stood facing the door with her hand on the door frame. "I wonder if you can lock pick so well in the dark."

"Not something that I want to find out."

"Maybe you don't. But I do."

The door slammed shut and locked itself. Her footsteps crunched against the gravel and grew quieter the farther she traveled from the shed. This mysterious girl clearly reveled in tormenting the campers. I tried to use my phone's flashlight, holding it toward the door while simultaneously attempting to unlock it, but the mission was futile as my hands were too clumsy, and I kept dropping either my phone or the bobby pin.

I slid down the smooth surface of the door until I landed on the floor. By then, all sounds of outside movement vanished, meaning I was trapped in the shed. Our interaction left me reeling; my body felt warmer than usual, more shaky and clumsy.

***

FIVE YEARS EARLIER

It was the night before the last day of camp. I was resting in my bed, breathing in the warm air and listening to the chirping of the crickets. It was the first time that they'd made an audible appearance all summer long. They were cool little insects, able to jump three feet forward, and when they chirped it almost always guaranteed rain was on the horizon. A superstitious belief—Mr. Black had dropped facts about crickets once.

As much fun as summer had been, I missed my parents. It seemed like everyone else was content, too, asleep in their bunks, but a knock came on our door, disrupting the peace. My two cabinmates didn't budge. The next knock came louder and more insistent, and so, reluctantly, I got up to answer it. Lauren stood on the other side of the door, rocking back and forth on her feet.

"Hey," Lauren whispered. "Is Jessie in this cabin?"

"She's asleep."

"Do you think she'll be mad if I wake her up?" she asked.

"Probably. But I won't stop you."

Lauren poked and prodded her, but it was impossible to wake Jessie. I had tried countless times throughout the summer and all I got in return was Jessie's loud snores and an occasional flailing of her hands. Lauren gripped Jessie's wrist before she got a whack to the face. She gave up, but before she stepped out of the cabin, she said, "It's Emma, right? A bunch of us are hanging out as it's our last night here. Want to come?"

"Let me grab a jacket."

"It's still warm out," Lauren said.

"Cool. Let's go, then."

She was right. Even though the sun had set, my skin felt like it had an extra layer of warm and fuzzy protection, like a woolly coat. Each breath was refreshing and pure, flowing freely in and out of my lungs.

It helped that by "a bunch of us," Lauren actually meant herself and a guy called Mike. It was easy to sneak around when the counselors' cabins were on the opposite side of the camp. We could do anything and be anywhere, but we tracked along the outskirts of the camp.

My fingers trailed along the smooth and waxy leaves of the nearest trees, pinching and tearing them. No kids screamed, ran, or laughed; it was as if the camp was devoid of humans. Lauren and Mike walked ahead a couple of steps. The evening was my favorite time of day because there was no structure or pressure to do anything but be yourself.

"I wish we could stay here longer," Lauren said, slowing her pace so that I walked next to them.

"Same," Mike agreed.

"Summer is time to spend with family. You guys see each other every day at school," I pointed out.

"Why did you move to Boston anyway?" Lauren asked.

"Dad said it was because they wanted a fresh start . . ." My parents lied. Their fighting didn't stop when we moved to Boston. It had been six years and they still acted like they were on the verge of divorce. "I don't think we'll be living together much longer. I want to spend as much time with them as possible before . . ."

"They divorce?" Lauren said.

"Yeah."

"I want to be a camp counselor when I'm older," Lauren said. "It's the best job in the world. Dad says it's a great way to build character or something, but I don't care about that. I love being *away* from them."

Something far at the corner of my eye moved. Or was I imagining things? If we were caught out of bed after hours, we'd get into trouble. They'd tell our parents, and then when I got home, I'd be grounded, ruining the few days with my parents before school. Holding my breath, I came to a standstill. Lauren gripped both of our wrists and dragged us into the woods to hide behind the first line of trees. Something tumbled against the trail, the stone crumbling beneath quick footsteps.

Without so much as a word, Mike raised one finger and pointed up. We climbed the skeleton of the trees. Once we stilled, there was no more rustling of the leaves. The trees stood eerily still in the summer air. In between my shallow and quick breaths, there was a sharp scent of soil. Trying to deepen my breathing, I concentrated on the ground, where the dirt around the tree was lumpy with roots, and tried ignoring the part of the branch that cut through my cotton shirt.

I was overcome with dizziness and when I closed my eyes my thoughts spun round and around in circles. I'd never climbed this high in my life. My knees and hands *needed* to touch the dirt, but my shaking limbs wouldn't let that happen. Over the sound of my heart thumping I couldn't hear what Lauren or Mike said to me. When I did manage to peek over at them, they were descending from the tree. No words tumbled out of my mouth to ask for help, and they didn't offer.

When I finally dared to attempt to get down by myself, I reached up to grab the branch above me to keep myself steady and saw a wasps' nest. If I moved, they would wake up and sting me to death. I was deathly allergic.

Lauren and Mike left me to suffer for hours up in that tree, and to no surprise, it started to rain.

The crickets' chirps guaranteed it, after all.

✦

I startled myself awake gasping from that memory/nightmare. My body's normal response to stress was napping, but now I had to work on getting out of the toolshed, working in the dark because my phone was at ten percent. I had shoved it in my bra, considering our uniform shorts didn't have pockets.

"This, this is why I *hate* camping."

THREE

I managed to escape the toolshed after thirty minutes, and meandered around the nearly deserted camp. I headed to the check-in point where we registered, outside the main building. Grabbing my luggage, I noticed a plastic bag with a mattress protector and sheets, and another with brand-new swimming gear. My mom had planned this to the smallest of details.

A prickling sensation appeared at the base of my neck. A sense of danger lurked when that shiver appeared. The first time I'd felt that rush of anxiety was the night Lauren and Mike left me to fend for myself in the tree. Now it was a nonsensical terror as it was the middle of the day, yards away from the outskirts of camp where the trees stood, but it wasn't something that logic could remedy.

Trying my best to look as casual as possible, I met the eyes of a few worn-out strangers fixated through a window of the recreation building. I should have stayed in the shed—that was a far better option than listening to whatever instructions, camp spirit, or other garbage spilled from that room.

Abandoning all intentions of actually attending the welcome session, I slipped into my cabin, after searching for it for ten minutes because I forgot which numbers belonged to the Beavers.

"Here, let me help you with that." The sudden voice made me jump.

"I think I can—nope. It's an impossible feat." When I turned around, there stood a frail-looking pixie-like person with short, spiky hair. "I might be the least athletically inclined person ever to exist, but even I could flick you away with my thumb."

"I'm sensing a challenge."

Compared to the bag, she was tiny. "Are you considering accepting?"

The girl snatched it from my grasp and held it like it weighed nothing at all, leaving me with my mouth gaping open. She leapt into the air to plop the bag into the compartment above my bunk, then she hopped back down with a broad grin.

"You might want to sit down," she suggested, amusement evident. "People tend to get testy when standing. And we can't have that grouchiness during our first-impression stages."

"And after we've gone through that hell?"

"Be your typical grouchy self." She had mad psychic abilities. "You have that look about you. That aura. I dig it."

Up I went via the ladder to the bunk, and the girl flitted up next to me, eventually pulling my pillow onto her lap. I folded my hoodie next to me and muttered to myself, "I solemnly swear not to judge a book by its cover again."

"That might save you a lot of time," she agreed.

"You're judging me right now," I accused.

The girl placed a hand over her heart and broke into tinkling laughter. "I have a feeling we're going to be the best of friends, Emma."

"How do you know my name?"

Deadly serious, she said, "I'm a psychic."

"Wait, what?"

"Relax." She flicked a tag on my hoodie. "Name tag on your clothing?"

"It says Lane," I said, raising an eyebrow.

"You were in my year at school. You sat in front of me in home economics. Always made me tie your apron. Never could return the favor, Ms. Lane, but you always let me sample your food, and it was always amazing."

One of the side effects of deep depression was memory loss, so I wasn't surprised I didn't remember her. "Nice to see you again . . ."

"Gwen," she filled in for me. "No one takes notice of me at school. It's Gwen Black."

"Nice to meet you again. If it helps, I barely even noticed myself then."

"I can understand bizarre tendencies. After all, I am from a rather insane family. And that's being polite. But this, name tagging clothes? No, this doesn't make sense. You must explain."

"You never know when someone might want to claim something as theirs," I said.

"That's your reason? I don't see you being at all devoted to the art of clothes shopping."

"It's a travel day." I looked down at the camp clothing, then at the grey sweatpants I had previously worn, tossed on my other pillow.

"Speaking of, why aren't you at the assembly?" Gwen asked.

"Why aren't you there?" I countered.

"Like I said"—she grinned—"destined to be best friends, Emma."

"You've been here at Mapplewood before?"

"Uh-huh. My name is Black, after all," she said.

"Your parents own the place?"

"Guilty as charged; it's the family business. I'm still technically a camper, but my older brother and sister are counselors."

"At least now I'll know someone cool around here," I said.

Over the next few minutes, campers walked by the cabin window, letting us know that the assembly was over. Thankfully, no one from my cabin came back right away.

Gwen hopped down from the bunk bed and chatted about how it was such a coincidence that she, too, didn't plan on staying at Camp Mapplewood for the season, and the time passed quickly. Her parents insisted that she spend the summer with her siblings, Walter and Vivian, before the latter went back to college. Mr. Black roped his brother Manny into being the camp nurse for the summer too. The entire place was run by various members of the Black family when you included Gwen's mom, who was in charge of the kitchen.

Looking up at me with big eyes, Gwen asked, "Would it be okay if I put my number in your phone? You know, for after summer? To cement our friendship?" She hopped up and down on her feet, preparing to beg. She looked at my very pointy boob, where I had shoved my phone for safekeeping. It was an awful hiding spot. I took it out of my shirt and slipped down from the bunk bed so we faced each other. "I promise not to be too overbearing with emoticons."

"I don't mind, I guess . . ."

As quick as a flash, she snatched my phone from my hand and typed rapidly. When I got my phone back, her number was in there, coupled with several hearts beside her name and even a perfect picture of her grinning at the camera. Gwen grabbed me for a death hug. By that, I mean she hugged me so damn tight that I thought my ribs were going to crack. She might have gotten the hint when I started coughing and spluttering about seeing the light.

"I'm going to get my stuff organized before lunch, maybe set up my bed," Gwen said. "Don't be a stranger."

"You live next door," I pointed out, but she wasn't appeased. "I mean, you did say we were going to be best friends."

"Oh, and Emma? You should really hide that phone."

As she spun around and walked out of the cabin with a quick, graceful lope, I saw a strange, orange flower pinched in her hair.

Gwen was right. As much as I wanted to, I couldn't go around with the phone shoved down my bra. There had to be a hiding place in the cabin, somewhere a counselor wouldn't think to look until I was good and ready to break the rules. There was no point trying to get myself tossed out on the first day, especially when there would be no one to pick me up. My dad would be hours away by this point. As much as I wanted to see his overly sparkly blue van outside of camp, the image of his worn-out face after hours of traveling spurred me to scour the cabin in search of a good hiding spot.

Under my pillow? Too risky. Other than my luggage, the only personal space I had was the bed, and even then, it was only the top bunk. Our bathroom was small and already cramped with all our personal stuff and the as-yet-unpacked generic cleaning supplies that had been placed there before we arrived. Under my mattress? I tested the spot, lying on the bottom bunk and looking up. It was visible between the wooden bars. I knocked Abby's pillow off the bed, and when I stretched out to grab it, a higher than usual floorboard beneath Lauren's bed caught my attention. With a prod, the floorboard moved. When I shoved it to the side, a little hole appeared. No one would think to look there. After bundling the device into a hoodie, I hid the phone inside the hole.

✦

Come lunchtime, we didn't have to scavenge for our food. When I shared that thought out loud with the woman serving us, she gave me the strangest expression, piled a splat of mushy goop on my plate, and told me to beat it. I didn't have the energy to get anything other than potatoes after her apparent dismissal.

The canteen was already full to the brim, so I sat down at an outdoor picnic table with my tray. The rest of the Beaver group soon came out and spotted me. They made themselves comfortable with

Jessie and Abby sitting on either side of me, Lauren opposite me along with Kendra, and the guys to my right at the other end of the table, speaking among themselves. The only person from the Beavers who wasn't there was Gwen.

"Is this, like, a thing?" I asked, nudging Jessie as soon as she sat down. "All the other groups are meshed together. But the Beavers are staying united."

"We're genuinely friends, that's why," Jessie said.

"Is Gwen still back in your cabin?" I asked.

Lauren scoffed and fixed me with a look that resembled a goblin, like the idea of being friends with Gwen was absurd. She wore the same expression as she had on the day she'd left me up in that tree all alone. How didn't I recognize that face straight away? Sure, blocking out that memory was the only way to move forward, but when we were grouped together by Mr. Black, and then when we were in the cabin, she hadn't looked familiar. Knowing who she was now? It would be hard to forget.

She took a sip of her apple juice, maintaining eye contact with me. Did she remember doing that to me? There was no way she could know how leaving me up there had impacted me since then, but that didn't mean I wanted to forgive her. Not until she apologized at the very least. When Jessie opened her mouth to answer, Lauren glanced at her, shutting her response down. There was a gleam in Lauren's eye, as if she liked the power she held over her friends, but, more importantly, she wanted to impress me for some illogical reason. Behind proud eyes, she didn't realize that she was, in fact, doing the complete opposite.

"I don't know how Gwen's a part of the Black family. Her brother and sister are cool. She's too weird to be one of them." Lauren looked around and raised an eyebrow. "Especially her hair. Did you see it yet? She's a freak. She dances everywhere she goes. How weird is that?"

"She seems pretty cool to me," I said.

"Trust me." Lauren took a sip of her drink. "She isn't. That's why she's not sitting here. Doesn't matter what she's like, though. It's pretty much guaranteed she's getting that camp counselor position next year after Connor leaves. Look at how the rest of the camp is run. Julie Black, Philip Black, Manny Black, Walter Black, Vivian Black . . . next year Gwen will join them. How is that fair to anyone?"

"Essentially, you isolated her." I deduced. "Who does she sit with at school?"

"Why do you care?" Lauren asked.

I picked up my tray and stood. "Even if I don't know Gwen very well, or at all, I know she's damn better than your bossy ass."

Lauren stood up to face me. "Like you've even spoken to her."

Ignoring her, I turned in search of my new friend. Lauren reacted immediately by squirting apple juice all over my camp shirt. One second my head faced the ground, and by the next I had flung my tray right into Lauren's face, hitting her square in the nose. Mash toppled onto her T-shirt. Maybe a little blood spurted from her nose.

"Oops."

"I am going to murder you," she snarled, wiping mash from her top. "I am, literally, going to kill you."

"Literally literally, or literally?"

"What?"

"Like, literally, it won't happen at all, or will you literally take my life?" I said.

"Who do you think you are? I could ruin you. Absolutely ruin you. Just like I did to Gwen fucking Black."

To say that I was disappointed in the response from the Beaver group would be an understatement. Most of them were nice nerds who didn't like confrontation, if the horrified expressions on their faces were anything to go by. Mike, well, Mike had always been a follower, just like when he was twelve, leaving me stranded in that tree during a rainstorm, maybe because Lauren had told him to or maybe they'd come to that decision together. Either way, it was my bet that Lauren had taken charge in deciding to leave me there. And Abby was always the quiet girl from what I could recall, so not much had changed there. Shockingly, Jessie, despite the many thoughts she displayed in her letters, didn't have one word to say in response to the scene. What the hell happened to her after I left York?

I tried my best at cleaning my shirt in the canteen bathroom, but the scent of apples wouldn't go away, and the stickiness on the fabric refused to loosen its grip. I ended up tying the shirt in a knot so the lower part of my stomach was on display. For a second I hesitated, but the more I thought about it, the more I realized people wouldn't give a crap about my stomach as much as I did.

Lauren's casual remarks about Gwen infuriated me. That wasn't the worst of it; it was the fact Jessie and the rest of the Beavers didn't make a move to oppose what Lauren said about Gwen or the rest of the Black family. Either they shut down and couldn't stand up to Lauren or they condoned her ongoing behavior to isolate Gwen.

Jessie crossed my path as I joined the crowd heading out to the next assembly. "These people are my friends. You can't create drama because your mom left you here for the summer. It's not their fault that they don't like Gwen. Some people don't get along. That's life, Emma."

"It seems like the only reason they don't like her is because of who her family is. That's not right." I pulled my elbow out of her hold.

"Look, Lauren's always wanted to be a counselor. She's been talking about it for years and there will be only one spot next summer. Of course she's fuming. She has no chance against Gwen."

"It's still bullying, Jessie," I scoffed. "You're sharing a room with Gwen, right? Maybe Lauren and Gwen can switch rooms. Bunch you guys together."

"Lauren wants to share a room with Abby."

"All right, you and I can swap."

"I want to share with Kendra . . ."

"Do I look like I give a crap?"

"No," she said, turning away so she faced where the counselors stood. "You don't."

"It's like you have an entirely different personality. Your letters made you sound at least decent."

"Look at you. Still the same depressed, lonely Emma Lane. You haven't changed a bit."

"At least I'll never follow someone like Lauren. She's a bully. And the fact you stood up for her and not Gwen says everything about you."

My skin itched, and I regretted sending Jessie those letters and exposing my deepest and darkest thoughts to someone I thought was a trustworthy pen pal. Moving as far away from them as I could, I waited for Mr. Black to assign the Beavers a counselor. Abby gave me an empathetic squeeze of the arm as I settled in beside her, safely away from Jessie and Lauren. The air was toxic.

"I hope we get Walter," Abby said, motioning to a bulky guy with curly hair. "He's competitive. His set of campers always wins in the head-to-head competitions between the groups. And even if his campers don't win, they don't get beaten all that badly. Plus, he's nice."

"No, don't think I want him. Is there anyone laid back? I want to chill on the sidelines, maybe cheer you guys on if I'm not napping."

"Maybe Connor? But if Walter's and Connor's groups are against each other, they're scarily competitive. Same with Walter's sister, Vivian. It gets . . . messy."

✦

Lined up against the wall, the Beavers and the Jellyfish were the two last groups to be assigned a counselor. One of the counselors was late, meaning Mr. Black would assign a group to the late counselor before they arrived. I didn't know the logistics behind pairing a counselor with a group, but I trusted that he knew what he was doing.

"First of all, Jellyfish," Mr. Black said, clapping his hands together. "You're assigned to my son, Walter, and Beavers, you're assigned to my daughter, Vivian. Because you won't have time to organize another activity, you guys can play dodgeball in here, after which you'll all receive schedules of your day-to-day activities at camp. If you have questions or concerns, seek out your counselor or drop by my office."

"Why is this clicking now?" I asked, glancing to my right at Gwen, who indulged my surprise. "You have, like, an unlimited number of siblings running this joint."

"Only Walter and Vivian." Gwen dismissed them, waving a hand carelessly toward the other campers. "My dad's brother, Manny, is over there—the guy with a permanent sulk on his face. He does this every year. He takes inventory of the faces he'll probably treat."

"Treat?"

"He's a nurse. Dad roped anyone he could into spending the summer here. So Manny's here part time."

"I can relate."

"Camp wasn't your plan either?" she asked.

"No," I said. "I wanted to spend the summer with my dad."

She placed her hand on my shoulder, offering a sympathetic squeeze. "He sent you here?"

"Nope. Mom has court-ordered visitation, but then she went on a cruise. Or a honeymoon. She dropped me off on the way and went off with her new husband. Her excuse was she wanted me to socialize more."

"Drama," she whispered to herself.

"Stupid, useless drama."

"Still, you met me."

"Mission accomplished." I matched her grin. "Is it worth being forced to play dodgeball, though?"

"Play and find out!" Gwen laughed.

That was the thing, I didn't want to play at all. Dodgeball required patience, stealth, and stamina, none of which I possessed. Besides, it brought back memories of standing in line against the wall in gym class and not having my name called. Being the last person standing usually decided which team I'd join. Shoes squeaked on the court and voices echoed in the large room, and remnants of that anxiety pooled in the pit of my stomach as we stretched out on the court. Dodgeball had never been fun; would never *be* fun.

The door opened with a loud bang, and it was impressive how a person could command the room as quickly as this girl did. With wavy black hair that ended an inch above her elbows and her head held high, she sauntered into the recreational room. The rhythmic clicking of her shoes added to the sound of the sports balls bouncing. Everyone seemed captivated by the swinging of her hips. She was beautiful, like the view staring out the window of a car on a clear night—no matter how impressive the landscape was, the stars always regained my attention.

Her eyes met mine and she scowled. I didn't know what I looked like to the common eye at that moment but I didn't scowl back, not straight away. She didn't look familiar. If I saw someone who looked like that in the past, I would certainly remember. The troubling thing was, that by the way she did a double take, it appeared she knew me.

Gwen's brother hooted and jumped up to his other sister, pointing in our general direction, causing her visibly sour mood to deepen. Vivian. Our counselor. I couldn't blame her. She was left with the Beavers. Our group name alone told her all she needed to know. We weren't about to be victorious.

"I still can't believe that Vivian Black is our counselor," Lauren said, her eyes sparkling.

"Nepotism at its best!"

"Tied that apple juice up nicely, didn't you?" she said.

"I did."

Lauren halfheartedly tossed a dodgeball in my direction. Gwen spun around like a ballerina in my direction, then, with her dainty hands on my shoulders, nudged me to the side so the ball missed me completely. The pair of us walked away to one side of the dodgeball line.

The Jellyfish gathered around Walter like ducklings, whereas the Beavers were too scared to approach Vivian.

"Come on, Em, she's mostly harmless," Gwen said, tugging on my hand. "I pinkie swear, okay?"

"Got to link pinkies for that to work, Gwen."

"Right, what was I thinking?" She stopped abruptly and wrapped her smallest finger around mine. "She's harmless."

"Do I have to go through the mind-numbing process of explaining the rules to you?" Vivian said.

I nearly choked on the saliva in my mouth because that familiar, heavenly, one and only voice belonged to the girl from the shed. No wonder she looked at me like that earlier. She was one who locked me in there and left me there to fend for myself. Gwen tipped up my chin to snap my jaw back into place.

"Run, get the ball, then throw it," Lauren answered, preening under Vivian's attention. "How hard can it be?"

"For the Beavers? Usually it's catastrophic," Vivian said.

"It's a cursed group," Gwen told me.

"We're the second largest rodent in the world," I muttered helpfully, turning around to stand at the end line, trying not to stare at the Jellyfish team—they had so much muscle.

Gwen patted my shoulder and said, "Dad would be so proud."

"If only we were the capybara, whatever the hell that is."

"The largest rodent in the world," Gwen quipped.

"Hilarious," I deadpanned.

Gwen matched the determination of the Jellyfish as she hopped up and down on her feet, readying herself for the match by drumming her fingers on my shoulders. The rest of the Beavers did not match her enthusiasm. Abby and Kendra stood with their arms crossed, while Jessie and Lauren didn't even look in the direction of the dodgeballs, too busy whispering to each other. The guys on our team stood frozen—their defeat apparent even before the game started. Vivian leaned against a wall with some magazine and a bored expression on her face. Walter boomed encouragement from the sidelines, riling his team up. The only indication that Vivian was involved in the game at all was the whistle between her lips. When she determined that everyone stood behind the allotted line, she blew the whistle.

"Run, Emma!" Gwen cheered, gracefully plucking a ball from the ground and launching it at someone.

"No." I refused, not moving an inch.

"Run, or you're going to get clobbered!"

"The floor looks comfy."

Gwen hit a six-foot guy cleanly in the shoulder, knocking him out of the game. "It'll hurt."

"Pain is less exertion."

"Man," Mike groaned, rubbing where he got hit in the knee.

I sidestepped a shot to my arm and let it bounce against the wall behind me but wasn't so lucky the second time as a red blur smashed against my left cheek. My knees buckled from the impact but I managed to stay upright. The court line, painted white on the floor, wiggled like a snake. The pain didn't even register, but then right below my eye felt warm, and the sting became prominent. Then the silence gave me a chance to notice I was sprawled on the ground.

"She's on your team." Mike's tone was accusatory. "That's just . . . that's just plain stupid, Lauren."

"Oops," Lauren said.

"I'll show you oops." I sat up, rolled onto my side, grabbed the ball, and flung it at the offending target. Lauren turned around in time for it to clip the back of her head.

A loud laugh came from the other side of the court over the chaotic screaming. Walter asked, "What the hell's happening on your team, Viv?"

"Self-sabotage," she said, her head inclined to the side.

"More like revenge," I grumbled, slumping over to the sideline.

"You weren't knocked out," Vivian told me.

"Mike can take my place. Can't you, Mike?" I asked.

He high-fived me. "Yeah, let's win this thing! We'll do it for you, Emma."

He ran onto the court, and a ball immediately whacked against his groin area. A range of *oohs* circled the court. Mike was left flat as more Beavers were thrown out of the game. Gwen swirled around, plucking dodgeballs off the ground and whipping them at the Jellyfish with perfect accuracy and lightning-quick speed. It was like her hands were the ideal catapult for the dodgeballs from hell.

I grabbed a bottle of water from the bench, not caring who it belonged to, and pressed it against my hot cheek.

"That's unsanitary," Vivian commented.

"So is your face."

The scent of roses surrounded me, and I felt the presence of a person delicately sitting beside me. "You must be so proud of your wit."

"It made you scowl, didn't it?" Even talking was painful. "Ow!"

Her finger prodded my cheek, making me hiss, splutter, and lean back so that I fell off the bench.

"What do you have to smile about?" she asked, eyes narrowing. "Your cheek is swelling."

"Why didn't you report me?"

"How long did it take you to get out of the shed?" she asked. Then, "You need ice."

"I'm fine."

She stared at me blankly. "You're fine?"

"One hundred perc—the heck! Stop. Dammit, stop pinching me!"

"You're fine," she mocked.

I pushed myself back until there was enough space between us so that she couldn't prod my cheeks again. Vivian wasn't the only threat in the room, though. I backed up too far and a ball hit the back of my head, forcing my head to slam down on top of my knee. The room went deadly silent, and I felt tears sting my wounds. My hearing took a little trip away to save itself from the destruction that seemed to find me attractive.

"Emma? You okay?" I grunted my response. "Shh. There's so much blood," Gwen said, returning to running her fingers through my hair. "I'll take her to the nurse, and you sort out . . ."

"You're not a counselor yet," Vivian said shortly.

"Does it matter?" her sister asked, sounding a little whiny. "She's my soon-to-be bestie."

"I'm fine," I claimed.

"I'm taking her," Vivian said. Another set of hands hauled me up to my feet. "And you, you're not fine. It's like you want me to prove to you again through mild clips to the face how not fine you are."

"Have I mentioned that you're evil?" I asked.

"Once or twice, yes," Vivian said.

With one hand covering my face, I linked my other arm with Vivian's. Walking across the camp with my face bleeding so much was mildly embarrassing. People stared a lot. It was like they'd never seen blood or someone battered by a bully with a dodgeball before.

What made the journey worse was how perfect Vivian was; she didn't have a blossoming black eye and a bloody nose. Everything about her—the composure, the limber walk, the glare that kept people far enough away but close enough to stare at her clear beauty—was perfect. Then there was me, the clumsy couch potato.

"I don't know how one manages to knee themselves in the face."

"You ram your face against an opposing bone and voilà!"

"It's been one day," she said quietly.

"It's all going according to plan," I said. "Enough of an injury to send me home?"

She helped me up the steps and knocked on the door to the camp infirmary next to Mr. Black's office in the main building. "One day and you've already got yourself enemies. Maybe it is a good idea to get yourself kicked out. End the drama. Save your body the trauma."

"I told you so," I said.

The door swung open, revealing not the nurse, but the camp director himself. Mr. Black blinked slowly as he took in my face. Once his daughter nudged him to the side, he allowed us through, quickly clearing the bed of some new equipment.

My feet dangled off the bed, swinging back and forth in rhythm with my dizziness. Instead of a sharp pain coming in short intervals, a consistent dull ache took over.

"I had a bad feeling, leaving you and Walter in charge of dodge-ball." He directed his comment to his daughter. "How did this happen?"

"It's not my fault if the children . . . bicker. Besides, it's the name of the game."

"Children?" I asked.

"Yes, *children*," Vivian confirmed.

She couldn't be *that* old. "How old are you, exactly?"

"None of your business."

"Nineteen," her dad supplied.

"*Pfft*, please. You're a baby yourself," I accused.

Vivian faced the wall with crossed arms, refusing to acknowledge the two people in the room.

Mr. Black left the room to get an ice pack. We didn't move the entire time he was gone.

"I'll call in Manny, he'll help with the swelling," he said when he returned. "In the meantime, there's this."

"Thank you," I said gratefully, receiving the ice pack wrapped in a tea towel.

"You're welcome. Should I expect any more casualties?"

"No," Vivian said.

"Maybe," I answered. "Mike Hanley got hit pretty badly."

Vivian finally took notice of me. "Mike was hit?"

"Are you telling me I imagined Mike getting hit in the privates?"

It wasn't a moment later when Walter, along with his uncle Manny, carried the faint-looking Mike into the room and deposited him on the couch. Vivian didn't seem bothered that two of her assigned campers were harmed. Wincing from the pain, I positioned the ice pack against my cheek. "Poor guy."

"Are you feeling anything other than fine?" she asked, tilting her head to the side.

"Meh."

"You're insufferable."

"Meh."

"Dad," Vivian said, "have enough children been hurt now to put an end to this activity?"

In the end, Mr. Black decided that dodgeball was much too violent to be allowed to continue, and it needed to be replaced on the activity list with something tamer like handball or badminton. Manny gave me a pass to rest in his infirmary for up to an hour. Vivian left behind the schedule for me to look over, and seeing it made me wish that Lauren had injured me enough to send me packing and out of camp. Every morning we were to get up for breakfast at seven o'clock, which was served until eight. Summer sleep-ins? No longer possible. From eight we had arts and crafts until ten, then a team activity chosen by the counselor until noon. Then we had an hour of lunch. From two until five we had to participate in an exercise-based activity, either based in the recreational hall if it happened to rain, in the courtyard behind our cabins, or in water activities down by the lake. Then, finally we were fed dinner from half past five until half past six.

It was a jam-packed schedule, and I sure as hell didn't like the sound of it at all.

FOUR

A full week later, my face was still bruised and sore. I'd made it through the dreaded Fourth of July celebrations the previous day. The early mornings were impossible. I missed winter when my bedroom wasn't bombarded with a blinding light and was instead greeted by the welcomed darkness. Squeezing the last few minutes of comfort out of my bunk, I refused to jump down until the last possible moment.

Lauren grew more frustrated by my leaving the cabin in shambles. There were enforced tidiness rules: our beds had to be made, our gear stored away, and our cabin put to right. My usual routine was to topple my mattress, move my duvet onto the floor, spread my clothes everywhere, and move random pieces of furniture around. It was all part of my plan to escape. Except Vivian didn't react or report me.

That left me no choice except to target my cabinmates so they could complain. That morning, I took my time in the bathroom,

Lauren whispering angrily outside about how we were going to get docked points for being late to breakfast. I folded three ketchup packets that I'd stolen from the canteen the day before and placed them under the toilet seat.

"Emma!" Lauren shouted. "Abby still needs to brush her teeth."

"I'm done." I got out of the bathroom and sat on the bottom bunk, only noticing when Abby rushed into the bathroom that there was another person in the cabin. Gwen stood near Lauren—too closely for comfort—rocking back and forth on her heels. "Gwen, what brings you by? Were you two arguing?" I asked.

"Nope. Came by to make sure that you're up," Gwen told me.

"We'll probably be punished this time because we're so late," Lauren grumbled.

"You can go ahead without us."

"No, if I leave, you're going to trash the place. We'll get warnings if they do an inspection."

"Shit!" Abby yelped. "Oh my. . . . What the hell? Emma?!"

Lauren shoved me so I toppled back on the bed as she went into the bathroom. "Abby? What is that? Is that blood?"

"No! I hope not. What's that on the floor?"

"A ketchup packet," Lauren said. "That's it! Emma, I've had enough of your shit!"

"Emma, what did you do?" Gwen asked.

"Nothing?" I lied. When Lauren barreled into the room, I asked, "Report me?"

"That's what you want, though! I'm out of here. Let's go, Abby."

"Is that a no?" I asked as they stormed out of the room. "That was a waste of time."

Gwen flicked my ear. "Stop trying to get kicked out of camp."

✦

It was after our arts and crafts session that the Beavers were scheduled for our daily bonding activity. The only information Vivian had given us was that it would be held down by the lake.

I was never one to eat before ten o'clock. My body considered that time as one that it should be resting and fast asleep, and not a time when it should be conscious and consuming food. At breakfast, I'd been sneaking an apple into the pocket of my hoodie and leaving it there until I was good and ready to eat it.

Throwing the hoodie on over my camp T-shirt, and pulling my hood up, I followed the rest of the Beavers from the arts and crafts cabin and walked into the gorgeous day. The daylight made the bruising on my upper cheek glaringly obvious. The camp's nurse, Manny, said he couldn't do anything for my eye, not really. I had to massage around the bruised area, and after the first day or two, I switched from ice packs to pressing a warm cloth against my face. Despite it being a week since the terrible dodgeball incident, my face didn't look much better.

I hid a yawn behind my hand as we traveled through the woods to the lake. My shoulders were hunched, not to keep the hood over my face, but as a reaction to the environment. The sky was clear, so it was unlikely that it would storm, but my rigid back didn't accept that, nor did my buzzing brain. The trees stood unwavering, and that was the only reminder I needed of being confined and frozen in place, the numbness of my fingers clawing at the bark of the tree, my back aching from sitting on that high branch for what seemed like hours with bullet-like rain drilling into my eyes.

Vivian bumped my shoulder, disrupting my mildly panicked thoughts. "Walk faster? I don't want to have to keep looking over my shoulder to ensure that you're not dead." She ran a hand through her hair and complained, "Grab someone and walk with them. They can make sure that you don't trip and kill yourself."

"Even when I don't try, I can be a great burden."

"The fact that you're turning your face away is a dead giveaway. I'm sure you've got a ridiculous grin plastered all over your face."

"You're not far off," I offered, fighting the urge to do just that. "If I see how much I annoy you, I'll want to smile, and if I smile, it will hurt. Your pain will be my pain."

She tugged my sleeve. "As interesting as that fact is, look ahead and call someone over to keep you company."

"They'll want to talk," I complained.

"And that's awful because . . . ?"

"I'm not a morning person."

She studied me for a moment. "Clearly."

I didn't make a move to grab my only friend, Gwen, who happily walked beside Abby, chatting enthusiastically despite the not-so-subtle glares shot her way by Lauren. Gwen was good like that, creating a happy bubble that seemed impenetrable. It was nice seeing Abby relax for a little while, and it was nice to see someone other than me talk to Gwen.

Ever since our fight last week, Jessie had stayed away. She and Lauren walked with their heads close together. Even when I visibly struggled to stay composed, Jessie didn't come up to me; she didn't speak to or acknowledge me. It went to show that words on paper were ultimately meaningless, that the care and the time spent writing to each other for the past couple of years meant nothing. She was the one person who knew my deepest thoughts, my hopes, dreams, pitfalls, and anxieties. She could deal with me on paper but not in person, and it was an unexpected, crippling blow.

The longer I stayed at the back of the group, the more Vivian slowed down her pace, calling out instructions to her sister if we had to turn or for which trail to take. Even if she did huff once in a while, she stayed behind, bound by the duties of camp counselor to herd the campers safely in the right direction. Because I was paying attention to Vivian's annoyed antics and trying not to laugh, a branch whacked me across my face. The good thing was, it was the other side of my face. The terrible thing? Vivian cackled at my expense.

"This camp is going to be the death of me," I mumbled.

"You're still here, because?" she pressed.

"If you want me gone so badly, report me."

"I condemn idiocy."

"And how am I an idiot, exactly?"

"People who make declarations of plans and don't follow through. It's frustrating." She flipped her hair out of her face then tied it back, the long strands seemingly a bother. "It means you're unreliable. Untrustworthy and a waste of time."

"It's been a week. Give me some time, and maybe some credit."

"No."

Gwen glanced back at the sound of my laughter. She offered a cheeky thumbs-up that made her sister, for some reason, flounder. Vivian stormed ahead, leaving me in the dust.

The youngest Black family member danced over to my side. We stopped and she pulled the hood from my face back to take a closer look at my injury.

"What made Lauren do that to you?" Gwen asked for the thousandth time since the incident occurred.

"It sounds like you're insinuating that I did something to her first," I said, pretending to be offended, then admitted, "I might have thrown a tray at her face."

"Oh my God, Emma!"

"It was retaliation! She squirted apple juice all over me . . . do you know how sticky that stuff can be?" I shuddered. "So sticky."

"And why did she do that?" she persisted, looping her arm around mine. I didn't exactly want to tell her that Lauren was talking smack about her family, so I lied. "I can't remember. Something about pain and misery."

We followed the path that everyone else had already gone along until we reached a clearing protected by a mass of leaves, branches, and cracked twigs on the ground. Gwen hopped over the mess of branches quick like a monkey and helped me stumble across. She gripped my forearms and somehow managed to keep me upright when I fumbled around.

What I saw next was beautiful, and that came from someone who didn't appreciate things like dirt and water. This side of the lake had wildflowers surrounding the shore of the crystal-clear water. The water was so transparent that the smallest of pebbles was visible and the way it remained entirely still freed my mind of its continuous whizzing of problematic thoughts.

Ten brown, narrow log boats laid upside down on the wooden platform at the edge of the lake so they would be easy to slide into the water. One oar stuck out on either end of the logs and one orange life jacket was positioned next to each oar. What was strange about the oars was the red cushions tied to the ends of them. They had clearly been set up before we got here, and it was a small mercy that we didn't have to fetch the log boats ourselves. More inland, beside the tree line, was a two-roomed hut meant for changing, and a red portable toilet sat to the left.

"Looks like that hoodie will have to come off," Gwen chirped, delighted.

"Dude, I'm injured. I'm not doing this activity."

"Water's harmless, you overdramatic grumpy pants," Gwen said.

"Preventing further injury isn't being overdramatic or grumpy." Besides, there was a small boulder that beckoned.

"I think I'm going to have to set up a tally for how dramatic you and Vivian are," she whispered to herself. "Your first day here you kneed yourself in the face."

"Which was a subsequent response to being whacked in the back of my head."

"You've already gained enemies," she told me.

"That's what your sister said." I looked at her, suspicious of the playful tilt of her head. "She's been totally complaining about me, hasn't she? Is she my archnemesis in this camp?"

"Further proving my point," she sang.

"Damn, an archnemesis. That's going to be high maintenance."

Gwen slipped into the group surrounding Vivian as I sat on the boulder. The Beavers stood statue-like, afraid of what was going to come out of Vivian's mouth. We hadn't spent much time by the lake as Beavers—ironic, considering our name.

Studying the siblings, you could see only one physical characteristic that was the same—their brown eyes. Gwen's were sweet and warm, like the surprise you get when caramel oozes from a chocolate. Vivian's were different, a shade darker than butterscotch.

"Emma," Vivian called, catching my eye. "You stay there."

"Sir, yes, sir," I said, mock saluting.

"I mean it, you're not getting into the water." Vivian addressed the group: "We need to clear the air, as there's obvious animosity between us. It's perfectly fine to have your feelings. Not everyone's going to get along. That's human nature. Acting on that aggression means you have no impulse control. Today, you're going to be knocking your opponent off the log and into the water. This is your only chance to act like animals. Savor it because you're not going to be afforded this opportunity every time you don't get along."

Lauren complained. "What if your opponent is not participating?"

"Way to be subtle," I muttered.

"Then you'll help me demonstrate," Vivian said.

Vivian and Lauren went inside the hut, where the lockers designated for our swimming attire were, and changed into their bathing suits, gearing up for the event. After they came back out and started to put on their life jackets, Lauren's cheeks reddened when her shaking hands couldn't put it on, forcing Vivian to help buckle her up.

I flung my hood over my head again as Mike lumbered onto the boulder quietly.

"I'm sorry about what happened to you last week." He scratched the back of his neck. "You offered me another chance at playing dodgeball. I got hurt. You got hurt, again. It couldn't have gone any worse."

"A giant mess," I agreed. "But I don't see why you're apologizing, Mike."

"You didn't deserve to get hurt," he explained. "And I don't know if you remember, but a couple of years ago . . ."

I left you stranded up in that tree?

"I remember," I said.

"I'm sorry about that too."

"I appreciate that, Mike."

Vivian and Lauren flipped over the log at the end of the platform and slid it into the water. Once settled inside, they stood up within the confines of the narrow log boat, testing the balance of the oars within their grip. The logs were heavy, so the occupants could move however they wanted to knock the other person into the water.

Mike and I were too far out to hear what Vivian was saying, so we hopped off the boulder and went to stand beside the rest of the Beavers. I didn't want to miss a thing. Lauren visibly shrank with each word from Vivian.

"Lauren must have a death wish," Mike muttered.

"I'm pretty sure she wants to suck up to her. You know, for that counselor job next summer or whatever."

"But she got rejected last year by Vivian. There were multiple crying fits but . . . rumor has it that Vivian went on a rampage last summer after Lauren asked her out for the millionth time, and tore down a cabin. I think it was your cabin, actually. You're number thirteen, right?"

With one gigantic hit to the shoulder, Lauren was flung out of the log by at least four yards, grunting in the most ridiculous fashion—until her head went under water for a moment.

"I wasn't ready," she shouted, wiping her eyes and spitting water out of her mouth.

"I asked you three times," Vivian said.

"You swung when you knew I was blinking!"

"Fine. Let's say I accept that excuse." Vivian reached out to grab Lauren's hand. Before she pulled her up, she wore a feral grin. "Would you like to go another round?"

Lauren spluttered. Vivian spoke, "I take that as a no."

Now that the demonstration was over, the rest of the Beavers paired up and tended to their own logs. Since I was not part of the exercise, there was an even number of campers. I stayed a few steps away from the platform until I was sure that Gwen wasn't partnered up with Lauren, and once Gwen hopped onto the same log as Mike, I returned to the boulder to watch the violence from afar and got around to eating my apple. Vivian sat at the edge of the platform, legs beneath the water, watching her campers like a hawk.

Seeing as she made it her mission to block my way out of camp, I had only one option left, and that was to expose my phone to a counselor or someone in authority who wasn't *her*. As if sensing my thoughts, Vivian glanced over her shoulder in time to see me take a bite out of my contraband apple. I winked and chewed happily because she'd already proved that she wasn't going to do a damn thing about it.

"You've sat long enough," Vivian said. "Up, bathing suit—you're going in the water."

It was one of the tightest things that I'd ever put on. The awkwardness of the fabric of the bathing suit was a creative punishment. The only good thing was we had our own lockers inside the hut by the lake with our own swimming supplies, so we didn't have to wear them all day long under our camp shirts and shorts.

I waddled uncomfortably toward where Vivian stood on the plat-form. Without a word, she tossed the life jacket into my arms, and when it was over my head, she spun me around and tightened the straps with a tough tug. When we flipped over the log and slipped it into the water, that's when it hit me that we were going to actively *whack* each other. My muscles barely held up my arms, never mind heavy oars.

Vivian hopped into the log boat with ease. She turned to me and offered her hand—a Trojan horse gesture? Luring me into a false sense of security before she pummeled me with all her might? I took her hand, marveling at the white crescent-moon design on her black painted nails, and stepped into the log. If Vivian hadn't gripped my forearm and held me steady, the rocking back and forth would have thrown us overboard. I missed the warmth and softness of her hand when she let go and handed me an oar.

I gripped the oar and braced myself for a walloping. Vivian, out of nowhere, casually sat down and untangled the cushion from the oar. "You don't think I'd set out to intentionally harm an already injured camper, do you?"

"Thank God."

"Just because you're injured doesn't mean you can't at least float in the lake for a while."

"That's . . . thoughtful of you."

"Do you feel different out here?" she asked. "It's the first time since you've come to camp that you don't look like you want to punch everything and anything. You seem relaxed. Steadier. Your shoulders aren't hunched. There isn't that annoying frown on your face. You're smiling. Don't tell me you're now content at camp?"

My fellow Beavers were splashing and crashing over one another in the lake, and it was at least entertaining.

"Do I still want to leave? Hell yes."

"But . . . ?"

"But . . . it's not so bad being out on the lake." My body wasn't rigid and my muscles didn't spasm in anticipation of threats. From Vivian's brown eyes to the clear lake there wasn't a hint of greenery. She spotted my safe spot before I did. If camp was like this twenty-four-seven I wouldn't have minded staying in the least. "Do we get to come down to the lake a lot?"

Vivian dragged her oar through the water and then quickly whipped it up, splashing me in the face. "I think we might in the future."

We relaxed in the log boat, floating to the VIP section of the lake with the best view. There was a sweetness to her under all that antagonism and the fancy words she used. At the end of the day, she wasn't that much older than us, one or two years at most, but she carried herself like a true adult who knew what she was doing.

Even so, I still needed to show that phone to someone in authority who wasn't her to get myself kicked out of camp.

FIVE

When I woke up the next morning, there was no desire to pull more pranks by moving furniture or placing ketchup in the bathroom again. My idea was simple: wake up, fetch my phone from under the floorboard, walk around camp, and *job done*. My temporary stay would be no more. It was inevitable that I'd be kicked out. All I had to do was confess to breaking into the shed and then I'd be gone. I had proof, after all.

I could have called my dad at any point, but the problem was Mom. I didn't want to create a shit storm in their already volatile relationship. Getting in trouble at camp meant my mom would have to deal with the fallout; she was the point of contact. Spending the rest of the summer with her and Ethan on their honeymoon? It didn't sound fun. But it was a hell of a lot better than putting Dad in the middle of this mess. He'd already saved me too many times.

The sound of shuffling around the room woke me up. The noise encouraged me to snuggle farther into my pillow. It was my last day, I was going to sleep in regardless of the repercussions. My cabinmates left and got their breakfast, obviously not concerned about my stomach. I didn't account for said mates to be so pushy about the morning arts and crafts activity.

"Come on, Emma, get up," Lauren groaned an hour later, tapping my leg. "They punish by cabin, not camper if someone's late."

"We can't force her up," Abby said.

"We'll all be punished because of her. You know that, right? Emma?"

I wiggled away from her. "Cool story, bro."

"Get the hell up." She pinched me. Really hard. I kicked out boldly, hoping to get her in the face. "I'm not kidding. I will . . ."

"Touch me again, and I'll end you. I'll ask Vivian to do another logrolling session. There's so much animosity in this cabin. Can't you feel it?" I said.

"Lauren, let's just go," Abby urged.

My bunk shook when Lauren jumped off. There were a few more minutes of shuffling until they left, slamming the door shut behind them. I fell back to sleep rather quickly. It was short lived. One moment I was dreaming about following a rabbit down a hole, violating some copyright from the movie *Alice in Wonderland*, the next, there was an earthquake. My eyes snapped open as I flung the covers off and swung my body over the edge, breathing far too heavily for it to be healthy. Something grabbed my foot through the sheet, making me screech.

"Oh my God, hell, it's haunted!" I yelled, jumping off the bed, tumbling to the side.

"And I'll continue to haunt your dreams if you don't go to arts and crafts," a familiar, silky voice said.

"Black," I grunted, watching as she played with some key chain. The angle of her hand changed so the thing with wild googly eyes looked down in unison with hers at me, sprawled on the ground. "Is that a beaver?"

She made it snap its mouth. "Indeed, it is."

"That's creepy as hell. Or cute? I don't know."

Vivian stood up from Abby's lower bunk and stalked toward the door. "Two minutes, get dressed."

My phone. The plan. I could bypass this mess.

The door slammed shut behind her. I quickly tugged a clean camp shirt over my head and hopped around as I pulled on some shorts because I wasn't risking her barging back in while I was in a state of undress.

After brushing my teeth, I pulled back the curtain and peeked out. Vivian leaned back against the railing of cabin's deck with closed eyes, looking both peaceful and beautiful. She was lost in her own world and she couldn't possibly intercept me getting the phone. I could walk out of the cabin without her knowing if she stayed right in that spot. I spun around and crawled under Lauren's bed. My hand slid along the floor until it came to the edge of the loose floorboard and I pried it out of the way. Reaching inside the hole, I pulled out my spare hoodie and flopped it onto the floor. As it unfurled, my lips turned downward. There was nothing inside.

"Time's up," Vivian said impatiently, already by the door, watching me.

Instead of throwing the hoodie away and onto the bed like I should have, I pulled it over my head. "Let's go."

"You're acting strangely."

"Your face is strange."

She ignored my comment and walked ahead, muttering something under her breath.

The sun was blinding, and I was freaking out because my phone was missing. Lauren was the only person I could think of who might have taken it, but how did she even know it was there? Maybe she wanted to speed the process along and kick me out sooner personally? Not that I could blame Lauren after our daily morning routine. Abby wasn't a suspect. Not yet, at least.

The only other person I could think of who knew of the phone and had the means to steal it was Vivian. I studied her from behind, looking to see where she could've hidden it. There were no pockets in her shorts, no bulge in her socks, and she wasn't carrying around any extra bags or anything. In an odd way, it made sense if she'd taken it. Maybe that entire conversation the day before about being disappointed in my attempts to get out of camp were to rile me up and set me up for disappointment when I went up a level and used the phone to get kicked out.

"Stop checking me out." She sighed.

I couldn't stop the snort, and Vivian stopped abruptly. "Ow?" I rubbed my face, taking a couple of steps back. "Can I see the key chain?"

"No. You're the most annoying person," she said.

"*You* dragged me out of bed at who knows what time . . ."

"Eight o'clock," she supplied.

"Treated me like a dog, stole some of my possessions, and now restrict me the fun of learning how to replicate that adorable beaver-sock-key-chain thingy?" I finished my rant, giving her my best foot stomp. "Who the hell do you think you are?"

An eyebrow quirked at me, and she looked smug as hell. She let go of my arm. "Daughter of the camp director, that's who. I'm a lot of things, Emma, but a thief isn't one of them," Vivian said. "You seem stressed."

"Oh, you know, I never did get to take out my frustrations on anyone yesterday."

"How tragic."

"How do you think I would've fared?" I asked.

"You wouldn't have been sent to the infirmary . . . you would've been sent to the morgue."

I couldn't help but laugh. "You know, Vivian, despite that vague death threat, I think you really like me."

"And how did you come to that conclusion?"

"I'm still here at camp."

Other than the fact that arts and crafts was held too early in the morning, it was the one activity that didn't make me panic, as long as I avoided the larger than life windows that had a stunning view of the entire camp. Inside the building there was a colorful mess that wouldn't let my gaze linger out the window for too long. Each group had a shelf in the big unit that was dedicated to their projects. Newspapers stretched across the long table that was in the middle of the room, but there were no jars with paintbrushes or trays full of paint—there was a bunch of socks and buttons.

Mr. Black had hired Marissa, an art student, for the summer for arts and crafts. I liked her. I truly did. Then she ruined it by announcing that I was on my first formal warning for being late, and if I got three, I'd be kicked out of the camp. While getting kicked out of camp was precisely what I wanted, that didn't mean I wanted to get dressed down in front of everyone.

"We've already begun, find a seat and start making a sock animal that you can attach to these key chains. You can collect them when you leave," Marissa said. "Remember, the puppet has to be small enough to attach to the key chain!"

Taking a seat as quickly as possible, I tried not to interrupt the work already in place.

"Stop with the puppy dog eyes," Vivian whispered, sitting down beside me. "It's beneath you. Maybe it's a good thing that you're in arts and crafts."

I pulled a sock from a bucket. "I know I'm going to regret asking, but why?"

"You need to work on expressing yourself."

"Hah-hah, very funny."

Starting below the heel and cutting the ankle part of the sock from the foot part, I snipped it, trying to make the rounded curve for an owl's head. My hands were shaky, but I didn't nip my fingers. The opening of the sock would be the bottom of the owl's body. The toe part of the sock cut away fine, the very tip, and it formed two teeny-tiny wings for my owl. With the remaining section of the sock, I cut up the side to open it up, and then cut a rough circle that formed the base of the owl.

"Cute."

"It's a deformed ostrich or something, Gwen. Not cute."

She prodded me on the shoulder and slipped me an apple under the table. "From now on, I'm dragging you out of bed—no more warnings. You can't get yourself kicked out. And don't get caught with that apple. I'm going to ask you something once, okay?"

"It doesn't sound like a nice question." I took the body part of the sock and turned the right sides together. Gwen diligently handed me a thread and needle. "Don't ask."

"Are you trying to get yourself kicked out?" she asked.

"Dammit, Gwen."

"What?"

"I told you not to ask."

The needle pricked my thumb, and I glanced around to see if anyone other than Gwen noticed. She good-naturedly thumbed behind her toward the sink and proceeded to prod me until I found the strength to get up from the stool. Most of the Beavers group acted like meerkats, necks straining to see exactly what I was doing, except Lauren who was too busy studiously making her sock animal beneath the table board. Or she was too busy going through my phone.

The cold water sprayed against my thumb, washing away the blood.

"Emma," Vivian called, her tone too casual. "You need buttons for the eyes."

I chewed on the inside of my cheek. "I think I'll stick to one eye. Name him Mike or something."

"Hey," responded an offended boy.

"I meant Mike Wazowski," I explained, plucking the box from the shelf.

"Who?" Mike asked, blinking at me stupidly.

I studied him for a moment. "Nope. If you don't know who that is, you don't deserve to know. Stop looking at me like that. It's your own fault, you uncultured swine."

The lid came off the little box and as it did, I tripped over something invisible, and the plastic lid flew like a Frisbee in one direction, followed by at least one hundred buttons pooling on the table and around my feet. Finally, the apple slid from my hoodie pocket. Marissa let her disapproval be known. My body stilled, then slowly, I raised my head and looked at her, taking in the wide eyes and parted lips, like she didn't know what the hell to do.

I bent down. "I'm going to . . ."

"Emma," Marissa said.

"I'm sorry. I'm *really* clumsy."

"She really is," Vivian said.

"I don't need a character witness," I said, throwing a handful of buttons into the box and missing entirely so that they fell onto Marissa's shoe. "Maybe I shouldn't do this. I won't invade your sock because that'd be weird."

"You're on kitchen duty," Marissa blurted, shocking everyone as she plucked the apple from the ground. "I knew I heard crunching noises this week. I knew it."

My finger tapped against a button. "What?"

"Yes, that. For a . . . week. There. Now you all know to not mess with me . . . because I'm a—"

"Cruel, cruel woman," I muttered.

"Two weeks," Marissa said. "No food outside of the canteen. Be on time for activities. You broke the rules, these are your consequences."

"Today is *not* my day."

"Two and a half weeks."

"What the fu—"

Gwen's hand covered my mouth, preventing me from cursing. Marissa shook her head, walked to the side of the room with the apple in her hand, and dropped it in the trash can.

Gwen brought me back to the table so that I sat across from Vivian, who looked much too delighted at the situation. I quickly sewed a beak and one eye onto the owl and shoved it in the counselor's direction.

"Send that owl to me when you get me an invitation to Hogwarts and out of this camp."

"No," Vivian said. "You're stuck here forever."

"You want me here to make you more of these owl key chains," I teased.

"Hmm. No, that's not it."

"Why, then?" I inquired.

"Does there need to be a reason?" she asked.

"Absolutely."

"What's the reason for you wanting to leave camp?"

There was no way in hell that I'd admit to being afraid of literally everything there was about Camp Mapplewood. "All right."

"You're going to give me an answer?" Vivian asked.

"Nope. I'm standing down. I was serious, though. You can keep little Mike there as a reminder of me when I'm out of here," I said.

"A token of your dishonor."

"Exactly."

We finished the sock-animal key chains half an hour earlier than anticipated and sat waiting to see what we would do with the remaining time as Vivian and Marissa chatted outside. Vivian sauntered back in and positioned herself in the space in front of the long table. Prolonging the silence, she dragged her gaze around the room, as if looking for inspiration for something to keep us occupied, until eventually her eyes landed on me. That seemed to spark an idea.

"Draw each other," she said as she gathered pages from the edge of the table and handed them out to each camper. "Use any style you want. Realistic, cartoony . . . you've got twenty minutes. Your time starts now."

Gwen and I spun around in our chairs to face one another and began to draw. It was my favorite activity at camp, but that didn't mean that I was any good at it. Soon after we started, I gave up and posed with a pencil between my upper lip and nose. Gwen took it seriously, peeking up at me briefly and then returning her attention to the page below.

Twenty minutes flew by, giving us ten minutes to clean up so as to not leave a mess for the next group of campers to come in. As we cleaned, Vivian gave us one key chain each. Vivian gathered the pages, not bothering to flick through them, and ordered me to pin them up on the empty bulletin board to show off our artwork for the week. It was like I was four years old and buzzing with energy, wanting to show off the work I did that day to my mom and dad.

Gwen's depiction of me was scarily accurate. The picture was a true reflection of my face, somewhat-healing black eye and all. I put Gwen's drawing first because it was the best of the bunch. I pinned the rest up on the board, subjectively choosing the order. When I got to the last page, it was as though I swallowed a fire pill and forgot to drink something cool because the inside of my stomach raged and sizzled. The word *LOSER* was stabbed into the page, drawn harshly with deep indents. It was the title of the piece, which showed one girl drawing another one who was covered in green and had black hair that was rattlesnakes, *Gwen* hastily scribbled beside her.

Holding the page behind my back, I turned around and snagged a pen from a cup on the table behind me, watching as Lauren made funny faces behind Gwen's back. The artwork was supposed to be anonymous, but it was clear as day who had drawn the picture. I sheltered the page from view with my back as I crossed out Gwen's name and replaced it with another in massive writing so it couldn't easily be crossed out.

"What are you doing?" Vivian asked, making me jump and shift guiltily.

"Nothing. Did you know that your sister is insanely good at drawing?"

"Show me what's behind your back."

"The last artwork to put up." I stabbed the pins quickly into the page against the board, but before I could swan off back to my section of the table, Vivian blocked my way.

"That's . . . interesting," she said slowly. "Which one is yours?"

"If I wanted anyone to know I would have put my name on it."

Vivian casually pointed to the second picture on the board. "*Bob's Burgers*–styled Gwen isn't yours?"

She'd caught me. "It's pretty rad, right?"

Vivian ignored me and turned her attention to the last page that I'd put up. At first, she didn't seem to know what to do but she narrowed her eyes and took a closer look at the page. She got another pin, jammed it into the center of the page, and left me to my own devices. For good measure, I stuck another pin into Lauren's picture and then helped Gwen tidy our station, mentally preparing myself for my upcoming punishment as Marissa left the arts and crafts building to tell Mr. Black that I was now assigned to kitchen duty.

SIX

Mr. Black signed off on my punishment, which saved me from participating in half of the activity where Vivian had us play soccer down at the exercise court. Being sent to the kitchen was more of a blessing than a curse. I spent from four thirty to five thirty transporting the already-cooked food from the kitchen to the service area in the canteen behind the glass barrier. While the other cook cleaned up in the kitchen, Mrs. Black and I prepared the service station, making sure that we had all the utensils we needed to serve the campers and the appropriate menu on the blackboard behind our heads. I wore one of those nets on my head to prevent my hair from going into the food. A fish, caught in a net, helplessly wiggling until death—the perfect symbol of my time at camp.

The food was divine, and that was the smell alone. Every time my hand reached out to taste something, Mrs. Black pulled it away, looking especially pleased when I complained about my mouth salivating too much to control. When the last of the food was put into the containers behind the glass barriers, ready to be scooped onto plates to serve, the campers came barging into the room, eyes crazed with hunger.

"See, Mrs. Black, the smell alone is driving them insane."

"I'm beginning to wonder if you got yourself placed here on purpose," she teased, placing a set of keys to the canteen and to the kitchen into my hand. "I trust you with those keys. I'll need you to come in some mornings to set up for the day. But I'll always let you know."

I picked up a soup spoon and pointed it at her. "No more chaos will follow me around. I'll keep them guarded. Seriously, how do I get placed here again after my two weeks are up? Another warning? I don't think I can afford a third."

Mrs. Black gaped at me. "You have a second?"

"Unless Marissa paired the food and lateness together into one warning?"

"It's been less than two weeks, Emma," she scolded, genuinely put out. "How, dear? Just . . . how? I'm more than willing to have you in here with me. You only need to ask, Emma."

Each of her children could be found within her features. She shared their brown eyes, except hers shone with motherly care. She had Walter's slightly curled hair, Gwen's high cheekbones, and Vivian's dimpled smile. I tapped my finger against the wooden spoon as I thought about my own parents. I got my height from Mom, standing at a whopping five-two. My blue eyes were different from Mom's green eyes and Dad's brown. My hair changed with the seasons, with golden brown hues in the summer, and growing darker in the winter.

Mrs. Black handed me a plastic container with a sample of the trifle dessert made for the staff. The campers were left with healthy options, like apples and bananas. The taste of the jelly, custard, and cream together? Nothing could beat it. It was what I always imagined a mom's cooking would be like. The spoonful in the little plastic container was gone in seconds. I threw the black container into the trash can to my left and prepared to serve people their food.

Mrs. Black and I stood behind the hot glass barrier and made sure that the GLASS IS HOT—DO NOT TOUCH sign was up because campers had an awful habit of pressing their palms against the barrier, either jabbing their fingers in the direction of the food they wanted or leaning against the glass.

The canteen was large, and the equally large windows didn't shut out the sun, making the already hot working environment that much worse. Standing beside Mrs. Black and being introduced to the ways of the kitchen from cooking to service made up for that by a mile.

Round canteen tables, fit to hold a handful of campers each, were spread across the room. Behind the service area, and through to the kitchen, was another door to the staff dining area, which was only for the cooks and senior staff. Then back in the canteen, there were the counselors' tables at the far left of the hall, where they had distance from their camper groups but were available if the campers needed to chat with them. Most of the time the counselors were left alone.

A collective sigh of relief coursed through the campers as the counselors barged into the room. One shoved past the campers and lumbered up to the counter. Walter's gaping mouth made it seem like the food was worthy of the gods.

"Mom, I need everything," he begged, putting puppy dog eyes into full effect.

"Tell Emma what you want, Walter," she said.

"I know you," he said. "You got a walloping on the dodgeball court. That's sore looking."

"You want this Vileplume Pokémon–looking thing?" I motioned toward a few mushrooms.

His eyes sparkled. "I dibs this camper. I dibs you. You're mine. Okay? Mine."

"Gay," I said, thumbing toward myself.

"Dibs in a you're-my-favorite-camper-this-year kind of way," he corrected.

"You can't call dibs on campers, Walter," Vivian said, roughly knocking his tray to the side. "The same as him but significantly less."

Walter nudged his sister. "She's a Pokémon fanatic. Guess what I brought with me today?"

"No, Walter." Vivian let out a tired sigh.

"Yes, Walter. You, the camper who I have dibs on, you're sitting with my pack of Pokémon cards and me. Mom, Mom, Mom, can she? Yeah? Forget Gwen—you're my new best friend. I'm way cooler."

"How old are you exactly?" I asked.

"Twenty . . ."

"Huh."

Mrs. Black inclined her head, quietly telling them to get out of the line. The siblings awkwardly stood off to the side as I piled more food onto plates.

"Emma, my children seem to be fond of you, so no more getting into trouble." She studied me, then smiled warmly. "Go."

Walter cheered and high-fived me. I never admitted it, but it stung badly.

Nothing could disperse the mood I was in. I had great grub and I got to inflict annoyance on my counselor by having a passionate Pokémon tournament with her much larger, almost giantlike brother. If she continued to ruin my chances of getting kicked out, it was only fair that I spend my time at camp around her being annoying.

Walter was as giddy as me. He rambled about how he never had anyone to play with because his family was a bunch of grumps. Gwen was the exception, but she was a camper, so she didn't count.

He placed the cards on the table.

"According to the counselor rule book, fraternization with the campers is grounds for dismissal," Vivian said conversationally.

"We're playing Pokémon," I argued on behalf of her brother.

"I'm only stating the rules," she said. "Go find another table to sit at."

"Don't go, Emma." Walter turned to his sister. "Define fraternization," Walter said, sticking his tongue out in concentration.

Vivian typed the word into her phone, and while it made sense that a worker shouldn't be restricted from their phone during lunch breaks, it rubbed salt in the wound. "'To associate on friendly terms with an enemy or opposing group, often in violation of discipline or orders.'"

"Well, by that definition, we aren't breaking any rules," I interrupted, thinking. "We'll stick with the other. To associate with others in a brotherly or congenial way."

"Personally, I prefer Emma's definition," Walter said.

"It's the dictionary's definition. I'm only the humble supplier of that information."

Vivian's glare burned into my cheek. "How do you know that?"

"I honestly don't know. Awfully convenient, though."

Walter playfully pretended to shoot a gun. "Yes, Em, here's to platonic friendship and keeping to the rules!"

"To congeniality!" I said, shooting my finger back at him.

We must have sat there for half an hour, awkwardly stuffing food into our mouths as we played. We tossed playful threats back and forth, garnering ourselves an audience. The pressure was on. There was no way I could lose in front of my fellow campers, not when I had been humiliated already with the warning in the arts and crafts activity.

There was only one prize card left for me to get. The end loomed and sweat formed across Walter's forehead. The tense atmosphere was bulldozed when cold arms wrapped around my body and a chin rested against my shoulder.

"Your friends aren't pleased with you," Gwen sang, squeezing me tight.

"The Beavers? Why?"

She gave me another squeeze and sat down beside me. "You ditched them."

"I'm avoiding Lauren. Is there a way I can change cabins?" I said, putting my cards down.

"Not unless there's bullying involved," Walter said.

It was like his voice blared throughout the canteen, daring the campers to react to his words and to rebel. One second, I was scooping custard into my mouth, and the next, something orange blurred across my sight. Instinct took over, and the spoon that was supposed to go inside my mouth whipped out, forcing a yellow chunk to splat against Vivian's cheek while simultaneously deflecting an orange from hitting Gwen's head. Then, the dreaded words came.

"Food fight!" cried a cracked voice.

And thus, chaos ensued.

Walter flipped the table over, Pokémon cards flying everywhere.

"Aw, man." He scooped the available cards up and slipped them up his sleeve for safekeeping.

"I know that I'm going to be blamed for this," I whispered to myself.

"Probably," Vivian conceded, smashing jelly right into my face.

"Why? God, why?" I cried out, licking my lips.

"I was the first victim in this mess," she hissed, glancing over the table and quickly sinking back down as grapes flew over our heads. "To not retaliate? That's a weakness."

Holding a tray in front of my face, wincing as food smashed into it, I turned my head to the side and was met with a yellow-cheeked Vivian, doing the same. And to think as a temporary cook and server that I could've sat in the isolated lunchroom with Mrs. Black and avoided this entire mess. We were at war. The Blacks and I were squished beneath a table, holding trays like shields, feeling the vibrations running up and down our backs as the table was hit with a magnitude of food.

I thumbed at the mess that was me. "What happened to turning the other cheek?"

"This," she said, pointing at her cheek.

I wiped a finger down her cheek and licked it, ignoring her wide stare and humming in appreciation. "Your mom makes the best trifle."

Walter shifted the table. "Dude, I know."

"Do you think your mom will share her recipe?"

"Sure! She's always wanted a protégé."

"I'll send in an application for that position." Vivian was too quiet. "If I'm not stepping on anyone's toes?"

"No, you're not," she muttered, shaking herself out of her daze.

It came to the point that I was worried that the table would crack under the strain the constant lashing of food caused. I crawled forward with one hand, the other still holding up the tray, trying my best to cover my face, because it'd hurt like a bitch if anything splattered against my still-bruised cheek.

When I finally managed to stand, a hand dotted with crescent moons on the nails gripped my available wrist and used my weight to pull themselves up. There was a calculated expression on Vivian's custard-covered face as she scanned the area like she had all the time in the world and wasn't in the center of a war zone.

"Let's get one thing clear," she murmured, tugging me along and stepping over several banana peels.

"Maybe we can leave the heart to heart until we're outside," I suggested.

"No."

"Okay, rant to your heart's content," I said.

"Stop mentioning my heart."

"Is yours beating wildly too? Mine's going to combust at this rate. Is it preparing me for exercise? I don't do that. It knows that."

"What did I say?" she asked, irritated.

"Stop mentioning your heart."

"Hearts. Stop mentioning hearts." She tugged at me harder.

I readied my tray for impact. "Okay. I think you've gone off track. What was it that you wanted to say? Rambling isn't something you do."

"The singular, and only, reason I'm helping you is because of your track record for causing destruction—be it to yourself or your surroundings. No excuses for getting kicked out."

"That's sweet of you."

"It's like disarming a bomb."

"Exhilarating? Highly heroic? Memorable?"

She shoved through the canteen door with her shoulder and immediately dropped my wrist. "A necessary, doomed, and reluctant act for the many."

That answer was so Vivian.

Peeking back through the crack of the door, I saw Gwen on top of Walter's back, arms and legs wrapped tightly around his body. The guy's face looked a little purple, probably from oxygen deprivation. His chunky arms blocked all impacts, leaving him looking like a rainbow, whereas Gwen was as clean as a whistle. They weren't going to want to escape any time soon.

Once the door shut, the noise suddenly stopped, leaving an unnerving silence outside. It was a relief to not be in the war zone, but now we were *outside*. I wanted to spend my lunch cooped up inside to relax for a while without the dreaded goose bumps or the strain at the back of my head from being alert at all times.

"Shouldn't you be . . ." I looked at the canteen door, then back at Vivian. I scrambled to keep up, walking faster than I was used to. "Stopping the food fight? Or battling through it with your brother or something?"

She kept walking, not fazed as I caught up. "No. I rescued a vulnerable camper. That's enough."

"*Pfft*, rescued? You're making me out to be a damsel in distress." When she turned to me, smirking, I waved my hands in her direction.

"Hello? I saved your sister from being knocked out by an orange. I got this whole escape thing kick started."

"Yet you didn't follow through."

"What happened to not fraternizing with campers?"

Now that made her speed up. "I can't be blamed if one chooses to follow me."

I slowed down until I came to a stop. "Okay. Point taken. Message loud and clear. Sirens are blaring."

The keys to the kitchen were still in my pocket. I figured that I could do something to help reign the food fight in, especially before Mrs. Black finished her lunch and came out to see her canteen in ruins. I turned to walk back. The more steps I took, the more it felt like a return to war. I plucked one of the two trays left on the ground outside the canteen as a hand grabbed the collar of my shirt and dragged me backward.

"What? I'm going to help—you can't *drag* me away."

"Would you look at that? I am."

"Why do you care that I'm out here and not in there?" I asked, scuffing my feet into the ground to slow down her progress, but she was strong and kept pushing forward.

"Because I owe you one," she said. "Did you see who started the food fight?"

"No." Only the orange blur came to mind. Anyone could have thrown it. "Why is that important? It's not a big deal, right? Food fights are expected when you group a whole bunch of teenagers in the same room with nothing better to do. They didn't have the entertainment that was Pokémon."

Vivian finally stopped walking. "Look, I was here as a camper and not a counselor last year. Someone decided it would be a great idea to ask me out in front of everyone."

"Oh, being asked out publicly is the *worst*."

"Exactly. With the swift rejection, a food fight broke out and three campers were given warnings. None of whom started the fight."

I was overcome with a memory of Mike and I standing at the side of the lake, watching as Vivian and Lauren demonstrated how the logrolling session would work. *She also got rejected last year by Vivian. She cried. There were multiple breakdowns, but* . . . Mike's voice carried into the wind.

As far as I knew, Lauren had never been kicked out of camp. If I had to guess based on Mike's gossip, Vivian was referring to rejecting Lauren. Going by how Lauren operated, she could have been the one who started the food fight last year in retaliation for the humiliating rejection. How did that scenario relate to this one? Going by Vivian's wringing hands, the topic made her uncomfortable.

"I've done you no favors, Vivian. I've made your job hard, which would be a hell of a lot easier if you let me escape camp, by the way."

"Like you said, you stopped that orange from hitting my sister."

"And how did getting me out of there benefit me exactly?" I asked.

"How can you be blamed for a food fight when you have an alibi outside of the canteen? There will be an investigation. Mark my words."

I tried to piece together the information I had. "This might have been a form of gratitude in a way, but you did it so that I wouldn't be kicked out of camp. Vivian, you are so damn confusing. Conniving? Evil. Why do you want to keep me here so badly? You're willing to cover for me? Even for something you and I both know I didn't do in the first place? That day, in the shed, was the threat to your authority so ego bruising that you have this vendetta against me? I'm impressed. You're an evil genius in the making."

"One would typically consider ensuring your stay at camp a favor. It's not my fault if you're outside that 'typical' range."

"I am out here." And was totally unsure if I appreciated being dragged out of the canteen. "But why aren't you back in there, Vivian?"

"I'm dirty enough as it is. Now, if it's all right with you, I'm going to go and shower. I'd advise you to do the same."

"Why would I be singled out and blamed?"

"You, Emma Lane," she said, fixing the collar of my T-shirt, "where you go, trouble follows."

Vivian walked in the direction of her cabin, leaving me to decide where I wanted to go—back into the war zone or to my peaceful and deserted cabin. The keys to the canteen rattled back and forth, springing Mrs. Black's hopeful face to the forefront of my thoughts. Could I disappoint her so quickly after she trusted me? Did I want to? The answer came not from my head but from my stiff limbs. Besides, taking responsibility for something that I didn't do didn't sit well with me.

The stickiness and scent of apple juice covering my body made the decision easier for me. I went back to the cabin and hopped in the shower, taking my time because it was rare that my cabinmates weren't on the other side of the door urging me to hurry up. Steam filled the cabin, soothing the rigidness of my shoulders and creating a foggy illusion of being back home. I traced along my collarbone, where Vivian's fingers had touched. The tingling sensation and warmth radiated through my entire body.

Vivian allowed the choice of getting kicked out on my own merits; whether that was her intention or not, it didn't matter. It would be more satisfying this way, seeing her face, as I did, as something so undeniably worthy of being expelled for that she had no choice but to kick me out.

I owed her one.

SEVEN

Throughout the next three days, campers and counselors alike were called into Mr. Black's office to give their accounts of the food fight, like it was an official investigation. All of the gossip at mealtime was about who was going to get caught and what kind of punishment they'd get. I overheard Mike saying that the last time a food fight of this magnitude happened at camp, those campers were expelled for life; that their kids' kids' kids wouldn't even be allowed at Mapplewood. That couldn't be true over a stupid food fight? Vivian said they'd only gotten warnings. It sounded like the perfect way to be kicked out of camp, but the only thing that went against me was the witnesses, and if they'd seen the camper who was actually responsible, I would be discredited immediately.

Mr. Black wanted to figure out who caused the mess without derailing the day-to-day activities for the rest of the camp, so we continued our schedules as normal, waiting for our time to be interviewed by him, which meant I was now stuck doing Beaver activities with Vivian and the rest of my group.

Looking up at the twenty-foot climbing wall made acid crawl up the back of my throat. If I knew we were going to do rock climbing today, I would've taken my meds. Ever since that day when I was stuck up in that tree, if I did as little as step onto a chair, I was frozen in fright. An overwhelming sensation of cold liquid spread across my chest at a rate that worried me. The wood on the exterior of the climbing wall was worn down, almost rotten, like a core of an apple after only one chomp had been taken—brown, bruised, but still standing. Alarm bells rang in my head, urging my feet to take several steps back from the daunting activity.

I bumped into someone as I backtracked from the wall and heard an oh-so-familiar scoff. A grimace made its way onto my face, as I expected hell to be unleashed upon me. "Oh, damn," I muttered, already knowing who it was by their scent alone. "Sorry, didn't see you there."

"It would help if you walked forward, not backward. Even in the easiest of things, you're incompetent." As I stared up at the climbing wall, a video played in my mind, revealing what would happen if my body was forced to climb it—cue screaming like a banshee and a possibility of crying. Vivian narrowed her eyes at my sudden movement and dragged her gaze from me to the wall, and back to me again. "You desperately hate anything that involves movement, don't you?"

"If I say yes, will you not make me do it?"

"Everyone has to do it."

"Then why point it out in the first place?"

"When you squirm with discomfort, it adds a certain joy to my day."

Vivian was clearly determined to show me all the horrible aspects of the camp in the first few successive weeks.

Sure, we might've been outdoors, but this particular climbing exercise was a single pitch route. We were safeguarded by a rope that was clamped at the top of the wall and helped from the ground by one person applying tension to the rope to reduce the distance to the ground. We were to climb the route with the rope connected to our harness, allowing us to kick off against the wall and drop as the belayer withdrew the tension.

We picked one person to race against and one person to be our personal support from the ground. I wanted to race with Gwen, but she needed a suitable rival to exert her monkey-like nature up the wall, and that person definitely wasn't me. Mike took up the challenge. Her face was a picture of exhilaration as she sped up the wall. She trusted me to get her to the ground safely under Vivian's supervision and help. When it was my turn to go up, I found myself procrastinating by slowly putting on the harness, hoping time would run out before I had to climb the mountain that was the wall. The only Beaver left to race against was Jessie.

"Hey, Emma." Jessie sauntered up to me. "You're looking a little pale. Maybe you should sit this one out. I know how heights scare you."

"How do you know about that?"

"You look exactly like you did on the day when you were dared to go over the wall to get the ball. It's not like our harnesses will be connected or anything. You can take your time. And don't forget about how often you went into detail in your letters about how much staircases freak you out."

"I'm fine."

"Sure, you are," she said. "Have you been called into Mr. Black's office yet?"

"No, why?" I asked suspiciously.

She kept her attention on the ground. "What are you going to say when you go in?"

"The truth." The second to last pair of campers started climbing the rock wall, making me grimace. "The whole truth and nothing but the truth."

"And what truth is that exactly?"

"Oh, I see now." I laughed. "Seriously?"

"What?" Jessie's eyes opened wide and she tried to look innocent.

"You guys started it. *You guys started it?*"

"No," she denied. "No, why—what? No?"

"Lauren threw that orange at Gwen," I stated confidently.

"How did you know?" She panicked. "Emma, you can't tell Mr. Black! He'll make Lauren leave camp. After last year, he said there would be severe consequences if a food fight happened again. We might get disciplinary warnings. You don't want that, do you? The Beavers disbanded like that?"

"Thanks for the confirmation, Jess. Really appreciate this talk."

Looping my fingers underneath the harness, I waddled away from her and her gaping mouth.

What started out as a hellish camp with my childhood best friend turned out to be a hellish camp being tormented by her friend and my ex-pal watching from the sidelines.

I pondered what to do with the information. Revealing the food fight culprit had all the positives, maybe including forcing Lauren to leave Gwen the hell alone. Ridding the camp of Lauren solved a lot of problems. Vivian watched patiently as Abby and Bennie jumped off the last hold and unbuckled the harnesses from their clips.

"Next," she said.

Jessie bypassed me and started to clip on her harness. "Come on, Emma. You're my partner. Everyone else has already raced."

"Why would I want to associate myself with a bully sympathizer?"

"I'm not a bully sympathizer," she said.

"What would you consider yourself, then?"

"Not a bully sympathizer, that's for sure," she huffed.

"You should probably act differently than one then."

I reluctantly stood beside the wall, and silently protested the activity by refusing to connect the clip to the harness. Although, when I didn't get dressed for school, Dad still forced me onto the bus in my pajamas. The same determined glint was in Vivian's eyes, and so I slowly backed away from the wall.

Vivian ended up in front of me, doing the harness up herself. "Can't we be civilized people and talk about this?" I said.

"You're climbing the wall, Emma."

"That may be civilized but . . . but it's not polite."

My foot only obeyed my mind when I met Jessie's eyes, which looked at me with anger and pity. I wasn't about to confront those emotions, and the quickest way to escape her was by climbing as high as I could. That proved to be impossible as the farther I climbed, the more strain was put on my body.

"Slow down, Emma, you'll make yourself sick," Jessie warned, breathing heavily.

"If I slow down, I'll throw up, and you'll be the target if it happens."

"Don't vomit on your opponent," Vivian demanded, sounding disgusted by the very thought. "That would be worth a formal warning, and you don't have one of those left to spare, Emma."

"Projectile vomit isn't exactly a choice."

"Please don't throw up on me," Jessie pleaded.

"It's not my fault if the reaction to a real phobia is vomit," I said.

Jessie gagged. In my haste to get away from her, I had climbed higher than I anticipated. At first, the vomiting talk was just that, talk, a joke. It felt like my eyes were spinning uncontrollably. Climbing that high *was* an accomplishment. I knew that in the back of my mind; having made it up this far was nothing short of a miracle. But everything after that, the lack of successful breathing, and the way the earth spun, tarnished the minor minute of victory beyond belief.

It didn't help to know that there were people waiting for me to complete the task so we could leave and go eat lunch. Basically, the entire group was on the ground, watching my every move. Their whispers grew louder and louder, like I was stuck in a cave with echoes bouncing from wall to wall, and my chest grew heavy, each heartbeat thumping harder until it was the only thing I could hear.

"You can do it, Emma. Nice deep breaths," Gwen called out soothingly. "I'm here. You can trust me to get you down safely."

Mike bumped shoulders with her, already belaying Jessie down from the wall. "Totally, you've done the hardest part."

Gwen nodded. "Now to get back down."

"I quite like it up here," I claimed.

"The view must be spec-tac-u-lar," Vivian drawled. "I suppose if you cannot do this, I can send someone up to get you. It appears you don't have the skill set to accomplish this simple task."

"What . . ." Rage boiled my blood. "Skill set? I'll show you skill set. Who even says skill set outside of business meetings?"

Without being conscious of what my body was doing, I hopped like a pro from foothold to foothold and landed easily on my feet. Perhaps the landing was a little awkward. Perhaps there was a sting in my ankle, but I made sure it didn't show on my face.

I unhooked myself and limped away. "Stupid skill set. Stupid wall. Stupid . . ."

A hand was on my arm right as I dry heaved. It was Vivian. Probably the only person I didn't want to witness the aftermath of my momentary bravery. "Emma, you look worse for wear."

I choked back another heave. "I'm . . . go . . . now."

"Are you okay?"

"Super-duper!"

I ran off and vomited in the bush. But I'd done it. I'd made it to the ground. Even if Vivian did follow me and shudder in horror as I spewed my guts out. Out of nowhere, Vivian offered me a handkerchief, slipping it out of the inside of her counselor jacket, and rubbed my back as I drew in deep, long breaths while dabbing my mouth. All I could think about while I practiced one breathing exercise suggested by my old therapist was Vivian, and her weird and old-fashioned ways. She was a girl born in the wrong era, with her fancy words and her on-call handkerchiefs.

I was glad that I didn't skip coming to the activity after all, because I got confirmation from Jessie that it was Lauren who started the food fight. Even if Lauren wasn't the one who stole my phone, she *was* the girl who threw that damn orange at Gwen's head, who made fun of her behind her back, and who drew crappy pictures of her, making fun of her hair. Now I had ammunition to get her punished, even if she wasn't kicked out of camp. It was something, at least.

✦

When Vivian directed me to the office after the whole vomiting fiasco, her face was carefully blank, like a perfectly structured mask; it was too smooth to penetrate, and that's why I didn't pester her with questions about how Mr. Black conducted the interviews and whether or not she was still on my side that I hadn't started the food fight. It was a waste of time to attempt to pry the armor off when she wore it so well.

We entered the room, the only light being the fading sunlight slipping through the cracks of the blinds. Compared to the nurse's room, the director's office was much frostier. His office desk was black and sleek, and the surface reflected the hard gaze of Mr. Black's disapproving stare. The distant look in his eyes reminded me of Vivian's. Lauren sat slumped in one of the two chairs opposite his desk. Vivian hung by the entrance, obviously as curious as me as to why both Lauren and I needed to be in the office at the same time when every other interview had been conducted separately.

Instead of leaving, Vivian sat down on the couch at the back of the room. "I'd like to witness the talk, to add my own perspective. If that's all right with you?"

"That might be helpful, yes." Mr. Black tapped a pen against a notepad, the page full of notes. "What to do, what to do," he mumbled under his breath.

"Mr. Black, why are we here? Why am I still here? I already told you that I didn't have anything to do with the food fight," Lauren said.

"You're here, Miss Peterson, because according to campers' and counselors' eyewitness accounts, you two create a tense atmosphere among your peers. That is exactly the opposite of what we're trying to accomplish here at Camp Mapplewood."

"I haven't done any—" Lauren started.

"Respectfully," I interjected, "I disagree. She started the food fight. Lauren threw the orange at Gwen." I continued, keeping my tone level, "You know you did. Don't embarrass yourself by denying it."

"You're the one whose covering for yourself. Think about it. I'm not the one on their second warning." She turned imploringly to Mr. Black, a sickly sweet smile on her face. "Emma's saving face. That's all. Putting the blame on someone she dislikes."

"I was too busy winning Pokémon to focus on food. Or rather, the throwing of food." Like a balloon at the end of its air, my shoulders sagged. "Look, sir, taking accountability for something that I did do and being kicked out for it? I'm down for that. This mess? Sorry, no, I'm not going to be a pushover. It wasn't me. Bring in Jessie Anderson. She confirmed right before I came in here that it was Lauren."

"Emma's telling the truth," Vivian said. "She was too consumed by Pokémon to have even thought to have started the food fight. You truly do eat like a bear."

"I do not," I argued, facing her fully.

There was a stern clearing of the throat, breaking us out of our little spat. Mr. Black wore reading glasses and used a finger to skim down through his notes. He nodded to himself a few times as if reaffirming what thoughts he had. He clicked his tongue and motioned Vivian to the table. She stood behind her father, a hand on the computer chair, reading the same documents.

"These are the accounts of what happened? Some . . ." she said, pausing, ". . . some are complete fabrications. The tension is there between Lauren and Emma. That I can confirm. One thing for certain is that Emma didn't start the food fight."

"How can you be so certain?" he asked.

"Unfortunately, I sat next to them as she and Walter played Pokémon."

Before Mr. Black could respond, Walter opened the door to the office. It slammed against a cabinet full of wine, forcing a shelf to open and allowing papers to escape from the very top, making a whirlwind of temporary chaos. The gentle giant didn't appear fazed at the destruction he caused. He lumbered toward his stunned father before slamming his hands passionately against the table.

"Emma's innocent! We played Pokémon," he shouted.

"There was mention of Pokémon." Mr. Black inclined his head.

"Before you ask, no, we're not bumping uglies." His eyes turned stricken at the hardening of his father's eyes.

"No fornication," I agreed, scrunching up my nose.

"Nope, none of that too."

His dad said, "Walter . . ."

"Mom gave us permission to play Pokémon," Walter whined.

"Your mother?"

Vivian looked out the window and grumbled, "Unfortunately, yes."

By this point, Mr. Black looked like a lovesick fool. Someone like Julie, with a genuine, kind soul, deserved that epic love. It was profound to see, especially since my parents didn't share that kind of understanding or spiritual connection.

"Action needs to be taken both for Lauren's role in the food fight and your animosity toward one another, especially when you turn against each other in team activities. What was it? Dodgeball? It needs to be put to a stop. Why not deal with the both of you in one go? This conflict needs to be solved, and what's better than isolation?"

"Kicking her out?" I offered.

"No, Dad," Vivian hissed, snapping her head in his direction. "That's not punishing them, that's punishing *me*."

"You'll be taken into the woods for a one-night camping trip. Only the three of you. If a solution to your antics doesn't arise, then you'll spend another night. And again, if it's not sorted, and so on."

My eyes began to sting because, yes, fright consumed me. My breathing became deeper and quicker, but it wasn't enough. I couldn't breathe enough to sate my lungs.

"Are you okay?" Vivian's muffled voice asked.

"Fine," I stressed, clambering out of my seat.

Walter's big hand landed on my shoulder. "You look pale. Maybe you should sit down?"

"No, I'm fine. I'm . . . I've got to go . . . now."

Wildly, I grabbed the handle of the door and swung it open. Before I walked a yard, Mr. Black said, "Follow her. Make sure she's okay."

The wood of the cabins, sticks in the fire, and the bark of the trees surrounding the premises was all around me. Leaves jostled in time with the wind and the sun burned a deep amber. I could only think of one place where everything wasn't so open—the shed. All I knew for sure was that a ball lodged itself at the back of my throat, and my tongue was useless and felt like it would be sucked down my throat, creating an image of me choking to death. I repeated my earlier actions, hairpin, unlock, storage shed door open, and finally I was safe inside its metal walls and cold metal floor.

I knew that the upsurge in my heartbeat, the sudden overwhelming sweating, and twitching was a panic attack. I was unable to touch the ground and branches stabbed my lower back, and there was Lauren's uncaring face, leaving me all alone in the dark and rain.

A hand slid against my cheek, cupping it. "Emma, look at me. Come on, look at me."

My wild eyes shot up, meeting ones of molten gold, my thoughts intensifying by the second. "I'm f-fine," I gasped, pulling back.

"You're not," Vivian said sternly. She tilted my chin upward so I faced her again. Nothing was menacing about the way she looked at me. There was only confusion. "You need to breathe, Emma. Look at me."

"I can't."

I brought my hand up to my neck, trying to make the ball smaller by massaging it.

"Your thoughts," she said, softly, "those thoughts running rapidly, they're what-ifs. Possibilities. Uncertainties. What are you certain of?"

"I don't know," I said, swallowing hard, again and again.

"You do," she encouraged.

"Please, just l-leave me alone." I turned my head to the side so maybe she wouldn't see the tears brimming in my eyes.

She took my hand in hers and placed it against her chest. "You're certain that my heart's beating, in case you were wondering. You do have an obsession with my heart, remember? It's there, providing life. Now, what about yours?"

I remained quiet when she pushed my hand back over to my chest. Her hand remained on top of mine.

"It's beating fast but it's regular," she told me.

"Isn't fast irregular?"

"The point remains, you're not dying." She cupped my cheeks again, continuing to breathe in and out, purely for my own benefit. I tried mimicking her. "Good. That's good, Emma."

Vivian changed her position from kneeling in front of me to sitting beside me. She brought my hand between two of hers and continued to take deep breaths, rubbing her thumb across the top of my hand in time with the movement. We sat there in the silent dark except for the air escaping and clawing its way back into our lungs.

I knew three things for sure: One, despite Vivian's frosty exterior, she genuinely did care about the welfare of her campers, which I should have known from the first time she brought me to the nurse's office. Two, even at my most vulnerable moment, I could lock pick like a pro. Three, the nonsense with Lauren needed to end before things escalated beyond food fights.

"How do you feel now?" she asked quietly.

"I'm fine. My throat . . . it's still weird."

"Emma, you've just had a panic attack." Vivian's grip on my hand tightened. "It's not weak to admit that you're anything but fine."

I pulled my hand back. "I should go."

"Does that matter?" She sighed. She scanned the inside of the shed with a casual shrug. "You shouldn't have broken in here. Yet you did. Not once, but twice. You shouldn't have taken your phone. You did. You shouldn't be at camp, but you are."

"What are you getting at?" I asked, feeling uncomfortable.

"Stay and explain why spending time in isolation with Lauren caused that reaction."

"I'm not scared of Lauren," I denied, scoffing.

"Fine," she drawled, still not looking at me. "I accept that answer. So, the question is, what did prompt it?" Vivian waited patiently.

"If I tell you . . . promise you won't laugh?"

"I promise to conceal amusement, yes," she agreed.

"I'm afraid of camping." I paused. "Everything to do with camping."

"You know, that explains a lot."

"It does?"

"Indeed."

"You seem so fearless," I commented.

"At some point, you've got to smile at the shadows, Emma."

"Smile at the shadows," I repeated. "Sounds scary."

"Try it sometime and see."

"I'll let you know how that goes," I promised.

"I'll be there with you, remember?"

"Oh, right, yes. *That's not punishing them, that's punishing me*," I mocked her from earlier in the office. "I'll go and do this isolation thing with you guys, but I can't promise that I won't freak out. It's one thing being in the cabins. It's another to have only the tent between me and the trees."

Vivian patted the side of my knee and stood up. "Now that I'm aware of your issue, I'm sure that if you do have a problem, we can work it out between us."

"I have my anti-anxiety medication back in my cabin. I've been trying to stick to the techniques my therapist gave me because I'm mostly off the meds now, except to relieve some short-term anxiety. The techniques have been mostly working, but I guess being at camp has thrown me for a loop."

"Understandable. Come on, let's drop by your cabin first. You can take your meds to calm down if you need to, then we can go grab something quick to eat and get a campfire going."

I took her hand and let her haul me up, not letting go right away. "Thanks for . . ."

"Anytime," she said, squeezing my hand. "It's tomorrow night's problem."

✦

It had been a long and draining day, what with the climbing wall, being called into Mr. Black's office, and the panic attack. My thoughts raced through my head—endless loops of gruesome deaths in the woods. There would never be a day when I'd feel comfortable sharing those flashing images and worries with anyone. As Vivian promised, we ate our food quickly as most of dinner had been spent in Mr. Black's office and the shed. By the time we went into the canteen, nearing half past seven, it was void of people except for Mrs. Black, who cleaned behind the counters. Vivian didn't leave me to fend for myself but sat with me at the counselors' table and made sure that I ate. Although we didn't speak more about the time we spent in the shed, it was nice to have her there.

Just because I'd taken my medication, it didn't mean that I couldn't also self-soothe by taking control of my breathing. In deep, hold my breath, exhale, and prolong the time to inhale again by a couple of seconds. By repeating this technique during dinner, the stress that lodged itself in my body drained away. I was bigger than this fear. I was bigger than this anxiety. There was a whole other world that didn't involve being overwhelmed.

An hour later, sitting by the roaring fire with Vivian across from me, the embarrassment of *sprinting* out of Mr. Black's office dissipated.

The Beavers sat on logs surrounding the larger-than-life camp-fire, roasting marshmallows. We were so spread apart that the crackling of the fire drowned out everyone's voices except for Gwen's, who sat on the same log as me. The only reason I was there was that the fire pit wasn't on the outskirts of the camp nearest to nature and its dirty elements. It so happened to be set up directly next to the main building. Gwen and I were huddled together for warmth, and there was safety in numbers.

Gwen took the stick from my lap and stabbed a marshmallow onto one end. "I'll roast you one."

"How are you so energetic at this time of night?" I asked.

She leveled the stick over the fire. "Emma, it's barely nine o'clock."

"We've been going nonstop all day," I insisted.

"The more energy you use, the more energy you have. Want to talk about what's making you so grumpy?"

"Nothing's bothering me," I said, the words sounding hollow even to my own ears.

"You're a bad liar." She leveled her own stick above the fire, now holding two with ease. "The good news is, you haven't been kicked out of camp. Selfishly speaking, of course. But you look like a kicked puppy, and that doesn't sit well with me."

I paused, not wanting to offend her. I pulled the stick back from the flames. "Your dad's putting Lauren and me into isolation."

"That explains your face. It also explains why my sister is more grumpy than usual."

"I think she's wary that I'm going to do something stupid."

"Are you?"

"No."

"Maybe you should tell her that?" Gwen suggested innocently.

Gwen took my hesitation as me being clueless about how to eat the marshmallow and forced me to watch as she peeled back the outside and slowly nibbled on the gooey mess underneath. Despite my aversion to junk food, I copied her and hissed in pain—it was much hotter than I expected.

"Can I ask you something, Emma?"

"Shoot," I said, hoping to ease her nerves.

"Do you have any friends?"

I snorted. "Yeah, totally."

"Who?"

"You."

"I don't count," she denied but sounded pleased.

"Of course you do, we're besties now."

"I'm glad." But the timid behavior continued. "You're wonderful. Crabby. But wonderful."

"Thank you?"

"I don't want you to miss out on showing people that."

I shifted so I could face her. "I don't understand, Gwen."

Her marshmallow stick drooped. "You're wonderful, and I don't want to hinder your interactions with others. I do appreciate you and . . ." Was she trying to friend breakup with me?

"Let me make something clear," I said. "I hate people and you're a person I don't hate, and I appreciate you too."

"Do you like me more than my sister?"

The marshmallow goo slithered its way down my lips. My brain jittered to a stop, leaving my lips agape. Gwen couldn't really think that I liked her sister romantically, could she? Did my heart speed up around Vivian? *Sure.* Did I maybe stare too long at her face when we spoke? *Yes.* She had a pleasantly symmetrical face. Did I sometimes want to reach out and hold her hand? *Of course.* Only to look at her phenomenally styled nails. Did all of that mean that I had a crush?

Maybe.

"Emma? What are you doing?" she asked, sounding amused.

"Nothing?"

"Seriously, Em."

My body slid off the log until I was sprawled on the ground, looking up at the sky, where soft oranges and pinks were long gone and we were left with scattered clouds. For a moment, I felt like I was lying in my tiny backyard in Boston. It didn't matter where you were in the world, the sky remained constantly far out of reach and beautiful in its flux of colors and constellations. It was an ever-changing, thick blanket of comfort that felt alive and watchful with the moon and sun taking turns patrolling the earth.

I rolled onto my side and threw my stick into the fire. When I turned around, I was face to face with the girl I wouldn't be able to escape for an entire day. Or two, if we didn't sort our crap out.

"Emma," Lauren said. "I want to apologize and clear the air before tomorrow, so it doesn't get awkward."

"We're already going to be stuck in the woods together for twenty-four hours, talk to me, then."

"I'm being genuine here," she said roughly. "I don't know about you, but I really want to get a job here next summer. That means I need to be impressive, act mature. I'm already on thin ice because of some shit last year. This trip with Vivian—it's embarrassing, okay? I want to impress her, not annoy the shit out of her."

"I thought you said it would be impossible to get the job because of Gwen?"

"I don't want to ruin my chances. Can't you accept my apology and move on?"

I cocked my head to the side. "For appearance's sake?"

"Exactly."

"Nope."

"Emma!" she shouted after me as I jumped to my feet and left the campsite.

"Emma," I mocked under my breath.

While everyone was busy enjoying themselves by the fire, I stormed into the cabin and started flipping mattresses, tearing pillowcases off pillows, and tossing duvets from the two other beds. There was no sign of the device anywhere, and now I had destroyed the room. I set about remaking the beds while doing another quick scan under the mattresses, and the only things I found were a single sock under Lauren's bed and a random hair tie or two near Abby's bottom bunk. My phone could not have disappeared into thin air.

After changing into a baggy T-shirt and random shorts, I climbed up onto my bed and sank into the mattress, not bothering to collect the duvet from the ground because it was boiling in the room, especially after the exertion of cleaning up the mess I'd made.

The door creaked open, and it didn't surprise me one bit who came inside.

"What can I do for you, Miss Black?"

"Don't call me that," Vivian murmured, sitting on Lauren's bed on the other side of the cabin beneath the window, crossing her legs. "Why aren't you outside with everyone else? According to my thirty seconds of extensive research, you shouldn't be left alone to get lost in your thoughts."

"You set that up, so I'd be busy?"

There was a moment of silence. "It was one factor that played into it. Also getting the campers tired so they'll be easier to manage tomorrow while I'm gone." She sneered. "You know what I don't get? You're surrounded by your phobia, but you're attending this camp. Paying for it, even. It doesn't make sense. It's essentially mental torture for you."

I sat up and swung my legs off the side of the bunk. "Do you have a point?"

She tipped her head to the door. "You'll writhe in uncertain thoughts when you could be dancing with the others or eating. Doing something other than self-assigned torture. Come back outside."

When Vivian mentioned dancing, I thought it was an attempt at a joke. But there they were, dancing around the fire like idiots to the music that blasted from Vivian's phone, no coordination or graceful moves. Except for Gwen; she could make eating a messy burger look refined. I didn't have time to escape, because the next thing I knew, Gwen had dragged me into a twirling mess that was both dizzying and exciting. Unfortunately, the spell wore off when people acknowledged my presence, making my movements stiff and awkward. Yeah . . . no more dancing for me.

When I sat down, Vivian joined me. After a moment, I said, "Being a counselor must suck."

"I wouldn't use that word. But I'd rather spend my time doing something else."

"Why don't you?"

At first I thought she wasn't going to answer, but then she said, "I could."

"You want to be here?"

"In a manner of speaking." She tapped her fingers on her leg and looked up at the stars. "I could be working behind a counter, getting paid minimum wage, or I could work for free here, save my parents money, and continue college without disruption. I chose the less complicated solution."

"I'd rather stock shelves than deal with us all day," I commented.

"That thought has entered my mind on more than one occasion."

The pace of the music slowed down to a raspy woman's voice that blended in with the whooshing of the campfire. The smoke that wisped high in the air diluted the usual earthy soil smell of the camp. The soothing fire-song combo made the branches of the trees lashing and crashing against each other sound like the beat of drums. To the rustling of the leaves and the odd camper who snapped a twig under their shoe, it all added to the elemental-styled music that somehow didn't freak me out.

"What do you do at college?"

"Social studies."

"Do you want to become a social worker or something?"

"Yes."

I thought back to earlier, and a measured caution entered my mind. "Vivian, would you do me a small favor?"

She looked cautious. "What's the favor, then?"

I pulled the keys to the kitchen from my pocket and dangled them. "Could you . . ."

"No, I'm not fetching you a bite to eat."

"I was going to ask if you could keep them safe for me? Give them to me when Mrs. Black can't prep in the mornings? Only when I need them."

Vivian studied me for a moment before snatching them out of my hand. "Fine."

"Aren't you going to ask why?"

"I assume you don't trust yourself with them and wish not to disappoint my mother. I'll bite." She placed them in her bag. "Why?"

"My phone was stolen."

She looked away slowly. "What did you just say?"

"My phone was stolen?"

"Are you being serious right now?" I nodded. "That's what you accused me of stealing. Now, I'm going to go ahead and venture a guess that you think Lauren stole it. It's another drama that we'll have to sort out on the isolation trip. That's more work for me. If she didn't steal it, that means another pile of work for me to find the device."

"Or your sister took it."

"Gwen wouldn't do that." Vivian raised the volume of the music on her phone and leaned in close to my face. "She better not come crying to me about you not trusting her because you will have me to deal with. Have you got that, Emma?"

Gwen twirled around like a ballerina while the rest of the Beavers danced together in one big tangled mess of limbs, swaying back and forth in a huddle to the soothing music. Vivian's quick assessment of the situation was nothing short of accurate. There was no way Gwen would lie to me like that.

Eventually, the Beavers got tuckered out from their dancing and Vivian called it a night, sending us off to our cabins, reminding everyone that she would not be available the next day and that after breakfast they should meet Walter and the Jellyfish near the exercise court behind the cabins. That night as I tried to sleep, the crickets chirped and chirped and chirped, and I hoped that it didn't mean that anything remotely similar to the first time I remembered hearing their singing would happen.

EIGHT

The next day started off poorly. My breath came out in quick bursts and my blood pumped abnormally fast through my body. Extra adrenaline ran its course, preparing me for what my body perceived as danger, which started as soon as I thought about venturing outside and into the woods for the isolation camping trip. Before packing my anti-anxiety meds, I took one, greedily gulping back a bottle of water that I was pretty sure belonged to Abby. Even throwing on clothes was a feat—with my jerky movements and spasming fingertips, well, the shoelaces didn't stand a chance. Lauren was subdued, too, the two of us painfully aware that we'd have to spend the next twenty-four hours locked in the death grip that was this punishment.

While I stood outside waiting for Vivian, my necessities slung over my shoulder, the cabin door next to us creaked open and a small fig-ure stepped out. Wild, black hair stuck out in all different directions, and a pair of sleepy eyes bored right into mine.

"You listen here, doofus," Gwen said, rubbing her eyes with a closed fist. "Don't be stupid and fight with her."

"I'm a lover, not a fighter."

"You threw a tray at her head, Em." She wrapped a hand around the cabin handle and said, "Don't take the bait. Give yourself the chance to stay at camp. I'll come after you if you get kicked out."

"My house is free all summer long."

"Quit joking, because that's *not* an option," she mumbled, slamming the cabin door shut behind her.

Maybe I'd find out who stole my phone, put that investigation to rest, and get myself kicked out. Or I could completely overcome all my fears due to constant exposure—that worked for allergies sometimes. There would even be time to reflect on my choices since coming to camp.

The air was cold, the sun not yet having the chance to warm the ground. I would've fetched a hoodie but I didn't want to face anyone that morning unless I absolutely had to. Ever since last night when Lauren tried to fake an apology, we hadn't spoken. I felt sorry for Abby having to put up with our arguments and long, awkward silences. She sometimes intervened when we fought and politely told us to not say anything at all if we had nothing nice to say, or made small talk to replace the heavy atmosphere that came after our arguments.

"How does this forced isolation usually go?" I asked as soon as Lauren stepped outside, curiosity getting the better of me.

"Why are you asking me?"

"You said it yourself, you were on thin ice last year and you're still allowed here. Maybe you're sneakier about it this year? Put the fear of God into your victims to keep them quiet? What is your secret?"

"I don't bully anyone," Lauren scoffed. "Whatever. Vivian's going to make us talk. That's all."

The gravel leading up to our cabin crunched. Lauren straightened up and tilted her chin upward, like we were in a military camp. It reeked of desperation. I adjusted the cap on my head as Vivian strolled toward us with a backpack and one large, black bag, not looking like she was in any hurry to get our camping trip started.

"You're not going to claw each other's eyes out, are you?" she asked, sounding bored.

"No," Lauren said earnestly.

Could she cut the military pose already? "Kill me now."

"That's the opposite of what we want on this isolation trip. One of you, carry that bag for me," Vivian said, dumping a black duffel bag on the ground before walking away. Lauren grabbed the bag from the ground, and like ducklings, we trailed after her. "The isolation camp is on the other side of the property. It'll take about ten minutes to walk over there."

"At least someone doesn't want me dead," I said.

"That can easily change," Vivian said over her shoulder.

"Will it be warm when you rip my heart out of my chest?"

"Don't mistake bloodlust for—"

"The fun kind of lust?" I interrupted Vivian. "What a shame."

"Hurry. Up," she said as she gritted her teeth. "Both of you."

Before we headed into the forest, we grabbed three sleeping bags from the supply room beside Mr. Black's office in the main building. We walked the same route that we took to the logrolling activity. Sitting in that weird log boat with Vivian was a fond memory, as was being able to watch Lauren get thrown off like a rag doll. The path was familiar, so I didn't freak out too much. It helped that I'd taken my meds that morning. It also helped that the sun was rising instead of setting—at least during the day if leaves rustled you could easily see if something was there or not. At night was a whole other story, when the loss of natural light kept me on high alert. Or when things like scurrying raccoons or foxes in search for food under bristles of wispy moss came across as badgers menacingly clawing at the bark of trees.

The trek was mostly quiet. I thought it'd be more awkward than it was, but everyone was lost in their own sleepy thoughts.

A short few minutes later, Vivian kicked a twig, and it sailed through the air snapping in two once it connected with the giant maple tree that could give the perfect coverage for our tents. Its ancient branches stretched away from the rest of the evergreens and looked out of place near the center of the clearing. If that tree could survive for so many years in this clearing, then I could survive a night or two. Twisted logic, maybe, but a thought process that kept me calm.

We entered the perfect camping spot. There was a flat space of ground and shelter from the abundance of leaves above us. The only problem was the whole space was bare—as minimalistic as it could get in terms of camping gear with only two logs that didn't look comfy at all. I made a show of looking around the space, trailing along the circle of the area, kicking the rocks and stepping on the acorns scattered across the ground. Vivian didn't offer any sort of explanation as to why there was no camping gear set up and ready to use. Usually the counselors were pretty good for setting up stuff beforehand for their campers, like the log at the lake or having the art supplies ready at the tables.

"Where are the tents?" I asked.

"You think we have prepitched tents because isolation punishment is such a *common* occurrence?" Vivian countered, placing a hand on the tree and leaning against it. She nodded toward the sleeping bags, the overnight bags, and the duffel bag we'd dumped in the center of the little enclosure. "No, no, Emma. Your tent is in the black duffel bag. You two can start setting it up. And I'd hurry if I were you. The sky's looking a little grey."

"And you? What are you going to do?" I asked.

"Supervise," she answered casually.

I looked to Lauren for some backup, but she had already grabbed the duffel bag and taken out the pieces, laying them out in a line. Kneeling down on the ground despite everything in my body screaming to ignore the order, I tucked in to help. My face scrunched up at the crackling sound that came from my knees pressing against the dry, leaf-carpeted surface. Connecting directly with the earth and especially below a tree line, and I was still breathing fairly normally? The reality of being out here was a much better experience than when I was in the toolshed imagining all the things that could go wrong.

Lauren prodded a rod into my shoulder and said, "How do we do this?"

"Lay the tarp down," I instructed, pushing myself back so instead of kneeling I sat on the ground directly. "The plastic sheet thing," I told her, waving my hand in the direction of the grey-colored piece. "It's to protect the tent from the moisture of the ground so we won't get wet when we sleep. Then put the tent over it."

"Aren't you going to help?"

I leaned back and used my hands behind my back to keep upright and stared up. "Since *someone* forgot to pack instructions, I'll be the brains; you can be the brawn."

There was a small and deliberate cough from Vivian's direction.

"Fine," Lauren agreed.

"That was too easy," I said. Lauren ignored my comment and instead placed rocks at the corners of the tarp to keep it in place. "Like suspiciously easy."

"You look sick. And I can be a decent person," she said.

"Nope. You've got some twisted ulterior motive. If it was someone like Gwen who offered to put up the tent, I wouldn't think twice about the reasons why. But you? There's definitely something going on."

"What next?" Lauren asked.

"Connect the numbered poles." I tossed the first rod in her direction.

She grabbed it midair. "You haven't liked me since day one. Admit it."

Well . . . that was an accurate accusation. While she tended to the poles, I took the tent out of the duffel bag and placed it on the tarp. "Are we actually going to try and sort our problems?"

Lauren said, "Answer me, would you?"

"All right. I didn't like you, Lauren."

"Why not?" she asked, her voice strained. She struggled to compose herself. Her hands gripped the poles and she attempted to piece them together, but every time she tried, she missed. Her fine motor skills simply didn't exist. It reminded me of how I became useless under pressure or stress. Me not liking her actually bothered her.

I took the rod from her grasp and connected two of the poles quickly then laid it across the tent.

"I hold grudges," I admitted. "You left me up in that tree. You never apologized for it either. You've been a bad taste in my mouth ever since."

"God . . . that was *forever* ago, Emma."

"It feels like yesterday. Being here at camp? My body's reliving the experience over and over again. I don't want to talk about that, though." Not with Vivian so close by, and it was embarrassing for me to still be haunted years later by it.

"Isn't that the point of this trip?" she asked.

"There's something more important to talk about. The way you treat Gwen," I eventually answered openly.

"Do you have a crush on her or something?"

"No." I laughed. "She's totally my soul mate, though. My platonic life partner in crime."

"If I liked Gwen from the first day you met me, would you like me?"

"Why is it so important to you that I like you, Lauren?"

"I don't know," Lauren answered. "I don't know why."

Lauren stilled completely at her own words, and it was as if she came to some sudden, world-collapsing realization and proceeded to stare down at her hands. She was obviously having a moment, so I let her be, and set up the rest of the tent.

Without bothering to ask Lauren for help, even though it would've been a hell of a lot easier to coordinate the bending of the poles, I managed to straighten the tent and raised it up, and it resembled a tiny space to sleep in.

"Finito," I announced, spreading my arms wide. Lauren didn't move. "You can set up the next one."

"There's only the one, Emma," Vivian said with a condescending pat on my shoulder.

"Oh, for God's sake," I muttered. "The tent is tiny. All three of us are expected to spend the night in such a cramped space?"

My fingers ran along the entrance of the grey tent until they came to a zipper, which I hastily drew down.

"No," Vivian snapped.

"What?" I stepped inside, bending down so my head didn't touch the mesh flaps.

"You're not going to nap the day away." Fingers gripped the hem of my T-shirt and hauled me back outside. "First rule of isolation—"

"No naps?"

"No naps," Vivian confirmed, instead letting Lauren go into the tent, without so much as a twitch to haul her back out. "Help me collect wood."

"Preferential treatment much?"

"She won't be in there long." She tossed me a backpack. "Expecting different treatment than her co-camper? Unacceptable behavior. There'll be plenty of jobs for her to do today." She wore an evil grin. "At least you listened."

"You dragged me out of there. No warning. Just full on maneuvered my body," I said.

She bent down and studied some sticks on the ground. "But did you go back inside? No. You didn't. You're semitrained. Congratulations. You might be the key to leaving isolation."

"You mean"—I hugged the sticks to my chest—"being the bigger person?"

"Perhaps. The sooner it's done, the sooner we leave and sleep in our own beds. Alone."

I rolled my eyes. "I'd still have to share a cabin with her."

"Sounds like a you problem."

According to Vivian, we needed small sticks because she didn't bring any tinder to easily set aflame. The weather was dry enough to try and build a campfire from scratch. It was the ultimate bonding activity according to her dad. We didn't wander that far away from camp, yet she stayed by my side as we collected light, snappable, dead, and downed wood.

I dumped the wood into a pile a foot away from the tent and our bags, and then Vivian organized it in an orderly fashion. Pretty soon after I sat down, she called me over to help organize the kindling. We gathered a bunch of rocks to circle the pit to keep the area as clean and neat as possible; the stones would hold heat and block out the wind.

As Vivian prepared to light the fire, I propped the last of the wood in a pyramid, allowing the tinder to have air. There was enough space around the campfire that we didn't need to get into each other's personal space, but it worked out that way regardless. Vivian's warmth seeped into my body, and she comforted me without ever opening her mouth. I melted into her like ice cream in a warm porcelain bowl, like I belonged next to her and she belonged next to me. Of course, then she leaned in closer to the pit and started to gently blow where she'd placed the lit match, and a strand of hair fell dangerously close to the pit.

"What are you doing?" she asked me, snapping me out of a haze in which I hadn't noticed that I was in fact holding the lock of hair back and out of the way of the fire.

"Being chivalrous and protecting your luscious hair?"

"Thank you?"

"You're welcome."

"How are you holding up so far?" she asked as the fire successfully caught.

Still kneeling, I held my hands out close to the flames and responded, "So far, so good."

"Let me know if that changes."

Day turned to late afternoon. Surely the campsite, being the size of two camper cabins, was enough room for three people, right? *Wrong.* After Vivian and I set up the fire, she dragged Lauren out of the tent and ordered us to take turns keeping it going, forcing us to remain in close proximity. The awkwardness of sitting next to Lauren was worse than when we argued back and forth. At least when we were in the same cabin as each other we could drift off to sleep. Out here in the open, there was no escape. Not unless Vivian allowed it.

The only thing that made the entire experience endurable was the smell that came from wrapping a piece of bacon around the end of a roasting stick, then slowly rolling it over the hot coals. Mine turned out perfectly crispy and edible, but I had to share with Lauren because she charred hers beyond recognition. All the while, Vivian enjoyed her abundance of bacon strips all by herself.

My panic hadn't reared its ugly head, not like the day before. Dark and ugly clouds loomed above the canopy, waiting to unleash hell as the sun disappeared. There was nothing fascinating about the dark-grey sky with its scattered stars. From beneath the abundance of green, yellow stars banded together, the background of dark blue illuminating them spectacularly.

The loud crack made me jump, especially when I thought a tree had fallen to the ground. Turned out, I was only being paranoid. The boom of thunder made my neck crane to look around the branch of the maple tree above my head; the strikes of lightning that crossed the sky were clear as day.

"It looks like there's a possibility of death tonight," I said. "Look at those clouds. Are they fluffy? Nope. They've been created to suck our souls out of our bodies."

"It's rain," Vivian said dismissively, although she looked skeptically up at the sky.

"Rain meant to *slaughter* us."

A flash of hot white materialized across the girl's face, making it clear how dark it had gotten in the past few minutes. All day the sky had been grey and boring. Her expression was blank, like the sudden gloom and absence of light hadn't affected her in the least.

"Perhaps the conditions are worse than I thought," she admitted.

"We should totally head back, right?"

"No." By the blank expression on her face, I knew there wouldn't be any reasoning with her. "As much as I'd like to put off sharing a space with the bane of my existence," she murmured, walking by me, "it's not possible."

A drop of water splat right into my eye. "You're sharing it with two people. You said bane. Singular."

For a moment she froze. "As much as the hum that is your voice annoys me, you haven't been consistently doing so, year in and out."

"I'm not at the top of your most hated list?"

"Why doesn't it surprise me that you sound proud of that?" she said.

"Because you like me."

"I like that you're helping me set up the sleeping bags." Vivian slowly widened her eyes. "Oh wait. Would you look at that? You're not."

"Right . . . helping."

While we set the bags up properly, Lauren sat outside, staring up at the clouds and about to embrace the rain. There wasn't enough room for her to help and she knew that. I envied her ability to get what she wanted without an ounce of effort.

Vivian's scowl as she motioned for us to get into the tent to brave the storm made it abundantly clear that she despised her life right there and then. A sense of self-loathing suffused my brain as we all attempted to get inside the sleeping bags, knocking elbows and wearing scratch marks when we finally lay down.

The drizzle became harsh and unforgiving, forcing us all to remain in the thinly veiled tent. It was strange, lying within the confines of a sleeping bag and staring up at the grey fabric, hearing the whistle of the wind and the punitive pelt of water against the tent. The weather didn't bother me, not as much as being in the center of two girls: Vivian striving to be as far away as possible, like I harbored a horrible disease, and Lauren, squishing in uncomfortably close.

When a finger tried to loop itself around mine, maybe the hardcore flinch was overly dramatic.

Lauren wasn't asleep? "What the hell?"

"I thought Jess was exaggerating about your antisocial behavior," Lauren harped, glaring, her chin tilted upward.

"I could be the most sociable person to exist and not want to hold hands with you. Wait. Why didn't you fight me for the middle spot? I heard rumors that you liked Vivian."

"I didn't like Vivian," she spat out. "What does that have to do with anything? What is it with you? Were you not loved enough? Is that why you wrote those letters? Can't talk to anyone in real life properly?"

I crossed my arms across my chest so that she couldn't grab at me. "That's what they say about bullies, and that's more your thing than mine. And no, I don't know how you know about those letters, but haven't you ever heard of keeping in contact with people the traditional way?"

"I have friends. We hug and whatever. It's so obvious that you have no friends. You can't even hold a conversation without turning into a raging bitch. No wonder Jessie hates you now."

I shuffled farther into the sleeping bag, the movement painfully loud within the tiny space. Once my chin was burrowed into the top of the material, I stared at nothing—because it was all blurry as an overwhelming discomfort flooded my system.

By this point, the rain had petered to tiny drops, rare to hit against the tent. My body moved without much thought as I stepped outside. Cool air filled my system and it helped, a little. I knew it wasn't the smartest move to be outside when it could potentially rain again, but it was the only thing that relieved my anxiety.

Lauren mentioned my letters.

My letters.

Had she read them? Did Jessie let her read them? They were years' worth of frustrations—my highs and lows and everything in between. They were more akin to a diary than letters. If Lauren had in fact read them, she probably knew me better than Gwen or even my own mother. Why did she want to hold my hand? There was a pattern to Lauren's behavior, and it was disturbing. Vivian rejected her and she targeted Gwen. I rejected her, and she had access to my letters. What would she do with the information? Jessie and Lauren having read them was bad enough, but what if they spread them around camp?

"What do you think you're doing?" Vivian asked, making me glance over my shoulder. "You look worse for wear."

"I needed some air," I explained, and hoped she wouldn't pry.

"What's wrong?"

"Shhhhh." I cocked my head to the side. "Do you hear that? Seriously. Listen."

"F-i-n-e," she dragged out, purposely elongating the word.

We both heard it, unmistakably.

Without much thought, my feet trudged toward the forest line. For the second time that night perhaps there was a lapse in judgment— the first being leaving the tent in the first place. The sound crackled somewhere in the distance, but walking toward it was preferable to sharing a confined space with Lauren.

Instead of walking around in the forest at night, I could've been at home, fast asleep on the couch while Dad watched TV from the armchair. Me revisiting camp and seeing Lauren again, my letters exposed to her, my phone probably stolen by her, it all would never have happened if Mom was a grown up and let me stay with Dad. The resentment was like an adrenaline boost, almost to the point where I ignored Vivian hissing my name as I walked farther into the forest.

Eventually, she caught up and grabbed my hand, keeping me still. "Typically, when you hear a noise in the middle of nowhere, you avoid it at all costs, not chase it like a dim-witted character in a horror movie."

"It's water, right? It's not the lake. It's rushing. It's loud. It's not a river."

"We're close to a waterfall; you are hearing the waterfall," she said. "Although how you heard that over the rain is beyond me. That's not why you left the tent."

"Lauren's attempt to mush our fingers together?" I said. "Like, I do not snuggle. I don't need that in my life. Maybe at a certain point with a certain person, but she's not that person."

"She attempted to snuggle with you?"

"She attempted to snuggle *with me*," I repeated, mimicking her disgusted voice.

She let my hand drop and then turned so suddenly that her hair whipped against my cheek. "Come on, this will be our only night here."

After standing still for a moment, I followed her. "How are you so confident about that?"

"Emma, not all is as it seems."

Vivian went to walk away, but I grabbed her upper arm. "You can't say something that vague and not fill me in."

"Yes, in fact, I can."

She pried my fingers from her arm and moved confidently toward the campsite. The warmth trapped inside swarmed my body almost immediately when I crept back into the nylon tent. My numb fingers somehow managed to zip the tent's fly back up. Trying to be as quiet and small as possible, I was shocked when I turned around to see Vivian snug inside my sleeping bag instead of her own. As much as Lauren could sleep through anything, me raising my voice to get Vivian inside her own sleeping bag was a no-go unless I was willing to put up with more of Lauren's subtle digs about my social capabilities, or lack thereof, and about my letters.

Vivian flicked her eyes to her right, telling me to get inside her bag or else. She placed her hand on the side of my face to keep my head in place after I wiggled in. She didn't say anything or offer any reason why she felt compelled to place her palm against my cheek.

"W-What are you doing?" I dumbly asked, eyes wide.

"Ensuring the sleeping pattern of my camper remains intact," she whispered back just as hotly.

"No offense, but I think my bedding material is more . . . fluffy. Not that yours isn't accommodating. It smells nice. Like roses. Must be the shampoo you use. Damn you counselors and your nice-smelling exteriors." I scrunched up my nose, liking the smell too much. "We get this off-brand, scentless crap."

Vivian flicked my ear, making me hiss. "You're offended by my scent?"

I pinched her hand. "Not offended, per se. It makes me a little angry. Don't scented candles make you angry sometimes? Like, when you smell vanilla, it makes you want to hulk out because it's so damn predictable?"

"The way I smell is predictable and makes you angry?"

"Keep up, I'm talking about candles, not your rose-smelling hair."

"Go to sleep, Emma," she said, closing her eyes.

"I will but . . . I'm not sure if I should say."

She closed her eyes again. "Then don't."

My breathing became shaky, because there she was, lying with her face inches from my own, eyelashes long and thick and dark, tempting the tip of my finger to run through them to see if they felt as soft and silky as they looked. Her lips were pretty in a natural, cupid's bow-kind of way. I reached up and touched her hand on my face to see if I was imagining that it was there and the fluttery sensation in my stomach was for nothing. Finally, glancing back up to take another peek at those eyelashes, she was staring at me. We stared at each other in an odd, silent argument.

A loud and horrid snore came from Lauren, making Vivian close her eyes and vibrate in concealed laughter.

"Vivian . . . I know my cheek is soft, but I don't think it's meant to be a pillow for your hand," I teased because, honestly, my heart pumped irregularly fast around Vivian and it was really unhealthy.

For a moment she said and did nothing. Then, as if she only noticed, she tore her hand away and glared at my cheek as if it was the cause of all the wrongdoings committed against her all her life.

NINE

I woke up alone to the sound of the crackling fire and the low murmur of conversation outside the tent. My stomach grumbled as I shuffled out of Vivian's sleeping bag, and it didn't stop making annoying noises until my head popped out from its slippery fabric. As I pulled down the zipper of the tent to escape the isolation, something caught the corner of my eye. It was the glint of a reflection right behind the top of Lauren's sleeping bag, of something digital, mechanical, and definitely mine.

Shoving the object within the pocket of my hoodie, I emerged from the warm environment to the cold of the morning. My freaking phone! All this time Lauren had my phone. Now that I had it back, there was no point in holding a grudge against Lauren. Especially since we were about to leave the isolation camp. Besides, she didn't have a charger. Surely it had died ages ago. There was no true damage done other than delaying my escape plan.

Placing my hat on top of my head, I walked across our little camp-site toward the other two campers. I asked, "We're not staying here another night, are we? The bedding wasn't up to my standards."

"Emma, allowing you to sleep in my sleeping bag rather than yours was nothing less than a blessing," Vivian responded.

"It did smell like roses," I conceded.

"Your obsession with roses and hearts might for appearance's sake make you look romantic . . ."

"Is that what you think of me?"

"You're nothing more than a hoodlum."

"Are we staying here or not?"

The question made Vivian direct her attention to Lauren, who'd been unusually quiet. She replied, "That's not up to me. Lauren?"

"I don't know . . ." Lauren trailed off. At Vivian's subtle eyebrow raise, she released a defeated sigh. "I guess not. No."

"And why is that?" the counselor prompted, clearly enjoying seeing her squirm.

"Look," Lauren started. "I'm sorry. The reason I've been awful to you is—"

"I know," I interrupted. Well, I didn't know why she was a bully in general exactly, but I knew what she did. She stole my phone.

Vivian asked, turning to me, eyes narrowed in disbelief. "I find that hard to believe."

"You know?" Lauren said, disbelieving me as I nodded.

"Yes. It's not a big deal. Everything is sorted now. I forgive you. So why don't we head back and forget the whole thing?"

Lauren, clearly not understanding, asked, "Forget everything and move on?"

My hat was moving awkwardly with the intensity with which I was nodding. "Yeah."

They seemed to silently agree to move on. We packed up quickly and trekked through the forest until we made it back to the main camping site. It was such a relief to see the cabins again. For some reason, a drop of disappointment ran through my system that I couldn't pinpoint. I'd panicked in the middle of the night, but it had nothing to do with my surroundings. It had more to do with Lauren and feeling vulnerable. My heart rate skyrocketed when Vivian touched me, but that was beside the point. I was still breathing—alive and well after spending an entire night out in the woods. Considering all thoughts prior to isolation were of me heading out of camp in a casket, it was a miracle that the means of my escape—my phone—was there and waiting to be used. Yet there wasn't that rush of accomplishment soaring through my veins.

With everyone wandering the grounds, including staff, it was time to do the thing I had promised myself, and apparently Vivian, since day one. I grabbed the phone from my pocket and started waving it around like a lunatic.

"What the hell do you think you're doing?" Vivian hissed, snatching the phone from my hands. "I thought you lost it?"

"I did." I frowned.

"We were isolated for a day. If you'd found it before, then you would've waved it around. Where was it?"

Lauren was mingling safely out of earshot with the other Beavers. "Under her pillow," I said. "Can I have it back?"

"No," she refused. "Sorry, you've bypassed the deadline to use this as a way of escape. Punctuality is important in all factors of life."

"Deadline? You imposed a secret deadline?"

"Not so secret anymore." She shoved the device down her top with a daring expression. "Going after this thing could be perceived as an assault. Think very carefully."

"I don't get you," I said.

"Good," she said, satisfied.

Watching her stride away from me with the device firmly planted in her bra, I wanted to punch a wall until my fists were bloody and raw. Magically, I'd found the phone without trying and then messed up the plan for when I found it: waving it around someone in charge who *wasn't* Vivian Black. How stupid was I?

Vivian joined the other counselors as they swarmed together outside of the main building, and all camp groups were standing bundled together outside of their respective cabins. As I slumped my way toward the Beavers, Gwen vibrated on the spot, alone. Even without Lauren's constant voice ordering the rest of them around, they followed her orders to ignore Gwen.

Gwen greeted me as though she didn't notice. "You're back!"

"Surprisingly unscathed and not scarred for life."

"You're *actually* smiling," she noted, tilting her head to the side as if it was the most peculiar thing. "You do have a pretty smile."

"It's not that rare of an occurrence, you know. What's been happening in the past twenty-four hours?" I said.

She nudged me. "Apart from Walter begging me to replace you at your Pokémon matches?"

"He has? That traitor," I said, secretly pleased.

"If it's worth anything, I'm an unworthy opponent," Gwen said. "And then nothing else exciting. We're due for a room inspection. Could be dreadful if you have something to hide. You've got T-minus . . . thirty seconds to sort that out. Could be less, because my sister is a fast walker. Look at her go."

Sure enough, when I glanced over my shoulder, all the counselors were making their way over to the cabins. Vivian glided over the pebbles, like the little pesky obstacles weren't a hindrance to her in the least. Especially at that speed, I would have tripped six times.

Taking two quick strides, Gwen stood in front of her own cabin with an expression that made the moment feel as though it were the end of the world. I tried to offer her a reassuring subtle finger wave, because little did she know, Vivian already had my phone.

Our cabin, unlucky number thirteen, was first. It wasn't all that surprising. Vivian didn't consider cabins fourteen or fifteen, and only had eyes for ours as she made her way over.

Vivian placed a hand on my chest and pushed me before I could enter the cabin. "I don't want the space to be overcrowded. Stay out here."

"Yeah, Lane, stay there," Lauren agreed, shoving me out of the way so she stood by the door instead. Vivian turned back around and promptly slammed the door in the girl's face. Lauren turned to me, not looking rejected, but looking almost shy? "Emma, about earlier . . ."

"I thought we agreed to forget about it. All's forgiven." Especially now that Vivian had whisked my phone away from me in a second flat. "It doesn't mean we have to be buddy-buddy, though."

"Maybe," she said, looking almost sincere, "we should?"

"Me and you? Friends?"

Before Lauren could reply, the cabin door swung open and Vivian marched out, holding my phone in her hand. Lauren's eyes nearly popped out of her head when she saw it.

Vivian shoved between us and held the phone out. "Which one of you ladies does this belong to?"

I frowned, wondering what she was getting at—all the while trusting enough to follow her lead and being thankful that my home-screen was text saying "Ahahaha you don't know my password" and that I had locked it down. No one was getting past my numerical code. Who would guess 1234?

"Never seen that thing in my life," I said.

"Lauren, it was found by your bed," Vivian said. "I don't know about you, but I find my father's rules to be fairly easy to follow. It seems you didn't take this warning seriously."

"That's Emma's, not mine," Lauren claimed, turning to face me.

"It looks like mine, but how'd it end up in your bed?" I pointed out. "C'mon, Lauren. Tripping me. Throwing dodgeballs at me. Squirting apple juice at me. Trying to frame me for the food fight . . . now stealing from me? Where does it end? The last time I saw my phone it was being carted away to be locked up in a gloomy, smelly shed or something."

"Come on, Lauren." Vivian shouldered her way through us. "You don't want a public spectacle."

The whispers began immediately, as the camper sulked after the counselor, who looked far more pleased than the situation required. Before I could whack my hand against my face because I had missed my chance to get kicked out, Gwen gripped my wrist and held it to her chest.

"Do you . . . do you think she'll be kicked out?" Gwen asked, squeezing the life out of my hand.

"Probably. Do you think if I run fast enough I'll be able to claim the phone as mine before they reach Mr. Black's office?"

"I think that you'd have a heart attack ten steps into running. Besides," she said and dropped my hand from her chest, "I'd tackle you to the ground. Speaking of violent tendencies . . ." She trailed off and led me inside my cabin to sit with me on top of the bunk bed. The rest of the campers were too busy talking about the public debacle Lauren made to pay attention to where we went. "Something just hit me and I don't think you're going to like it."

"You can say anything to me, you know that, Gwen."

"You know how guys pull on ponytails and treat girls like crap when they like them as kids?"

"Little shits. I'm familiar."

"Well . . . Lauren has been pulling on your ponytail since you came to camp."

Lauren *liked* me? The warm summer air felt like it had turned into an icy wind choking the breath from my lungs and forming a noose around my neck. Gwen's savage, bitter theory blast right to my bones and gripped my brain in its freezing claws. Wiggling my body didn't help shake the idea and sudden coldness from my limbs. Too late. The theory turned to ice and refused to melt.

"You know what, you're right? I didn't like that *at all*."

Gwen fluffed my pillow and snuggled against it. "Do you think I'm actually right, though?"

I thought about it for a moment. "No way. What about you? What if she likes you?"

"Hate to break it to you, Emma, but the way she treats me is way different than how she treats you. I'm someone to ignore, to poke fun of behind my back, someone to be the odd person out so there's a clique inside a very small camper group," she said, and pressed her hand against my mouth so that I wouldn't interrupt. "She's fully confrontational with you. Physical. Almost attention seeking. Don't you think?"

"I don't know . . ."

"Sit with it for a while," she said. "For the record, Emma? I don't ship it."

Neither did I.

✦

Before I knew it, it was dinnertime—that meant dressing up in an apron and a net hat and serving people at the counter again. Unlike the first time, there weren't any nerves because Julie was the nicest person to ever live. Her passion for food rivaled her love for her children, and either way, she was compassionate; the type of person who with her smile alone could make anyone feel at ease. Mrs. Black prepared homemade burgers and fries. The BBQ sauce she made to accompany the food smelled delicious.

"Do you know if Lauren Peterson was kicked out of camp?" I turned around to grab another plate.

"There was no mention of it at the isolation review meeting with Vivian this afternoon," Mrs. Black murmured. "You know, dear, if you have any problems, with her or other campers . . . you know where I am."

As I turned back around again to face another person waiting for their food, there stood Lauren, impatiently tapping her fingers against the counter.

"Hi, Lane." Lauren greeted me, clapping her hands to gain my attention. From the corner of my eye I caught Vivian looking at us.

"What the hell are you still doing here?"

"Let's just say, Vivian and I made a deal," she told me with a wink before sauntering off to sit with the Beavers.

She and Vivian made a deal. So not only did Vivian have my phone, she stole my escape plan, gave it to Lauren, and they somehow came to the conclusion that Lauren should stay at camp. Was the wink innuendo for something . . . sexual? I needed to bleach my brain. I couldn't get that image out of my head for the remainder of dinner. Gwen missed the mark by miles! As much as I didn't ship myself with Lauren . . . that didn't mean I wanted her to get with Vivian. Vivian deserved a decent human being. Someone she could banter with. A chill person to balance her out. Who was the chillest person I knew? What did it mean that my name was the first to pop into my head? The deal. That's what was important, not my panic at the idea of Vivian being with someone the likes of Lauren. Lauren and Vivian? Gross. Shipping? Who was I? Gwen?

With each scoop of food, my mind wandered—my plan to escape camp was ruined, and Lauren was sticking around. Now I had to deal with the whole letters scenario. With permission from Mrs. Black, I took a ten-minute break and waved Jessie over from her spot beside Lauren to an unoccupied table.

As soon as she sat down, I cut to the chase. "Lauren told me that you gave her my letters. No, Jessie, I don't even want to argue about it. I don't need to tell you how messed up that is. You already know. I've scoured my cabin time and time over, so I would've noticed if Lauren had them. That means you still have them, and I don't trust you anymore. I want them back."

"I . . . Emma, I actually don't have them."

"Look, I'm giving you a chance here before I report it to Vivian.

Give them back to me or you and Lauren will probably be kicked out for bullying."

"Emma," she said hastily. "Lauren has them! I swear."

"I don't care who has them. *You're* the one who's going to give them back to me because you're the one who breached my privacy. It's the least you can do, *pen pal*."

TEN

In the early hours of the morning, my stomach started to act like my cat, Thomas. He meowed constantly, demanding food, and he'd follow me all around the house until his mission was complete. And it wasn't even me who fell for his pouting all the time. It was Dad who fell for his adorable, charming headbutting.

The only problem was that our cabin didn't have snacks and the kitchen was locked. I had made the decision to entrust my keys to Vivian's possession, and I didn't exactly want to annoy her at three o'clock in the morning. I snuck out of our cabin and walked to the canteen. Usually, at night the main building's indoor lighting would make the entire camp seem bright and safe, but that night, it was the opposite as the lights weren't on.

That uneasy feeling didn't go away until I picked the lock of the canteen door and slipped inside, sliding behind the service area to gain access to the kitchen. Just as I unlocked the kitchen door, a hand covered my mouth and wiggled us until we were both inside before the door shut.

"Calm down, Emma," Gwen whispered, right into my ear. I proceeded to mumble underneath her cold hand. She released me and turned me around to face her sheepish expression. "Sorry, I guess the excitement got to me."

"What are you doing here, Gwen?" I asked, moving by her to head behind the counter.

"Following you, silly. What else would I be doing?"

"Maybe snoring the night away with the rest of camp?"

"I don't snore, Emma." She scolded me. "We don't even share a cabin," she pointed out, slipping into a seat at a round table. "Are you actually hungry, or were you hoping someone would catch you rummaging through the food stock? Please stop trying to get yourself kicked out, Emma. Mom adores you; you know that."

"If you can stay quiet for more than ten seconds, all questions will be answered." With the seconds left on the imaginary clock, I started making sandwiches with the supplies I got out during our little miscommunication—some ham, American cheese, and a bit of butter. I cut the sandwiches into halves then glanced up. "See?"

"I see," she said, eyes widening. "Is that why Mom gave you the keys to the place? You have chronic hungriness or something?"

"Nope, she trusts me."

"Yet you didn't use your keys to get in."

"I never said that I trusted me." I placed the sandwiches into some tinfoil and rolled it up until it was entirely covered. "I didn't want to lose them, like my phone, so . . ."

"Wait." Gwen got up and moved to the other side of the counter. "I don't know what to tackle first. Conversations with you are exhausting."

"Maybe we can start by mentioning the awesomeness of your mom?"

"No, start with how you lost a phone you're not even supposed to have or that you gave away the keys that were entrusted to you."

"Found my phone. Gave keys to Vivian."

"Where did you find it? You trust my sister?"

"Lauren had it with her on our isolation trip. How was that a clever idea in any way?" I shook my head and thought of my second answer. "I don't know. She's our counselor? There has to be some form of trust there. This two-in-one conversation is kind of confusing."

Shoving one sandwich pack into one hand and sliding another across the counter, I rounded the counter and motioned for Gwen to follow me out of the canteen. The door was one of those that automatically locked when it was shut. Keys only allowed access.

With both of us munching on cheese and ham sandwiches, the dead of the night wasn't as daunting, even if the only thing I saw were the shadows of Gwen's face.

We lumbered up to our cabins and stood at the railing of mine.

"Lauren took your phone . . ." Gwen coaxed.

"The only incriminating thing on that device is the way too many pictures of my cat, Thomas." Considering Vivian had access to phone chargers, those would be the only images Vivian could access as well. "I took the phone back, and naturally, Vivian took it from me. Your sister's strange, you know that?"

Gwen offered me an agreeable pat on the shoulder before she wiped a crumb from her lower lip. "What did she do to make you say that?"

"She shoved the phone down her bra."

"Vivian's always shoving stuff in there," she told me. "Pockets. Who needs them? Not her, that's for sure."

"She planted the phone in Lauren's bed during the cabin search."

"It's not like she didn't steal it."

"But why is Lauren still here? Sleeping right in that cabin." I turned around and nudged my foot against the door. "Like, right in there, dude. Sleeping. Drooling. Existing. Not kicked out onto the streets or anything?"

Gwen opened her mouth to respond, but the cabin door was flung open, the sound of it whacking against the wall stopping whatever thought she had in mind. It was Abby, her glasses awkwardly perched on her nose. When she noticed us, she adopted the queerest expression. It was only three thirty and she could have had at least another three and a half hours of sleep if we didn't wake her up. I was the worst cabinmate.

Abby waved her hand between us. "Am I interrupting something?"

"Did we wake you up?" Gwen said. "Sorry about that. I'm an early riser, and Emma was so kind as to keep me company."

"I *am* always kind."

"Sure, you are," Gwen agreed, tone pitched even higher than her usual bell-like quality.

"I'm sensing sarcasm," I said.

"You mistook that for sincerity," she told me, reaching over to pat my arm. "Don't be getting paranoid on us now, Em."

"You're a minx, you know that?"

Abby's eyebrows scrunched together. "I did interrupt something."

"Don't mind us. We communicate our thoughts in an unconventional way." Gwen rocked back and forth on her heels and nodded toward the camp's building. "By any chance, do you know what we're up to today? My sister refused to tell what we're doing for our bonding exercise."

"Archery." Abby yawned. "I'm going back to bed."

Gwen took a huge bite out of her sandwich. I munched on my sandwich, too, and despite it being the best damn sandwich to ever exist, it didn't help answer my questions about why Vivian suddenly wanted to make deals with Lauren. Maybe my time would've been better spent storming over to Vivian's cabin and demanding to know right there and then instead of staring into space. Or better yet, waking up Lauren. No. I had already disrupted Abby's sleep once, I couldn't in good conscience do it again.

After breakfast, the Beavers were brought to an open field with nine targets set up out in the distance. There was a clearly visible shooting line set up on the ground near us. Archery sounded cool, but the unknown deal made between Lauren and Vivian made it difficult to relax. I drew a bow up to my arm and plucked the string like it was a guitar, and watched as others jumped around in excitement about becoming "warriors."

Instead of leading the charge like she normally would, Vivian sat on a blanket on the ground nearby, out of range of the shooting but close enough to keep observation over the campers and our temporary teacher, some guy called Ryan, who Mr. Black brought in every year.

"Let me guess, this isn't quite your activity either?" she joked as I walked over to say hi.

Standing awkwardly beside the blanket, I said: "There is a reason for me wanting to escape the camp, you know."

"You're angry," she said. "I know."

"No, I'm not angry. I'm dealing with the cards that I've been dealt, I guess."

"I obliterate your escape plan and you're not angry?" Vivian asked.

"Why is Lauren still here?" I asked, keeping my voice low. "I think you didn't report her. Your dad made himself clear about what would happen if we did something stupid again. I even asked your mom and she had no clue either."

"How I deal with insubordination isn't really your business, is it?" she said, handing me an arrow that was lying by her feet. She pushed her sunglasses down from her head and covered her eyes. "For once, put in some effort. Maybe you'll find that you enjoy yourself."

I took the words for what they were, a dismissal, and wandered over to stand between Lauren and Mike, the only available space.

Mike offered to show me how to use the bow and arrow, but I opted to watch the teacher demonstrate in front of everyone because he was a professional.

We were to raise our bow arms only once the signal came. Then we'd all walk to the targets, score, and collect our arrows. We weren't allowed to aim in any direction but the target. The logistics of it all *looked* simple, but in practice, handling the bow and arrow was heavy and awkward. After watching the teacher demonstrate a few times, I let the string go, but the arrow shot off a good few inches and then tipped over on top of my feet. I tried again to fix the arrow to the bow, only someone gripped my arm.

"I don't think you're doing it right," Lauren said.

"I don't need your help, Lauren," I said, shrugging her off.

"Say that to your limp arrow."

"I don't have need of an arrow to be limp," I said pointedly, looking down at my lower region.

"It goes like this." She quickly fetched the arrow and stood behind me so that she could lead my arm into a proper position to aim the arrow. Unnervingly, her breath hit the back of my ear. "It's amazing what you can do in the right position."

"I've got it. *Back off.*"

"Wait." She placed her hands on my hips and slowly pushed my legs apart, making me freeze in place, unsure how to get her the hell off me. "Your stance needs to loosen up a little."

My hand gripped the bow a little tighter. "Lauren, I've *got* it."

And suddenly she was gone. *Poof.* Out of my personal bubble like she was never even there.

"Do you think the camp hired a qualified teacher for this nonsense?" Vivian snapped, managing to get Lauren's entire body to shift until she was back in her own spot, all the while glaring. "No. This level of disrespect won't be tolerated."

"I was showing Emma—"

"Emma looked ready to shove the arrow into your heart. Perhaps a lesson on consent should be retaught at the camp, despite its awareness every single year."

My body was frozen. The only thing I could see instead of the usual admiring look Lauren often gave Vivian was nothing but deep hatred.

I held on to the arrow and muttered, "You're better off limp."

ELEVEN

The day after the archery session I slept through breakfast, and continued to sleep through arts and crafts, not caring if Marissa gave me more time serving in the cafeteria. By the time I was ready to tackle the day it was already after lunch. Punctuality had never been my thing, and it wasn't because of a lack of concern for those who waited for me. That was the thing with having both depression and anxiety—they were an almost always hopeless argument between worrying about something that needed to be done but not having enough motivation to rid myself of what made my thoughts go hell-bent on keeping me up at night.

Again, being late was my own damn fault, but I stomped around Mapplewood clueless as to what we were doing for the afternoon. That was the problem with becoming used to relying on people to tell me what to do each day: they were human, like me, and made mistakes. Even someone like Gwen, who had boundless energy, couldn't be responsible for me all the time.

Vivian watched me closely as I made my way up the hill overlooking the exercise court. Gwen played with her soccer ball alone while the rest of the Beavers were partnered up and having a good time. Vivian didn't berate me for being late. Instead, she ordered, "Why don't you grab a ball and partner with Gwen?"

Everyone else in the Beavers had someone to kick the ball to. They stood at least five feet from each other and kicked a soccer ball back and forth. They used other body parts like their waist or shoulders to gain control over the ball. A few balls flew over the tops of their heads, and some campers went the direct route and headbutted them. Everyone participated. Everyone except Gwen.

"Bitches," I deadpanned.

"Bitches," Vivian agreed, crossing her arms.

"Gwen's the definition of a decent human being. They . . ." I paused, finally feeling a sting in my palm. I shook it out. "You think a guy shoving another into a locker is awful, but girls are so much worse. That devil incarnate and all those cowards who stand idly by. No one deserves to be ignored, especially not Gwen. I don't understand. Why? What's making them act that way?"

Vivian's eyes zeroed in on the three girls grouped together when one of them should've been partnered with Gwen. "It started last year after I left for college. It was only after becoming a counselor this summer that I realized it was like this at school for her too. That I realized it was like this for her at all."

Automatically, my hand reached out to touch her arm. "That sucks, Vivian."

"Much like you, I experienced an endless torment from sharing an enclosed space with Lauren."

"You shared a cabin with Lauren?"

"With much reluctance." My fingers grazed her arm. Slowly, she stepped away and sat down on the grass. She only began to speak again when I sat down beside her. "I had my ways of escape. In more ways than one."

"Are you purposely being cryptic?" I asked.

"Maybe a little." Vengeance rolled off her in waves as she clamped her hands against her thighs. "Lauren kept breaking boundaries that I had set. Much like she does with you. Persistently. When she finally understood that I wanted nothing to do with her, she didn't target me. She waited and targeted Gwen. My dear, younger sister never told me. All those calls and visits and she acted like her usual self. *Acted*."

"You only found out at camp," I mumbled, shaking my head.

"She refuses to engage in any conversation pertaining to it." Vivian released an aggravated sigh, only hiding her annoyance when Gwen waved up at us. "Then you were here, talking to her and making her smile. She gushes about you. It's disgusting. Emma, you're right, the bystanders are cowardly, but no one is more so than Lauren."

I rested my hands on my knees to stop myself from digging my nails into my palms any farther. "How did you put an end to it?"

She didn't answer me straight away. "That's a story for another day."

"Does this by any chance have to do with a certain interaction between you two in the canteen last year?" I asked, which she confirmed with a little nod, a silent implication that she had in fact rejected Lauren. Mike was telling the truth. "So, I get to hear this story?"

"You do. For now, go partner up with my sister."

"Wait, does this mean that you're not hooking up with Lauren?"

"What?!"

"Lauren said you made a deal."

"And you assumed we were . . ."

"Getting it on."

"No."

"Thank you for yesterday, for getting her away from me."

"No thanks necessary," she murmured. "And, Emma? Lauren and her ongoing activities . . ."

"Don't worry, Vivian. I've got it," I promised, not letting yesterday's invasion of my boundaries make me scared of that little witch.

When I shuffled down the hill, Gwen dropped the ball to the ground and kicked it in my direction. It assumed position right beneath my foot. With a kick at the ball, hitting it back to her, I made my way closer to her.

Every time my foot connected with the ball, an image of the ball connecting with Lauren's face settled in. It was all I could do to not make the picture a reality. When the ball rolled under my foot, I took a few steps back. It was time. With a quick sprint toward the ball, I whacked it in the direction of Lauren, Abby, and Jessie, following it with my eyes as it knocked against Lauren's stomach, winding the girl.

"Emma, what the hell?" Gwen asked, grabbing my arm. "I thought the isolation camping trip sorted you guys out? You said you didn't care about the phone thing?"

"I thought so, too, until she groped me yesterday," I said, realizing that maybe that was another factor in kicking that ball. "She didn't let go when I told her to, Gwen. Everything I say, she twists it, and honestly, sharing the same cabin space as her is making me lose my mind. *Besides*, she's a bully and she deserves a little of her own medicine, don't you think?"

Gwen paid attention to the ground. "I don't know."

Lauren came up to us, holding the ball that I'd kicked between both of her hands. "Here, Gwen, I believe this is yours." She shoved the ball in Gwen's direction, only to whack against my arm.

"Ours, actually," I corrected. "Thanks for fetching it for us."

"You're welcome, Emma." Lauren shot me what seemed to resemble a genuine answer. She focused back on Gwen. "Look, Gwen, we had a deal, remember? You leave everyone alone, keep to yourself, and don't bother us. But . . . I had a chat with your sister, so I'm going to leave *you* alone. She didn't mention anything about anyone else. Do you understand?"

Gwen's hands bunched tightly by her sides. "No? I don't under-stand?"

"She didn't kick the ball at you, I did," I said.

Lauren's forehead creased. "You did?"

"I did. And whatever shit you're threatening," I said, "Gwen, shush. I swear to God, it's nothing compared to when I kick your ass. Apologize to Gwen properly. Start treating her like a fucking human being—"

"Fine," Lauren interrupted, holding her hands up. Fixating her reasonably apologetic eyes on Gwen, she continued, "I'm sorry, Gwen. I guess it's time to let everything out in the open?"

"No," Gwen gasped, pushing my arm aside and shoving Lauren's shoulders. "You can go after me all you want, but Emma? No way."

"Gwen, what's going on?"

Eyes full of rage and pain, Gwen explained, "Emma, I've tried getting them back. But I couldn't. Jessie thought it would be a good idea to bring them to camp, I don't know why . . ."

"Bring what to camp, Gwen?"

"Your letters, Em. The letters you wrote to Jessie."

Time slowed down. All I could see was Lauren's triumphant smirk, the thought of Gwen silently having my back for who knew how long, maintaining the peace so my letters wouldn't be released. My hand zoomed quickly to slap Lauren in the face, but someone caught my wrist before the impact. Vivian sent Lauren and the rest of the Beavers on their way to the next activity down by the lake—everyone except for me and Gwen.

"Are you okay, Emma?" Gwen asked.

I cleared my throat, eyes stinging. "Yeah, I'm cool."

"What happened?" Vivian asked, still holding on to my arm.

"Gwen. You stand up for yourself and slay, and don't worry about those stupid fucking letters. I don't care about them anymore," I said angrily.

"Emma," Gwen said quietly, "I'm not a fighter. And they're *personal*."

"Who cares? Lauren's not going to blackmail anyone into doing anything. I don't understand. How did you know about them? What did she make you do so she wouldn't expose them? Don't tell me it has to do with that stupid counselor job."

"Do you remember that day when you planted those ketchup packets under the toilet seat? When I first came to make sure you were out of bed? I found some of your letters in our cabin and I overheard Lauren talking about some that she had in her cabin, so I went to get them back for you. She said if I said anything to you, she'd pass them around, and if I kept to myself, she'd keep her word and wouldn't tell everyone everything you said in them. She wanted the counselor position too."

"Letters . . ." Vivian said, her grip becoming tighter on my arm. "Were those letters on your phone?"

"No." Gwen and I answered at the same time. I continued on to explain. "Letters I wrote to Jessie over the years. It's nothing."

"They're deeply personal," Gwen insisted.

"I confiscated letters from under Lauren's pillow." Vivian's voice was lower, more confident. "When I inspected your cabin, I took those, too, because the letters had Jessie's name scribbled on the top. I meant to investigate the matter further, but you have nothing to worry about. Either of you. We can talk more about it later."

"I could kiss you," I admitted, probably more honest than I should've been.

"That's unnecessary," Vivian said.

"Well." I scratched the back of my neck. "Can I anyway?"

Vivian studied me. "I suppose you asking first is polite."

I planted a chaste kiss on her cheek. "And you securing those letters saved me years of embarrassment, so thank you."

Vivian walked away, waving her hand for us to follow.

Gwen squealed and whispered, "That's it. I'm putting on my captain's hat and getting you two together? It's happening."

"You're talking like it's fate or something."

"That's because it is! I'm fate's helping hand."

If I argued back, there was a good chance she had already prepared reasons for why I'd be wrong.

✦

Lately, when walking through the woods, my heart remained as steady as it could, considering the extent of exertion. Taking my anti-anxiety meds when I had activities near the woods trained my brain not to panic as much at the sight of trees. Instead of that suffocating feeling that came with seeing the green and brown meshed leaves, the fresh air rejuvenated my lungs. Nothing felt so free as when we pushed through the final branches and arrived at the lake.

There was no large hoodie to protect me from the twigs, sunlight, and face-to-face interaction. I looked like everyone else in our camp T-shirts and shorts. The big boulder by the lake no longer called my name because I *wanted* to be near Gwen and Vivian. I *wanted* to participate, especially because it was a lake activity.

The Beavers and the Jellyfish were sent into the huts to our lockers to get changed into bathing suits. After, we stood in a semicircle around the counselors as they explained the activity we'd be occupied with for the next two hours. We were to partner up and race across to the other side of the lake and back rowing mini drift boats. What was the prize? The satisfaction of winning plus some candy. It was so on.

Along the platform on the lake laid all the necessary equipment: the oars, life jackets, and then along the side of the lake were white, mini drift boats that looked like cute little fishing boats. It made me appreciate all the work that the counselors did when we weren't looking. I don't know how they did it and managed to get enough much-needed sleep.

"What if I decided to stay on land today?" I asked.

"You won't because you don't want to disappoint Vivian, now, do you?" Gwen insisted, pout firmly in place.

"Your sister doesn't *like* me."

"Think about it, Emma. She cares about her campers, but she doesn't get all personal with them like she does with you. You keep her on her toes. C'mon, why would she go through all the hassle to keep you in camp? And before you say for *my sake*, think beyond that!" She let out a deep breath and made me stand beside the last rowing boat. "I'm not going to be your partner if you keep up with this denial . . . I'm not going to be your partner full stop. Bye, Emma."

"Wait, what?"

The fact that Gwen strolled confidently toward Mike and asked him to be her rowing partner was nothing short of awesome. She had always loped around camp like she was too busy in her own little world to notice that she was ignored by the majority of the Beavers, but this time it was true confidence. There was no burden of keeping my letters safe, and Vivian had promised to sort Lauren out. Not too long after, Abby joined their little group discussion. Lauren's reign was *over*.

"Hey, Gwen! You're the best friend ever!" I shouted, and muttered to myself, "Even if you are a little delusional."

I grabbed the life jacket and pushed it over my head, like everyone else. I didn't bother to tie it up straight away. I was too concerned with who would be joining me in the isolated, little manual boat in the next few minutes. My watch pulled against a hair on my arm— of course I'd wear something incredibly inappropriate for a water sport.

"Just once at camp it'd be great if you didn't sigh like you're about to die," Vivian said, standing beside me.

"You have another month to accomplish that goal."

"It won't be something I'm actively attempting to do."

"But you'll cherish the occasion?"

Vivian hummed noncommittally and scanned the area, keeping an eye on the campers. "Maybe not as much as the ones you find insulting."

"Cute."

"You find me *cute*?"

Yes, but I wasn't going to outright say it. "Not you, well, yes, you, but I meant your behavior. Sometimes."

"I locked you in a toolshed."

"But didn't rat me out for being there. Cute."

"I forced you out of bed. Stole your phone. Might be intentionally keeping the keys to the kitchen away from you."

"With the underlying intention of keeping me out of trouble and at camp. I work with your mom because of that art incident. She's as cute as a button too."

She exhaled slowly, as if expelling the weirdness of the conversation. "You find my mother cute?"

"Look up the definition of cute."

Her nose wrinkled. "Is that all, then?"

"No. That's not all, and neither is fishing for compliments. But I believe I need to find myself a partner."

As soon as the words escaped my lips, I regretted them. Lauren was the only one left without a partner. Now that *was* frightening. Walter dragged over a reluctant Lauren and their speed was as slow as it was fast, but one thing was for sure, it was a painful amount of time given to overthink the circumstance.

"Emma, I noticed you didn't have a buddy so . . . here's one."

I fiddled with the untied jacket. "How *sweet* of you."

"No problem, dude." He wandered off again.

"Your life jacket isn't done up properly," Lauren pointed out, indicating her own. "Here, let me." Lauren reached out, but Vivian knocked her hand away. "Ow?! Damn, I was only trying to help."

"No unauthorized touching," Vivian insisted.

My lips pursed to stop from smiling, and I mumbled, "Cute."

Vivian grabbed the loose straps of my life jacket and walked that little bit away, tugging me along like it was perfectly normal and proceeded to tie them herself.

When she finished, she outright glared at both Walter and Lauren and then grabbed an oar from my boat. She placed the end on the ground and leaned against it. "Emma's with me today. Lauren, you partner up with Walter."

"Just today?"

Walter snorted. Lauren's eyebrows furrowed.

Vivian turned her glare to me. "Get in the boat, Emma."

"Just today, then."

I did as she said and climbed into the drift boat, with my newly strapped-on life jacket. The perfect knot may or may not have prompted my cheeks to heat up, from remembering how close she stood and her confident expression, like doing little things for me was expected.

As Vivian pushed the boat slightly into the water, I slipped off my watch and dangled it between my fingertips. When she noticed, she caught it dutifully and placed it with her own stuff beside a rock. The Beavers and the Jellyfish copied her, placing valuables into their piles of bags or clothes before hopping on board their drift boats. Normally, Jessie partnered with Lauren for group exercises, but this time she got in the same boat as Abby. Gwen hopped into the same boat as Mike, winking at me after seeing her plan had succeeded.

Walter led the charge by calling out instructions and giving a little demonstration with Lauren in their boat. Each person had two oars and gloves to prevent blistering on their hands. Making it across the water was pretty simple looking. Row in time with your partner, communicate, and you'd be fine. My chest hurt from attempting to keep in the hiccups that had started unceremoniously, distracting me from asking why Vivian brought a satchel onto the boat.

"What's wrong with you?" Vivian asked, eyeing me strangely.

"Has anyone ever died from hiccupping?" I asked.

Vivian, sitting opposite the bow end of the boat, leveraged both her oars into the water and took the position of backstroke. We were face to face. "I imagine it's a possibility."

I gripped the oar tightly. "Seriously?"

"I suppose I can look it up," Vivian said.

"With my phone," I mumbled.

"I very much doubt you're that annoyed by its lack of presence in your life," she commented, lips tilted upward slightly.

"Unless you're a mind reader." I winced again, cutting off my comment. "Dammit."

"Now, I don't believe you," she teased, tilting her head to the side. "You may be experiencing some chest pain, but hiccups? Prove it."

"Okay, your suspicious nature is over the top now. I like the lake," I told her with a laugh. I glanced around, expecting a camera and crew because it was such a wildly silly moment. "You want me to prove to you that I have the hiccups."

"Yes, Emma. Prove it."

Challenge accepted.

I waited for the spasmodic inhalation and continued to wait awkwardly. "What the hell? Why am I not hiccupping?"

"It's a little trick I learned growing up," she told me. "One of my teachers, you remember Mr. Philips? When I had a bad case of the hiccups, he dared me to continue to disrupt the class and get a detention, and all of a sudden, I couldn't hiccup anymore—even when I really wanted to. You're welcome."

We rowed together as though we had done it a dozen times before, when in fact it was my first time rowing a boat. Instinct kicked in and we worked together well, making sure we steadily kept up the same pace. Admiring our routine for a moment, I surveyed the lake, but it was total and utter chaos around me. Some campers were in shouting matches, an oar or two floated in the water, and other campers splashed their oars wildly in their attempts to make a turn. We were winning the race without trying.

A nudge to my knee brought my focus back to our own boat.

"Look at us?" I said proudly. "We're good together. We're winning this thing."

Vivian scanned the area quickly and trained her attention back on me. "No thanks to you."

"Hello? My arms make for a perfect noodle meal with the way they're working. I think I gained mega muscles."

"That wobbliness forces my perfectly normal arms to do the grunt work."

"Would you like me to withhold my part in this activity?" I asked. My arms were burning and needed a break.

"I've brought us this far." She brought the oars back into the boat, letting them rest across her lap. "You can bring us the rest."

My mouth dropped open. "If you're not rowing, then I'm not."

"Then we'll drift into the middle of the lake," she said carelessly.

I let my oars drop into the water, and as Vivian stared after them, I made a grab for both of hers and tossed them into the water too.

"In the middle of the lake, we remain." I mocked her.

"You have proven yourself unworthy of being my partner. Then there's the lack of evidence of your hiccupping disaster, and now we're without oars . . . are you *pleased* with yourself? I can't believe I opted to share this confined space with you."

"No takesies backsies now."

She murmured, "No, I suppose not."

Maybe throwing the oars overboard wasn't the brightest idea, especially when Vivian's brother and sister decided that leaving us to fend for ourselves was the best option. The other boats righted themselves and flew right on by us. The water rippled from the boats' wakes, and as the little ringlets grew smaller, the lake's water returned to unnervingly calm, and that, paired with the stubborn quietness of Vivian, did nothing to help the nervous twitching of my hands.

Vivian took my phone out of the pocket in her shorts and started going through it like she had permission to do so and we weren't on a boat, stuck unless one of us did something about it. She was clearly in no hurry to get the oars from the water. She had already guessed my easy password.

Vivian crossed her ankles and stared at the screen of the phone, then placed it back in her little satchel next to her feet. "When I said I found the lack of the phone's presence in your life annoying doubtful, I truly meant it. There are photos of you and your cat. That's all I could find. The cat and you."

"Thomas is the love of my life."

"Thomas?" Her thoughtful expression twisted. "You've never mentioned a Thomas."

"He has the most adorable eyes. Oh, and his feet. You should see them when he's sitting there, rubbing against the couch. I might have a video on there too."

"Insanity. You drove me toward it, and now there's a true possibility of my body swooping into the water and never coming back."

Well, I didn't want *that*. "I don't think me annoying you can turn you into a mermaid." She still studied the water, as if contemplating jumping in to get away from me. That thought alone made me sad.

"Sorry," I said. "I'm not used to . . . I don't know. Sharing interests with someone," I explained, bringing my fist up to my mouth to hide how much this type of thing affected me. "I mean, I thought people gushed about their pets to their friends. Or acquaintances. Counselors. People. I'm doing it wrong."

"Oh. He's your cat."

Such a simple and understanding response.

It made it a little better because she still didn't look at me, but at least the expression changed from its void. I'd never met someone like her before—someone who could hold an expression of both contempt and nothing at the same time. In one way, it let you know where you stood but left everything unimaginable too.

My legs wobbled as I made to stand. Her hand reached out to steady me, holding on to my arm as the boat rocked back and forth.

"I'll get the oars."

She more than likely never intended to get them herself. "I won't say no to that."

Eyeing the water, I asked, "What do you reckon? Are there mermaids floating around in there?"

"I don't hear any singing," she said.

"Right." I steadied myself again and glanced back at her. "Hopefully it doesn't, you know, tip over because of my heroic actions or anything."

"Emma, I'm warning you . . ."

"Look at me, in trouble with a counselor, again."

"You do that, and your phone is destroyed."

"As you so subtly pointed out, my lack of social life means having nothing important on there. I can swim, you know." The water didn't look so bad. "You can keep it. It would probably get more use that way, Viv."

"Emma," she said almost too quietly to hear. Her nose wrinkled at the nickname. "We can share stories if you wish."

"You want to hear about those letters, don't you?"

"Maybe."

"We have a deal, Vivian."

I didn't give her a chance to respond before I catapulted from the boat and into the water. She appreciated my conclusion that no, there didn't seem to be aquatic humans swimming beneath the surface. As I shifted one oar back up onto the boat, Vivian casually dug out a *spare* oar from beneath the seat and knocked my oar from my grasp. There was no need for me to have dived so heroically into the lake to retrieve our rowing devices. Pushing the wet hair from my face, I brought the oar back up and whacked it against hers. She easily disarmed me, flinging the oar out of my grasp and farther away from the boat.

With a laugh, she tapped her oar against my cheek condescendingly. It was a good thing I had the life jacket on and was floating, because it would've been a mess to keep myself above water and fight her attacks. With all the oars floating aimlessly behind me at this point, there was only one logical form of payback. My fingers gripped the edges of the boat as she watched with a victorious glint in her eyes.

"You know . . . I may not be able to sing, but I *can* hum," I told her.

She hummed teasingly back and inched closer. "Without that alluring voice, I don't think you're cut out to be a mermaid, Emma. Humming doesn't lure people to their death. Singing is an essential element."

"I beg to differ."

Like a bat out of hell, I used the edge of the boat to push myself up and on my descent back down, I gripped the side of her life jacket and plunged back into the water with her in tow. Already imagining her reaction, I stayed under the water for as long as possible, which was awkward. My chin rested against my chest as I floated upright in the water. She tilted my chin up and cupped my cheeks in her hands as she stared angrily into my eyes. Ever so slowly, the charged and ember flames of Vivian's eyes burned softer, and her fingers slid into my hair. My chest burned from holding my breath, and my legs grew weaker and hung nearly limp under the water.

If anything, the warm feeling of her breath, although destabilizing, was inviting. And as I leaned in ever so slightly, a splash of water knocked against my face. Vivian spun around and started to climb back into the boat. I had an odd sort of spluttering laugh as I processed what happened.

I almost kissed her.

And she knew that.

I grabbed the oars and shoved them into the boat without resistance this time. By the time I came back to full awareness of my surroundings and noted that Vivian's lips were in fact not inches away from mine, she was in the boat and holding out her hand for me to take. "That doesn't prove anything," she said, hauling me inside. "Pulling me out of the boat. It doesn't mean you're a mermaid."

"Right," I said, and motioned in the direction of where the rest of the campers had gone. "Are we following them?"

"I don't know about you, but I feel like showering. Plus, because of that stunt you pulled, I'm recruiting you to help me set up the scavenger hunt."

"In the woods?"

"Yep."

"Drat."

We rowed back the way we came and all I could think about was that almost kiss. The fact remained that Vivian pulled back. She slapped water right into my face and pretended nothing happened at all. She was Vivian, and I was Emma. She was a counselor. I was a camper.

The kiss didn't happen because Vivian came to her senses and I didn't. Did it matter who did what? The point was it *didn't* happen. All I had to do was go back and shower and then join Vivian *all alone* in the woods to set up for the scavenger hunt.

Oh boy.

TWELVE

The shower was heaven compared to the coldness of the lake. Vivian wouldn't let me go back to cabin thirteen. I wasn't trusted enough to be the only camper wandering around camp without supervision, so not only did I not get time to prepare for the alone time with Vivian in the woods, but I was stuck in a place where we would both be naked. Gwen was right. Fate had plans for us, and this time, it didn't need her helping hand.

The counselors' bathroom was a fairly small room with communal showers and a couple of stalls. We each went for the private option, steam filling the room almost immediately. The pressure was awesome, but the shower gel and shampoo provided didn't smell like roses.

"Vivian, what sort of shampoo are you using?"

"You already know the answer to that question," she said, and showed me the bottle between the open space at the bottom of the stall, snatching it away quickly when I tried to use my foot to knock it over to my side. "Counselor privileges. Sorry."

"You've got two choices. One, let me use that god-tier rose-smelling shampoo or two, face the consequences."

"Seems to me, Emma, that your version of revenge is grumbling every minute of every day."

"Then I'll do the opposite." Squirting the generic body wash onto a sponge, I stood directly under the showerhead and wailed as high as my vocal cords allowed, water surging against my face and making my voice all garbled. Almost as soon as my voice rang out, Vivian roughly knocked her shampoo bottle into my shower. "Now am I qualified enough to be a mermaid?"

"You could definitely kill someone with that voice of yours," she murmured.

Choosing to not take offense, even though she was *very* quick to give in, I used the shampoo, humming beneath my breath and closing my eyes. The steam carried the rose scent all around me, transporting me to a flower shop. The other stall's door creaked and not a second went by before the towel hanging on my stall door was whipped away.

I dared to crack open the stall door a little and peeked outside, where Vivian wore nothing but a towel. Her hair was sudsy, and it dripped down her chest and onto the floor. "I have no qualms whatsoever about walking over there au naturel and taking that towel back from you."

She hesitated. "You wouldn't."

"Opening the door . . ." I bluffed, at which she dropped my towel and flung her hand up to cover her eyes. Hearing my footsteps, she squashed her hand tighter across her face. I wrapped the towel around myself and prodded her nose. "You really didn't think this through."

"You wanted to smell like me," she said as an explanation.

"Yes, to be reminded of you when you're not there," I teased.

"The only time we spend apart most days is when we're in bed."

"A shame, apparently, because you wanted to see me naked." I laughed and headed to the changing room. "Go rinse. I'll meet you outside, fully dressed. No complaints!"

Once I dried myself off and got changed, I stood outside the hut down by the lake and dried my hair by looping it over my head and rubbing a towel against it vigorously. It smelled so nice. I hummed as I leaned against the cabin, watching as the campers were rounded up for head count. The cabin's door swung open and Vivian stepped out.

"Ready?" she asked.

I sidestepped her and hopped down the steps. "Do I have a choice?"

"No, not really," she said. "It's either we set up the scavenger hunt now or wait until Walter gets back, and I don't know about you, but I'd prefer to be indoors during the night."

"I would be indoors, sleeping . . ."

"No, you'd be scrambling around in the shadows, making sand-wiches." How did she know about that? She stopped next to two large, black bags. "Gwen has a big mouth. She told Walter, who, in turn, had her leftovers. Walter also has a big mouth and told me. It wasn't hard to piece together, Emma."

"Detective Black. Speaking of which . . . what are you going to do about Lauren? And can I get those letters back?"

"Gwen wants to speak to me before I do anything. And as soon as we get back, you'll have your letters."

"Thank you," I said, relieved.

Vivian brandished a map from inside a bag. She picked up the bag, putting her hands through the straps so that it sat snugly on her back. I ended up doing the same, and nearly fell over due to the bag's weight. Vivian brought me back to rights by gripping the strap, and released a condescending chuckle at my predicament.

Trailing after her as she walked back into the woods, I concluded that she carried the lighter bag. Not that I particularly blamed her. If I had a lackey, I'd use them too. I'd probably pick a much more phys-ically capable lackey, though.

"Emma," Vivian said as I bent down to unzip the bag. "We went to the same school."

"Like everyone else in this town," I pointed out, taking out a stuffed toy. "Only, like, half a year when I was fifteen. Most of it I skipped. I'm coming back for this bunny tomorrow and keeping it. That's not contraband or anything, right?"

"You won't be participating in the activity." She patted the top of my cap as she went by me. "We'll be monitoring the game. I don't want you cheating."

"The one time I want to participate in an activity, and you deny me that fun."

"Walter will be monitoring with us. I'm sure you can make your own fun."

"True."

We headed off again once I'd marked the bunny's position on the map. We left it looking cute sitting on top of a tree branch. With the weight of the bags and the amount we had to walk, the exercise kept me warm enough to fend off the coolness of the breeze.

"So," I said, clicking my fingers, "why did you bring up that dirty word?"

Flattening the map against her thighs, she asked, "What dirty word?"

I visibly shivered. "School."

"It had three hundred students and never did I once see you, not even in passing."

"Maybe you did but it didn't register. It's normal. Or maybe you didn't because you were a year ahead of me. I didn't know Gwen until I came to camp. To be honest, we could have met—interacted even—and I wouldn't remember. The details of that year are really foggy."

"Do you have a bad memory?"

"Only when I'm going through a rough patch."

"I see," she replied. "Everyone's phone, it tells you an awful lot of information about a person."

Finally catching on to what she was saying, I replied, "Yes. I was a perfectly content loner. The only time we could've interacted, at lunch, I was hidden away. Did the phone tell you all that, or did you assume my only friend was a chubby cat called Thomas?"

She spun around so that she walked backward. "Don't offend your only friend."

"Gwen is my friend. Walter too. Your mom. Wait, thinking about it, your dad too. I have a bone to pick with him about some capybaras."

Her footsteps slowed. "Capybara?"

"The largest rodent in the world," I answered, still having to speak to Mr. Black about the creature. "And I'm sure, given time, we'll be best buds too."

"You and me?"

"No, me and the capybara," I joked.

Unlike the last time I was deep in the forest, coincidently with Vivian, this time we followed the sound of the water until we came across a waterfall. All we had to do was follow the stream, shining flashlights as we made our way across the debris.

I snagged my phone from Vivian's open hand after she took it out of her satchel and danced my way to the top of a flat-looking rock. Ignoring her protests, I put on a random song. I remembered the way I'd felt dancing at the campground beside the fire, and decided this time it would be different; this time, the counselor would join in.

"You're not allowed your phone, remember?" Vivian told me, stretching out her hand expectantly.

"Sure," I said, ignoring her. "How the hell is this thing charged at fifty percent? It died when I had it. Lauren couldn't have charged it, right?"

"It was dead when I took it from you," she confirmed. "Essentially, her thievery was senseless. I, on the other hand, have a charger in my cabin."

"Interesting. Anyway, dance with me," I invited, rocking my head back and forth. "You made me dance that one time. Now it's your turn."

"To join you as you slip to your death? No, thank you." But she did sit at the edge of the rock and pressed her palm against the surface. It was then I noticed the jangling of keys. I managed to pull them out of her pocket and was blindsided by what came out with them.

"Oh my God. Vivian, you kept it." I poked the key chain between the eyes as I slipped down to sit next to her. "My little ostrich, my Mike."

"It's an owl. You named him Mike? What kind of a name is Mike?" she scoffed.

"From *Monsters, Inc*. Aw, he's the most hideous owl to ever exist. Who'd want him in their pocket all day long?"

"Me," she deadpanned. "He's not hideous."

"I made him; I'm only being realistic." I took the little owl from her hands and made it dance on her shoulder. "Even with one eye, he's drawn to you. Look! He wants you to dance."

I stopped making the key chain dance when I glanced at Vivian. Her face held one of the softest expressions that I'd ever seen her wear, something I thought was impossible for her to achieve. She moved her head closer to mine. I sat frozen with fear and excitement. She leaned in so her forehead rested against mine, and I shut my eyes. "Drawn to me?" she said, barely more than a whisper.

Vivian leaned in and slowly kissed my lips. We quickly pulled apart and took shaky, shallow breaths. Unable to contain myself anymore, I held Vivian's head in my hands and pulled her into a fiery and passionate kiss. Her hands worked their way around my body, feeling each crevice, each line along my physique.

I lay on my back as she matched my body's form by climbing on top of me. My hands ventured over her curved body, exploring. We pulled apart and opened our eyes. Staring deeply at one another, we breathed in tandem, our eyes searching; mine were full of wonder, hers of curiosity.

As quickly as it started, it ended.

Vivian shot up and slid off the rock until she stood inches away from the waterfall. "I shouldn't have done that."

Still lying on the flat rock, I held the owl up above my head and pulled on its wings. "But you did."

I slipped off the rock and we left the waterfall in complete silence, although I noticed that Vivian made sure the little guy was with us, and it didn't seem to matter that I was the one carrying him.

It wasn't like we could head straight back to the cabins and sleep away the awkwardness. We still had the rest of the scavenger hunt to set up. For the first time since coming to camp, my skittish limbs and darting eyes weren't because of the paranoia of being left alone in the woods. No, my heightened emotions sent my anxiety skyrocketing, and every time Vivian walked too fast, my body had a mind of its own to clamber across the terrain to walk right beside her. She slowed down for me and kept close, even if her shoulders were rigid.

We moved quickly and dropped sunglasses, a Frisbee, a sun hat, a beach ball, and flip-flops in quick succession, marking them on the map, and then headed back to camp. It was dinnertime when we got back, and the thought of shoving food in my mouth was a no-go. My stomach was a pit that had shut down for business.

Vivian left me behind, and it seemed that we weren't going to say anything to each other at all when she came out of her cabin with my letters in her hand. As I turned to crawl into my cabin and face-plant, she called out, "Wait. I know how being out there affects you . . ." She swung her backpack around and pulled out a chocolate bar. She handed both the letters and the chocolate to me. "I know you're not going to eat right away, but chocolate helps me sometimes when I'm stressed. Take it with you. Eat it *slowly*. Don't eat like a bear. I'll get Mom to put something aside for you later."

Back in my cabin, lying flat on my back, I ate the chocolate, snapping it into pieces so that it wouldn't be gobbled in five seconds flat. My hair engulfed my bed with the same smell that had filled the air as we'd kissed. With my eyes closed, it felt like I was flat on my back on the boulder, kissing, kissing, kissing.

✦

The Beaver and Jellyfish groups gathered around their respective counselors to hear the rules of the scavenger hunt. I stood off to the side, watching as they got handed a map, a compass, and a list of items they had to find. The group that found the most objects would win. I understood that because I was involved in setting up the game, I couldn't participate, but I wanted to give Vivian and myself as much space as possible now because when the campers went into the woods, we'd be alone again. She hadn't talked to me since she'd handed me my letters late last night.

Walter positioned his group at the starting line then tossed them a clumsy thumbs-up as he finally joined me by a tree trunk. He swung a jacket from over his shoulder and handed it to me. "Here, since we're going to hang by the finish line, you might need this."

My fingers traced over the word *Counselor*. "How very sweet of you, Walter."

"Nope. Wasn't me."

I glanced at Vivian, watching her instill total terror into her campers. "Oh."

"I could be with my little campers, searching for stuff, winning, destroying the masses," he said. "But here I am, under strict orders to be the buffer. Gwen, she senses disharmony with our favorite soon-to-be couple. She wanted to speed the will-they-won't-they process along. Her words, not mine."

"This isn't normal. A family shouldn't, I don't know, encourage their sibling's romantic interests or lack of interests, to pursue them."

"What do you mean, 'lack of interests'?"

"You shouldn't try to force anything on someone who doesn't feel anything, Walter."

"Hold on a second . . ."

"Seriously, man, let it go."

The Beavers and Jellyfish were set loose by Vivian into the woods.

I thought Vivian might make her way to the finish line without us, but that wasn't what happened. She waited for us to make our way over to her before she strode ahead of us, determined not to make eye contact with me, or any contact whatsoever. I trailed behind the siblings, not wanting to impose. That's what it felt like, and it didn't feel good.

The jacket was thin. Fluff lined the inside, so it kept my body heat inside. The lack of movement at night meant that we wouldn't stay warm like the rest of the campers. Hence the jacket.

"It was her?" Walter gasped, making me tune in to their conversation.

"Go ask her yourself," Vivian said rather smugly.

"It was you, Emma?" he asked in disbelief, slowing down his steps. "You made those fan-fucking-tastic sandwiches and didn't tell me?!"

"You would want a personal assistant," I guessed. "Why would I tell you?"

He bumped his shoulder against mine. "To please both of our bellies. Duh."

Unintentionally, we caught up with Vivian. I wasn't even mad that Vivian had told him that I'd made Gwen's sandwiches, which he had snacked on. She spoke about me willingly. Was that a good sign? "I'm already your mom's cooking partner. Gwen's, too, at night sometimes. Can't add another one of your family to the list. I might go crazy."

"Sure, you can," he joked.

"You'd owe me one."

"I'll owe you many."

"Can I cash in now?" I whispered, making sure no one heard us. He hesitated and then nodded. "It's not that bad. I left a bunny in one of the trees and kind of want it after the game. Make sure that I get it?"

"That's all?"

"That's all."

Walter began walking backward and swapped his energetic gaze between Vivian and me. The contemplation was there, blatant, but I didn't understand what he had to debate about. It was a simple ask, and a simple task. He'd get me the bunny; I'd make him sandwiches sometimes. It was a fair trade between us—not fair to the campers participating in the hunt, but what they didn't know wouldn't hurt them.

Walter was about to do something incredibly stupid. His clenched fists shook by his side. I almost reached out to grab him, but he shot off like a bullet, leaping between the leaves of the nearest trees and hollering as he ran, like a crazy monkey. I didn't even get the chance to raise my voice to stop his rash actions. He was gone like he was never there at all.

Hesitantly, I glanced up to see Vivian's jaw clenched so tightly that I thought her teeth might crack. This lack of conversation and out-right ignoring me was slowly eating away at me. The two of us brushed our way through branches and started climbing up the steep forest ground.

I threw my hood up so that I couldn't see the outline of Vivian's body, as if not seeing her meant she wasn't there at all. That worked perfectly fine until I slipped and fell backward, smashing into her, which forced her to release a grunt as she somehow caught me.

Faster than Walter left, I straightened up and shook my head, mumbling, "Sorry."

Once we made it to the top, she commented, "You're acting stranger than usual. You're jumpy."

"I'm afraid of camping and that so happens to include the woods?"

"No, it's not that," she deduced, like I was a puzzle waiting to be solved. "You've gotten much better at handling the environment. Improved remarkably. Something else is going on."

"Fine. I'll be blunt." Still wondering whether I should speak, I nodded to myself, accepting what was about to come out of my face. "You accidentally kissed me. Maybe it was my imagination. Maybe I kissed you. Now you're avoiding me—a silent rejection, and I take that rejection. There's no need to be scared I'll come on to you or whatever."

"Scared? You think that I'm scared? I'm not scared," she scoffed.

"I'm letting you know so maybe we can rip the awkwardness in half because I quite enjoy our conversations. Forget the kiss and move on?"

"If that is what you want, then that is what you can do, Emma."

"We're agreed?"

"Seems that way," she said, going back to ignoring me.

The finish line was up ahead, a firm and tangible orange string hung across two tree trunks, concluding the race between the campers, and seeing it also ended the most painfully awkward conversation of my life. Having said those words allowed the imaginary hand clasped around my throat to ease its grip until my breath came out in fine, firm lengths. Relief, such a palpable feeling in those few moments as I settled beside one of the trees and huddled within the rose-scented jacket.

I pulled the sleeves over my fingertips and dug my nails into the fabric. A string or two caught my nails, and so I was distracted, pulling a taut string like a cat for a few minutes, thoughts too dispersed to think clearly and eyes downcast as the string remained stretched.

"I think we're more alike than you think, Emma." Vivian leaned against the same trunk as me but stayed standing. "We're both incompetent at social cues. That doesn't mean we can't communicate clearly. It probably means we're more honest than most people."

"Are you saying that you mean everything you say?" I asked.

"Of course not. We're not completely dim witted." Vivian slid down the trunk and sat next to me, shoulder to shoulder. "Your style. It can be captivating. Charming. You don't play games. You wear your truth on your sleeve and expose vulnerability, emotions—it could be susceptible to weakness, but it's not. That's how we differ."

"You're saying that we're both idiots, but in separate ways?"

She placed her hands on her face and kept them there. "No."

I leaned forward, peeking beneath her hands. "Then what are you saying?"

"For the reasons I said—that's why I kissed you, and there's no way in hell that I'm repeating myself."

"I'm really confused. I thought we were forgetting about that?"

"I said that you could."

"But you're not?"

"It appears that way."

We sat beneath the tree's leaves. The warmth of our shoulders was the only thing that let me know that I wasn't alone. It was as comforting as it was scary. Vivian had said her piece; she responded and now it was my turn to answer her words.

"You make this hard," I eventually said, shuffling slightly away to give her space.

"No." She brought her fist up to her chin and set her attention on the finish line. "Perhaps. Yes. You're no innocent bystander either. I had a plan for the summer, Emma." Her tone was sharp, angry, but accepting at the same time, which confused me. "Do you know what I like about visiting camp? Familiar faces, routines, predictability in this old town. Two months. Then the rest of my time is spent without stories attached to my name. Strangers. A blank slate, figuring out what it is that I like, who I am, finding meaning in the world." Her knuckles whitened. "I'm not particularly fond of surprises."

"No surprise birthday parties for you. Got it."

"Camp is not the designated place for surprises," she continued, ignoring my comment by digging her fist farther into her cheek. "But there you were, stealing from the shed, getting hit by dodge-balls, getting phones stolen, panicking about the camp, obsessing with my heart, infatuating over rose-scented things, trusting me with the kitchen keys. Having Gwen *and* Walter care for you; even my own mother adores you. Me liking you." She removed her fist from her face and looked at me, hard. "Being into a girl? Perhaps that was a surprise, but not the biggest. I processed that and accepted it. Liking you? Emma, you make this hard."

"I have a suggestion, but I'm not sure if I'd be making this harder or not."

"I don't think that's possible," she said.

Her open expression made me continue with my thoughts. "Instead of forgetting it, maybe we can revisit that thing that happened."

The way her face, and damn, even her entire body, froze, I was sure that it was quite possibly the worst thing that I could've said. When she made a move to come closer to me, I freaked out and put my hands over my face. Ever so slowly, she leaned her head back against the trunk and closed her eyes. "It appears that yes, it is entirely possible to make this easier. It took you ten words to express exactly how you feel. I can hardly follow through with the suggestion to kiss you if you're barricading your face."

"I didn't specify a time for my suggestion."

"A one-time deal, Emma. Now or never."

"But it's my suggestion!" I squished my entire face between the space of my two knees, a little panicked. "How can you make it so that the terms and deal are yours?"

Her fingers tapped against my neck. "Compromise. That's how."

I turned my head so my cheek rested against my knee and met Vivian's eyes. "I've got a better idea than my suggestion."

She paused. "I don't see what's better than kissing you."

"Courting," I said.

Before she could even think about the word, never mind formulate a response, cheering, yelps, and a stampede of footsteps trampled their way through the forest until they tumbled out of the cover of the leaves and stormed their way through the orange string. Walter held up the stuffed bunny like a champion holding their trophy for everyone to see.

"That's your way of compromising? Removing the suggestion entirely?" she questioned, tapping my cheek to regain my attention.

"I mean, you're doing pretty well." I pulled at the sleeves of the jacket.

Something pulled at her lips; whether it was a smirk would never be revealed because she didn't let it enlarge. "That doesn't count."

"Preventing me from being cold doesn't count?"

"Affirmative." She didn't hesitate to answer.

When Lauren emerged from the camper huddle, it made me think of something else. "And swapping our sleeping bags to keep my discomfort away doesn't count either?"

"Preventing you from being harassed was the decent thing to do."

"I'm winning, then."

"Winning? This isn't a competition."

"According to you, I'm wooing you faster than you're wooing me. Faster. Better. Apparently, courting is my game," I said.

"I kissed you," she hissed, leaning closer so no one else could hear. "You say I make things hard. Emma, no. You have to breathe and it's hard."

"Hard not to kiss me again?" I received a slap on my thigh for that comment, but that didn't make my giddiness falter. I slowly stood up and offered my hand. She purposely stood up by herself and crossed her arms. "I offered you the chance to be in the lead. But no, by your definition, you weren't already courting me."

She placed her hand on my shoulder and gave it a nudge. "Go get your bunny."

"Speaking of, even Walter has bypassed you."

"Go," she repeated through gritted teeth.

I left her alone because she could only be teased so much, especially in the same area as the other campers. That little detail didn't derail my happiness at the productiveness of our conversation. We established a few things without getting overly serious and worked up. We deserved a clap on the back for not letting our frustration with each other ruin the flow of the conversation.

Since the Beavers and Walter came back, and we continued to have that conversation, the Jellyfish arrived worse for wear in muddy clothes. Walter had them all occupied, still clutching the bunny under his arm. He scanned the group repeatedly, forehead creased. I saddled up to the campers and immediately had my arm gripped by a cold hand and was greeted with overly hopeful eyes.

"Emma, my best friend, Emma," Gwen said, drawing me in closer so that she could hug me. "I am proud of you. My grumpy stumps were grumping together."

"Please, don't ever repeat that again."

"So proud," she sniffed, backing away and wiping a fake tear from her cheek. "Sorry, happy tears."

"What's Walter freaking out about?"

"We're one camper short."

"Damn."

That was how, a short fifteen minutes later, everyone was supplied with a searching buddy, a flashlight, spare batteries, walkie-talkies, and jackets. We were sent off into the woods to find the missing person. Walter's normally happy face was hard and tight, making the campers take him seriously, even if he had the bunny tucked neatly into his jacket so that the head popped out of the collar.

My watch revealed it was eleven o'clock at night, and even if it was summer, it was cold and dark, and no one was in the mood to actively search for the idiot who didn't clasp their arm with someone else's.

Vivian and I continued our banter. "Quite frankly, I'm impressed," she said.

"You were the one to admit your feelings for me first. I'm the one who should be impressed."

"No, not that. I would've expected this gallivanting in the woods alone from you, considering your late-night snacks."

"Impressed? Courtship point to me, then."

"You have fallen under the delusion that you're winning this courtship. Now, that's a typical abnormality from Emma Lane." Her lips quirked up deliciously and the next thing I knew, my back was pressed against a random tree trunk and her lips grazed against mine. "This, right here, this is reality."

"Just by walking beside you made me irresistible, apparently. That is a nice reality."

Before I nudged her back, I pressed the tiniest of kisses to her cheek and went back to my strolling, lips tingling and hands slightly shaking, making the light flicker from one spot to the next. Other than that, I was completely calm. Not counting my breathing.

I busied myself by studying the little, black walkie-talkie in my hand and went to the station that everyone was using to communicate. People rambled mindlessly into the device, clearly thinking their words were a source of entertainment, when in fact, it was annoying. "Okay. Spit it out."

"Fine," she drawled, taking the walkie-talkie and turning it off. "How do you determine you're winning? Is there a point system? Does one action have more worth? Have you devised something palpable?"

"I thought it wasn't a competition, Vivian."

"In your brain, it is, and who am I not to indulge in your childish games?"

I reached for her hand, and her instinctive move to tangle our fingers together made my cheeks hurt from smiling. "See that? Our first romantic stroll through the woods, holding hands. Clearly, I'm awarded the maximum of ten points."

"Ten points for a creepy search party?"

I squeezed. "And two points extra for the blush you're sporting."

After a two hour search, we found Jessie lost in the woods. Vivian and I found her stretched out across a boulder, staring up at the stars like they had the answers to all life's questions. Two wine bottles were on the ground beside her. It didn't take a detective to figure out why she was so loopy. She had stolen wine from Mr. Black's office.

We declared the mission successful into the walkie-talkies. I helped Vivian haul the drunk girl back to camp. She mumbled non-sense about me still being her best friend and mentioned how she regretted giving the letters to Lauren. The jumbled mutterings fin-ished once Jessie fell asleep in our arms. It was a bit of a relief that she felt terrible about the way she'd been acting since I came to camp. Maybe what she said in the letters was the person she wanted to be, but in reality, peer pressure derailed that path.

"Will she get in much trouble?" I asked eventually.

"Underage drinking, theft, disobeying her counselor," Vivian listed in answer. "It depends. My father likes to get into the reasons behind this kind of behavior. If he can help, he will. If it was an act of rebellion, then yes, there will be consequences."

"That's why he comes up with ideas like isolation camping?"

"One of his favorite punishments that so happens, more often than not, to fix the stem of the problem."

"God, Jessie's really out of it, right?"

"Jessie seems guilt ridden," Vivian commented in her attempt to casually gain information. She motioned for us to stop walking. We gen-tly leaned the girl on the ground and took a breather. "Not that I know of anything in the letters, but if they were that deeply personal . . . you two were best friends?"

I almost said yes but held back. "I would have said yes when I lived here, but I had nothing to compare it to. I don't remember much, and that's one of the reasons why I liked writing to her. She filled in the gaps for me. Meeting someone like you? It shows me that my idea of friendship is nothing compared to reality."

"From an outsider's point of view, sharing such personal thoughts with someone might mean she was more than just a friend," Vivian said. "That's all."

"No, it was never like that with us. She told me at the start of camp that she reads the letters every summer, and at first I thought it was kind of sweet," I said. "But she easily showed them to Lauren. It makes me wonder who else has read them all over the years? I think it's a messed up thing to do, sharing stuff like that. Even when friend-ships end, I couldn't imagine sharing something so personal with anyone else. I'm glad that I don't live around here."

"What are you going to do with them?"

"Burn them. Writing stuff down, it was something my therapist suggested I do. Well, she said to keep a journal, that it was a good idea for keeping track of my memories if I was having a hard time, but it felt kind of weird talking to myself, so I sent copies to Jessie. It became a routine."

"What happens now that your routine is . . ."

"Done for? Stop sending letters and start journaling properly, like I should have done in the first place."

It only took another five minutes of dragging Jessie through the woods to drop her off with Mr. Black in his office. He ordered everyone back to their cabins for the night and from the grunts and elongated sighs, it was clear everyone was relieved. As soon as we got back to the cabin, my cabinmates instantly toppled into their respec-tive beds, not bothering to change out of their muddy clothes or take off their shoes. I flicked on a lamp and undressed, even if it took me five minutes to take off Vivian's jacket. It smelled too damn good to get rid of willingly.

I climbed up onto my bed and rested my arms behind my head. Instead of drifting off to sleep like I wanted to, I lay there, wide awake. It wasn't a period of insomnia or worry. I kept thinking back to before Jessie went and got herself lost, and honestly, it didn't feel real.

THIRTEEN

The memory of Vivian's lips pressed against mine ran through my head repeatedly, and my eyes were bound to the ceiling of the cabin all night long. The thoughts created an impossible warmth within my chest that shot up into terrifying flames, the more the whispers of rejections slipped through the cracks.

The lack of sleep left me twitching, and the sheer determination of Vivian the next morning didn't help. She woke us up at six o'clock to have a quick breakfast and then we were tossed out to play volleyball of all things. She'd swapped the schedule from our morning arts and crafts to an exercise activity for some reason. She slammed the doors multiple times with the palm of her hand and threatened to take away our locks if we didn't get up. Thankfully the cabin was the target of her morning rage.

The sun was bright, and out came the cap I took everywhere these days. It was the one thing in the camp that I quite liked, other than Vivian. I wouldn't have been surprised if it had melted into my skin.

Vivian forced the guys to carry a lawn chair to the make-do volley-ball court. "You can set it down here," Vivian ordered, shifting her sunglasses down to cover her eyes and stretching out on the chair. It made a little sense why she was so angry that morning, having to get up and deal with us when all she probably wanted was a lazy day. It was the same for me, but it wasn't because I couldn't be bothered to do anything—it was that damn kiss. It was holding her hand. It was every-thing we spoke about that made my knees weak and head all fuzzy.

Since there were only nine in total in the Beavers, we made three teams of three. Mike and Mason were on my team. Gwen, Abby, and Bennie were put on the opposing team to play us first. The remaining three, Lauren, Jessie, and Kendra, would sit on the sidelines as we played on the little beach volleyball court at the side of the lake.

While Mike and Jessie set up the net for the game, I dragged Gwen over to where Vivian was lying down. I sat at the end of the lawn chair. The last time the three of us were together was when things came to a head with Lauren about the letters. Ever since then, there had been a shift in the dynamics within the Beaver group so that Lauren was the one on the outskirts looking in. Even now, while we three were close to the changing huts and the rest of the campers waited by the wooden platform, dangling their feet in the water and waiting for the net to be put up, Lauren sat in the sand all by herself.

"Have you two spoken about . . .?" I asked, not mentioning Lauren by name because of how close we were to the rest of the campers.

"Here's the thing, Em," Gwen said, clasping her hands together. "I don't want to tell Dad anything. It hasn't been *that bad*. Okay, maybe it has, but it's *not* anymore. What's the point in rocking the boat when we don't need to?"

"There's something you're not telling me."

"I'm working here for free," Vivian said. "As is Walter. As is Uncle Manny. Our mother's in the kitchen, our father is—"

"Point is,"—Gwen cut Vivian off—"we need every camper we can get to keep this place afloat. Lauren's family is influential, and if she gets kicked out, her family can destroy the camp's reputation."

"Are you not funded by some sort of board of education?"

"It's a privately owned camp, Emma. Reputation is everything—the lure for campers, the lure for sponsors, and her dad's company is one of the biggest. I'm good now. Why should I ruin my dad's business when it's not a problem anymore?"

"So that's it?" I asked. "She's getting away with *everything*?"

"Yes," Gwen said firmly.

"No." Vivian pushed the sunglasses off of her face and pierced her sister with a withering glare. "Lauren's not going to be around as much during the day because she is, in fact, being punished."

"Please don't tell me she's doing kitchen duty? That's my gig."

"Cleaning maintenance."

"I wish I could take a picture of you guys right now," Gwen said out of the blue. That was all the prompting Vivian needed to push me off the lawn chair using her foot. Gwen helped me to my feet, and when I was standing, she kept hold of my hands and wiggled them as she danced. "You guys looked so domestic sitting next to each other like that! Cute as buttons."

Awkward.

Clearing my throat, I said, "Yeah, until she *pushed me* off the damn chair. Come on. Have they got the net up? They've got the net up."

✦

"Okay, Emma, it's not as hard as it seems." Mike put the ball in my hands, smiling encouragingly. "Start us off by whacking the ball to the other side of the net to get a feel for it, you know?"

"I hope you're not competitive," I grumbled, reluctantly holding the ball.

"I mean, Gwen killed my nuts at that dodgeball game."

"Good thing she has no nuts for you to take a shot at," I said, looking down pointedly.

"Dude," he said, his cheeks reddening.

"I will put in the minimum amount of effort," I joked.

"That's all we ask." Mason high-fived me.

"Let's do this," I said, twirling the ball in my hand.

My promise went down the drain when I found it took a little more effort than I thought to bop the ball over the net. The game got a little crazy when instead of slapping the ball away from my face like a fly, I headbutted it and it flew over the net, getting us a point. The boys stared at me like they were prepared to kneel and appoint me the volleyball goddess. The other team groaned in frustration, and then there was Vivian, who, apparently deciding to pay attention to the game, cackled. That was enough volleyball to last a lifetime. Instead of savoring my team's reaction, I called for a break. Gwen moved forward so we met at the net while everyone else gulped down bottles of water.

"You haven't moved in fifteen minutes and now you're winning the game," she said, impressed.

"What can I say? I'm a natural."

"Emma and I are tag teaming Jessie and Kendra," she called out to her sister before dragging me off the court.

"What? This isn't wrestling—you can't tag team!" Mike yelled after us.

"Would you look at that, my friend requires emotional support," I explained.

Gwen forced me to the boulder overlooking the lake and court and made us lay down on top of it so that we couldn't see anything—the sun wouldn't allow us to open our eyes.

"Do you want to know a secret, Emma?"

"Is it as much pressure as I'm thinking it is?"

"Not this one," she sang. "My family are fundamentally dorks.

Charming, delightful, and impressive specimens, but ultimately, dorks. With one exception. Vivian. So it's rather strange to see how she's so awkward today. You're the embodiment of awkward and lazy. Today? You headbutted a volleyball, Emma. Full head movement. I daresay, almost graceful."

I scampered to my feet. "I think I'm going to do that some more."

"Emma," Gwen whined.

"Headbutting!"

✦

Most of our activities that week were outdoors stuff, nothing restricted to secluded areas. A couple of hours after the volleyball game we were brought back to the arts and crafts cabin. Thankfully, the temporary counselor, Marissa, had already left camp, having given the counselors her phone number if they needed more of her help.

But spending time in the kitchens with Julie was my favorite time of the day. I was learning stuff like knife skills and the proper amount of spice to add to vegetarian chili. One neat trick she taught me when we were doing steak for dinner was to dry the meat so it would sear properly. She got me to dab the meat with a paper towel and the end result was dark, crisp, and really flavorful. While Dad was awesome, he wasn't the best cook, and it gave me a lot of wiggle room to test things out at home. He'd probably think that I'd come home from a culinary camp. I'd probably find a way to get into trouble again to get on kitchen duty if Julie decided she didn't need my help anymore. I had to get through arts and crafts before I was meant to be back in the kitchen.

Mike the little sock key chain was set on the table beside my marker for inspiration for today's exercise. I'd had him since that day at the waterfall. He was a symbol, a token of that day because what would have happened if she hadn't sprung it on me that she'd kept him?

Kept him on her person? The way she presented him to me . . . gosh, it meant *everything* to me. He represented the start of our honesty toward one another.

There was a large poster on the table, and everyone had their own individual sections to attach to the edges. Vivian had briefly mentioned a consent exercise when we were doing archery, so here we were, making up our own slogans and words to remind "certain people" about its meaning.

"Emma, seriously, hiding your face won't stop me from pointing out how you guys are both acting strange," Gwen said, refusing to let the conversation drop.

"I disagree." I continued to hold my poster in front of my face.

"You're such a baby," Gwen muttered, placing her fingers along the rim of paper. "I shared a secret with you." She slowly dragged the page down. "My secret observations, Emma. I don't share them with anyone."

I placed the poster flat on the table and grumbled, "And you want me to do the same?"

She handed me a tube of glitter and nudged my shoulder with hers. "No."

"Then what do you want? Me and Vivian aren't acting strange at all, dude."

"I want nothing. I just . . . you're both grumpy stumps."

"Grumpy stumps," I repeated slowly.

"Yes, grumpy, but in separate ways, together the two of you are pretty adorable."

I placed the glitter tube into the front pocket of my T-shirt and went up to the shelves containing everything and anything concerning art. The thing was, it was so much stuff that I had no idea what to use first. I grabbed a plain old black marker and sat back down on my chair. At this point, Gwen was too consumed by her glitter bomb mess to pester me anymore. I drew a gigantic stick figure and a speech bubble, and considered my little project done. All I had to do was come up with short but effective words to push the message of consent home.

I rested my cheek against my hand and assumed a position so I could have a staring contest with the little owl and his one large eye. Despite Vivian going to extreme lengths to avoid me now, she'd kissed me. In the end, she'd kissed me, and that was her choice.

"I've been thinking about what you said, about how we should forget it, but I can't." Lauren sat in the chair next to me and played with a sheet of paper. "I get it. You're afraid of your feelings. Me too. I'm giving you this so maybe you'll be brave too."

Throughout her whole speech, I didn't blink once. "Say what now?"

"Read this," she said, shoving the page in my direction.

DO YOU CONSENT TO ME?

"Look, I'll forgive you for stealing my phone because I don't want drama. That's not cowardly. Then I found about you somehow blackmailing Gwen with something that belonged to me? So, no, no phone for you."

There was a moment of silence. "Emma, I think you're confused."

I prodded the page below me harshly. "This, Lauren, this isn't something to be joked about."

Grabbing the two posters, I made my way out of the cabin. Shaking my head, I plopped onto the floor of the deck outside the arts and crafts center. Those five words scribbled on a page didn't make sense.

I jumped out of my skin when I heard shuffling behind me. With a far too quick twist of my neck, the realization that it was Vivian did nothing to help the sudden shock that went through it. Rubbing beneath my hairline, I groaned, "I forgot that you were out here."

Vivian stayed in the lounge chair but turned her body so that she could see me. "You *were* a little hasty with the door."

"Lauren's acting . . . weird. She steals my phone. I give her an out and we forget about it." I held up the poster so that Vivian could see it, and it was quickly swiped from my hand. "Only, she doesn't forget about it. Now she wants my consent to use it? She makes no sense to me. I know what I can write on this thing now," I said, scribbling the words down on my paper.

Vivian sat up on the lounge chair with her legs crossed and looked over my shoulder down at the poster. "'Only yes means yes.'"

"Yup. Blunt as hell and everything else is no. Even silence. Uncertainty. Absolutely no."

"Emma, I think you and Lauren have your wires crossed."

"I'm pretty sure I have a firm grasp of her bullying tendencies, Vivian, being the target and all."

"Gwen did mention the exhausting part of dealing with your obliviousness," she murmured, reaching forward to place Lauren's poster in front of my face. This way, I was entrapped in her arms as her head leaned over my shoulder. "She has a crush on you. This message was supposed to be some sort of comical way of asking you out, I'm guessing, which is quite depressing. Her handwriting is deplorable."

My mouth dropped open at her explanation. My hand reached forward and calmly removed the poster from her grasp, only to bunch it into a ball and throw it into the trash can opposite me.

"You're telling me she *likes* me? That's impossible. I would've known."

Vivian chuckled. "No, you really wouldn't have."

"Why? Have *you* had a crush on me for that long?"

She shifted backward, panicked. Cute. "I think your stick figure needs one more leg," she said, dismissing me.

"No, that's the way he is," I disagreed, standing up. I perched the owl on top of her shoulder and turned around to go back inside, calling over my shoulder, "Mike misses you."

As soon as I went into the cabin three heads looked in my direction, and each had a spare seat beside them. Time slowed down enough for me to consider my options. One was Gwen, who was really riding that whole tell-me-everything-about-you-and-Vivian wave, which was a little awkward to try and talk about. First of all, Vivian was her sister, so that would be weird, and second, well, I'd never done the whole talking-about-people-I-liked thing. This was a whole new experience for me—liking someone and actually having them like me back was slightly terrifying. Even if I had happened to have a crush before Vivian, it wasn't like I had anyone to talk about it with.

The second person who paid me attention was Lauren, who my crush claimed had a crush on *me*. It made sense. The whole isolation trip was the biggest hint because she didn't want me to hate her despite all our grievances against each other. How was I supposed to know that the girl who left me up in that tree and hadn't thought to apologize, the girl who sprayed apple juice on me, the girl who tried to play it off like I started the food fight had a crush on me? That night in the tent, trying to hold my hand, the conversations after the isolation trip . . . that was another conversation I wasn't yet equipped to deal with because I'd never had anyone who liked me before, especially someone I didn't like back.

Then there was the last head faced in my direction: Jessie. The betrayer of all my deepest and darkest thoughts. She was the perfect person to sit beside! At first when I sat down, we didn't fully acknowledge each other. It wasn't until she turned around in her chair with a piece of paper in her hand that we made eye contact again.

Taking the offered page, I asked, "What's this?"

"Something you deserve," she said quietly.

It simply said: I'm sorry.

"You were telling the truth. You didn't have the letters anymore," I said.

"But you were right. I gave them to her, to Lauren," she whispered too low for anyone but me to hear. "I'm sorry."

"Can I ask why? I never did anything to you, Jessie."

"You came to camp. Your most feared place and somehow, even then, you managed to get a new best friend in a second flat. I thought it would be cool to hang out this summer. Catch up. It's why I kept those letters, you know? Why I brought them with me in the first place? You confided in me. I know this sounds really selfish, but you didn't need to anymore and . . ."

"You were jealous."

"Yes."

"I can't apologize for making new friends. It's something I thought I was literally incapable of. Imagine my surprise when Gwen wanted to be my friend too? Why me? Why not anyone else? There's a lot of people cooler than me."

Jessie disagreed. "She has good taste."

"Thanks for apologizing."

"Thanks for not punching me in the face. Or vomiting on me that one time . . ."

"It was very touch and go," I joked.

"We're not going to be close anymore, are we?" she asked suddenly.

"I'm sorry, I don't think I'm capable of trusting you, and without trust . . . friendship doesn't work. Or so Gwen tells me."

"I get it. I'm glad we talked anyway."

"Same here."

We went back to doodling for the rest of the arts and crafts time. Thinking about it, I'd made the right call. There was no returning to that friendship even after talking about something as hard as our *feelings*. But there was no point in holding on to resentment and rage.

The camp's environment already drained a hell of a lot of energy out of my body—I didn't need the extra stress from enacting revenge on my ex-best friend.

Glancing up from the page, I saw both Gwen and Lauren were peeking at me. Now, *those* conversations could wait until another day.

FOURTEEN

Two days went by and suddenly it was the eighteenth of July. Three weeks into camp and I found myself still dealing with the fact that I had a proper crush for the very first time. Having a crush on someone was one of the more optimistic and happy feelings in the world. It could be a small bubble that no one could trample on because those feelings were your own and a well-kept secret. For it to transform into something more profound and reciprocated blew my mind because it wasn't a happy little secret anymore; it was my reality, and the scary thing about escaping fantasy was the unpredictability of life.

And no one was more erratic than Vivian Black.

The spiderweb dangling from the corner of the ceiling above my bed didn't deter me from staring into space for a while after dinner, replaying every little moment with Vivian in my mind over and over again until it felt like a silly daydream. We'd had the choice of signing up for yoga in the recreational hall. Meditation in my bed was the superior choice. I turned onto my side at the same time Lauren shuffled around in her bed. Since when did she get back? Abby must've still been at yoga.

"Emma, you misinterpreted a lot of things that I think I need to explain," Lauren said quietly.

I became suddenly aware of our last conversation. "Vivian explained it to me. Don't worry."

"I'm sure she did." Lauren perched herself at the side of her bed and clasped her hands together. "We're compatible, Emma. One of those love-hate relationships that eventually lead to a romantic partnership."

"I wasn't aware that there was a love-hate situation," I admitted.

"Me either. Not until I could put a word to the constant tension between us."

"Yeah, that underlying tension that you feel? I think it's only you who feels it." I rubbed my forehead. Job applications that were denied over email, their rejections were to the point and snappy, right? That's what needed to be done here. "Thank you for your interest, but we're, I mean *I'm* not looking for what you're offering at this moment in time. Our interests don't align."

The immediate silence forced me to peek open my eyes to see the aftermath. Lauren stayed in the same position, her fingers tangled in her hair, frozen. "You haven't given me a chance. I know you said it was because of that day . . . when I left you up in that tree, but you treat Mike like it never happened."

"Mike apologized to me," I said.

"How about Jessie, then? I saw you two speaking the other day too."

"She apologized too. But that doesn't mean we're automatically friends again. It doesn't work like that."

"I'm sorry."

"You know, I might've believed your apology if it wasn't for the fact that you invaded my privacy. First it was my phone. Then you taunted Gwen with the letters? Be honest with me. Why?"

"Have you ever read a really great book and never wanted it to end?" she asked. "Reading your letters was like that for me. You go around camp with Gwen and distance yourself from everyone else, but when I read your letters, I got a look inside your brain. The way you talk about your mom . . . not accepting you for who you are. Ditching you, forgetting your birthdays, the arguing between your parents, hell, you even blame yourself for their divorce because you came out when you were twelve, Emma."

"I don't need a refresher on my life, Lauren."

"I'm sorry. We would understand each other. My dad . . . he's the same as your mom. The way you desperately hate camp and want to get out of here to spend time with your dad? It's the exact opposite for me. I want to stay here to not have to deal with him every day of summer. Keeping that secret every second around him feels like I'm slowly dying. But it's better than him disowning me for being gay. Camp has always been there for me. Every single summer without fail."

"I'm sorry that your dad is like that," I said, knowing that homophobic parents were really tricky. "Why get everyone to ignore Gwen?"

"It's always about her, right?" Lauren asked. "She has everything. Next summer, she could run this place if she wanted to with her entire family. She didn't need to read your letters to get to know you. Why should she get everything without trying? There needs to be a balance. If she got you, she couldn't have the rest of my friends too. Couldn't I have one thing to myself?"

"You treated her that way before I came into the picture, Lauren."

"There's only one spot for camp counselor next summer and this camp runs on nepotism. Why would she want to be a counselor next year if she *hated* it this year?"

"Why are you telling me all this now?"

"You asked and I wanted to be open with you, to show you that you can be open with me, too, that it's possible. Besides, there really isn't a chance of me getting that job next year. Not anymore."

"That's the deal you made with Vivian, right? Leave Gwen alone and you'll get the spot next year?"

"That's right."

The air in the cabin was suddenly overbearingly stuffy and too warm. The only windows in here were above Lauren's bed and in the bathroom—both much too far away. The only sound in the cabin was the rhythmic ticking of my watch. Nine o'clock couldn't come soon enough for Abby to come in to lend us the distraction of small talk about what happened at yoga. Would it always be this way? Me counting down the seconds while around Lauren now that I knew she liked me?

Vivian was in my position before and rejected Lauren.

"Hey . . ." I said, cutting through the tense silence. "When you asked Vivian out, you didn't actually like her, did you? You wanted an in for the counselor position?"

"What if I said yes?"

"I would say that this camp really isn't a healthy place for you to be."

"I'll apologize. I'll say sorry to everyone. To you. Properly."

"What's the catch?"

"You give me a chance."

"I'm sorry, Lauren. I can't."

"Can't or won't?"

It was both considering I had *something* with Vivian, but I couldn't say that. "I'm sorry, Lauren, but no. It doesn't mean we can't be civil though, right?"

If our roles were reversed and she rejected me, I'd want to be left alone instead of stewing in that awkwardness with her in a bed a couple of steps away. Even with her eyes on me, I thought I was sly as I slid out of bed and managed to haul Vivian's jacket back onto my body. Her scent felt like a protective bubble, warm and fluffy.

The door cracked open a little before it was slammed by a hand over my head. It was hard enough to vibrate and loud enough to be heard by anyone who was wandering outside. My stare lingered on the white knuckles pressed against the wall.

"Let go of the door, Lauren," I ordered, turning around.

"That's it, then? Reject me and run off to whoever you have waiting for you?" She leaned in closer, scoffing. "You're always sneaking out of here. I know you've got a bed buddy, who is it?"

"Speculation isn't a great form of detection, Lauren. Besides, you think you're entitled to that information because?"

"It's not about entitlement."

"Then what is it about? Because you felt entitled to my phone and my letters. Maybe it's the size of your ego after rejection? I'm sorry, but I don't like you that way. I'm sorry, but I don't."

"I'll find out who you're seeing," she declared, a feral look in her eyes. "And once I do . . ."

"What, you'll spray apple juice in my hair? Been there, done that."

"Emma, if you don't tell me—"

I shoved her away from me and didn't stop there. In the middle of her stumbling over a lone shoe, I moved forward and pushed her again with a grunt of effort. She couldn't find anything to grip to balance her weight, and consequently, she fell flat on her ass.

The cabin door opened, and as soon as Abby stepped inside, she noticed Lauren and was at her side in seconds.

"What the hell, Emma? Are you okay, Lauren? Honestly, you guys," Abby said. "Destroying the cabin every morning for weeks, the constant out to get one another during the day, I finally had peace when you both went on that isolation trip. You need to sort yourselves out. It's driving me nuts."

"I'm sorry, Abby," I said, and then removed myself from the situation and slipped out of the cabin and headed for the kitchen.

I threw the hood of Vivian's jacket over my head, dragging my feet.

Out of the corner of my eye, lights outside a cabin turned on, halting me in my tracks. Even though I was far away, I froze like a wild animal in oncoming traffic. The cabin door kicked open and Vivian came out, back arched like a cat amid a hunt, ready to scratch and claw at whatever came her way.

"Knock, knock." I announced my presence, rocking back and forth on my heels. Vivian startled.

"Do you ever not wander at night?" Vivian snapped. "It's contradictory—you're scared of camping, the woods, the animals, and then here you are, roaming the campground during the most dangerous time."

"Only the nights I'm not annoyed," I admitted.

"But you're out most nights," she pointed out.

"I'm in a constant state of annoyance. Why are you out here? Does it not freak you out that you're alone out here, in this cabin?" I asked. "I'm stuck with Lauren, and even that feels safer than being all alone."

"I like having my own space."

"Don't tell me it's a spider in there," I teased. "Is that why you're out of bed? A spider?"

"I'm simply tired. I'm sure you can empathize."

"Totally. It's usually because my brain is too busy thinking. So, the question is, what are you thinking about?"

"Wouldn't you like to know," she said slyly. "What about you? What will you do while wearing my jacket?" she asked.

I placed my hand on the cabin door's handle instead of answering her question. Vivian clearly had no intention of stopping me, and I needed to investigate. The room was dark, so I pushed the door open enough to let moonlight shine inside. Vivian's boots crunched against the stones, wandering away from the cabin. Out of nowhere, some sort of tiny black thing scrambled across the floor, making me trip over myself and scramble to get out of the cabin.

I spun around and grabbed the rail with both hands, steadying myself while panting. "What the hell was that?"

Vivian stood on the stones, arms crossed, scowling. As she mumbled something, I leaned across the rail closer to her. "What did you say?"

"You were right, it's a spider," she hissed, stomping her foot. "A tiny creature there to make my life a living hell. You want to win the competition, don't you?"

"At this rate, I don't think you can catch up." I tapped her fingers so that she'd let go. I leaned across the railing and tried my best not to place my hand over her hand, which was now clutching the front of my jacket. "Are you suggesting that I kick down your door like a knight in shining armor and save the day? Rather cliché, don't you think? Asking the girl who is literally scared of this entire experience?"

"It's an insect."

She wasn't going to sleep that night with it still in there. "You want me to kill that foul beast?"

"I'm asking you to politely ask my intruder to leave. You'll do that for me, won't you?"

The moonlight made Vivian's hair appear softer than any imaginable substance on earth. I heard myself speak before the thought even originated in my mind. "Fine."

I fumbled around for a few minutes, tossing stuff out of the way to get the spider into a tissue, then tossed it out the front door. Vivian was sitting with her legs under the last rail, swinging her feet back and forth off the platform, with her elbows leaning against the middle bar and her chin resting on top of her open palms. Her cheeks were rosy.

"What are you thinking about?" I asked.

"You," Vivian answered. She stood up from her position on the platform's wood and came toward me. She zipped open my jacket, nudged the glitter in the front pocket of my T-shirt to the side, and placed the owl key chain next to it. Then she grabbed my hand. She pulled me toward the door of her cabin and inclined her head inside. "I'm not scared of being alone out there, but I'd prefer some company. Your company."

The little owl's eye bulged under the moon. "You like me."

"Unfortunately."

Vivian pressed a finger against the side of the lamp beside her bed three times and a yellow light illuminated the small space. I was relaxed now that we were indoors, and walked backward toward the middle of the room until I felt the edge of the bed, then dropped down onto it. To the right, hung up on the wall, was a mural of a large maple tree, but instead of an overwhelming number of orange leaves, it had a variety of colors, like a rainbow.

It was a home away from home. I considered my bedroom back home my own personal safe haven, with trinkets and comforts that were mine. This cabin gave off that same vibe; it felt like I'd stepped into a portion of Vivian's brain, and it was terrific.

"You know about my late-night snacking. You totally waited out there for me to come strolling by."

Vivian kicked clothes out of her way as she made her way across the room and sat primly on the end of the bed, clasping her hands together. "Now that's what you call paranoia, Emma. You clearly haven't been getting much sleep. Don't make accusations that you can't back up," she teased, skirting her hand across the bedsheets, cheeks lifted into what I thought was a sly grin. "I've learned something about you today. Something pivotal to whether or not I want to continue this courtship."

"And what's that?" I asked, flopping back so that my legs hung off the bed but my head rested in the middle of it.

"You're brave."

My eyes closed. The camp made me feel the opposite, but being here with Vivian? She made me brave. "A spider is literally a tiny little obstacle in life, Vivian."

"You're brave because you didn't once mention heading back to the cabins and out of the woods before we found Jessie. The thought didn't enter your head at all, and even if it did, you didn't make it known." A contented hum sounded from my throat as her fingers ran through my hair. She continued, "Are you ever going to explain the reason behind your phobias?"

"It's silly," I admitted.

"Most things are when it comes to you, but I don't care."

I laughed a little. "Growing up, I loved the outdoors. I liked napping on a lounge chair or on a trampoline, feeling the sun against my face. One day, Dad decided it was the perfect night to pitch a tent in the front garden. It was endless arguments between my parents, so I jumped at the chance to separate them for a while."

"How old were you?" Vivian asked.

"Ten. Here's a secret: I used to love, and I do mean love, climbing trees."

"I'm finding it hard to believe you," she told me. "What happened?"

"Then I came to camp." I turned my head to the side as she was rolling her eyes. "Lauren and Mike wanted to walk around camp on our last night here. And when we heard someone coming, we climbed the trees higher than I ever have before. I swear, Vivian, it felt like the world was about to end. I couldn't breathe. Everything kept spinning around. So, I'm there, on a branch, frozen and unable to speak, and they hopped down and left me there."

Vivian's fingers circulated right beneath my ear and asked, "What did you do?"

I faced the ceiling again and closed my eyes. "Cried mostly. I was cold, wet, and miserable, and I couldn't do anything but wait it out."

"You're holding back something. You climbed up. Why couldn't you climb down?"

"There was a branch above me, one of the last ones at the top that kept wobbling."

"You were scared it was going to hit you?"

"At first, until I noticed what was on the branch. It was a wasps' nest. I sat there for hours, head craned upward, feeling the rain against my face, but I didn't care because I was petrified that the wasps would sting me to death. Even when the wind stopped, I felt like if I had screamed, or made any sound, the wasps would wake up or something and attack me. Your dad got me down eventually."

We heard the pitter-patter of light rain against the roof, then Vivian said, "I pity you so much that I'm even willing to let you fall asleep on the bed and not on the floor."

"What will the neighbors think?"

Vivian twirled a strand of my hair, shifting her position so that her face was above mine. "I'm sure they'll remain consumed with their straight outlook on life and won't give it a second thought."

"You're going to let me stay here the night?"

She took in a deep breath. "Concede to me winning the courtship and we'll see."

"Nope."

She tugged on my hair then stood up and started organizing her belongings. I assumed the only reason she didn't freak out was because it was her counselor clothes that were tossed around the place and not her personal clothing.

It took me longer than I'd like to admit, getting out of the haze she'd settled me into by playing with my hair, to get up and help her pack her things back into their respective places. It only took us a few minutes because it was clear that the room was usually kept tidy, and it helped that the only things I'd tossed while chasing the spider were easily accessible.

Vivian wandered over to me and unzipped the jacket, then took it off me and draped it across the chair by the desk. She came back and plucked the glitter and key chain from my T-shirt pocket. She placed them on the desk, too, not saying a word, then tossed me a pair of her pajamas.

All she had to do was rid herself of her boots, and then she climbed into the bed and waited. The only remaining light in the room came from her bedside lamp. One of my hands rested on my hips, and the other held the pajamas she gave me.

"I'll close my eyes," she assured me.

"I wasn't going to ask that, but good call," I muttered, shifting awkwardly in the middle of the room.

"You're nervous," she deduced, sounding a little amused. A moment went by where we both didn't say anything. I changed from my camp clothes into pajamas and went toward the end of the bed. She broke the silence by suggesting, "Think of it like a sleepover."

"I've never had a sleepover before," I revealed reluctantly.

"May I?"

"Yeah, sorry."

"Well," she said, opening her eyes and looking dead at me, making my heart skip a beat. "Have you ever imagined having one?"

"Of course."

Vivian patted the other side of the bed after pulling back the covers. I followed her silent instruction and slipped under the covers. Lying on my back stiff and unmoving wasn't part of the plan, but that's what happened. She made no move to turn off the lamp. She laid down on her side so that her cheek rested against her hand on the pillow, and smiled up at me. Slowly, like she was afraid that I'd change my mind and leave, she reached out with her other hand and gently cupped my cheek, turning my head to face her.

Her eyes practically sparkled. "Tell me about how you imagined a sleepover."

"Like the movies," I said. "Friends sharing secrets, not having a filter because they chose to be there. Popcorn. Not the cheesy kind or the other weird crap. Buttered. Proper popcorn, you know? Scary movies, blankets, I don't know."

"We might not have popcorn, we might not be exactly friends, but you have chosen to be here."

"And the secret sharing?"

"Anything you wish to share?"

"I consider you a friend. A best friend, maybe, if I'm not crazy."

"Best friends, courting each other." She hummed thoughtfully.

"I guess all that's left is the scary movie," I said.

"Find the remote, and by all means, we can watch something scary." She settled farther into the blankets and let her hand trail down my cheek, my chin, and my neck until finally she curled a hand around my waist and closed her eyes. "My secret is, I'd much rather stay in this position."

"Goddammit," I whispered to myself. "You're good at this."

"Good at what?" she prompted, smug as hell.

"Wooing. I think I might black out from swooning this hard," I said. "Damn. I don't think sleepovers have one participant staring at the other's lips. There was probably a lot of subtext in those movies. I'd probably know what to do right now if that subtext was, you know, plain and visible rather than hiding in the shadows."

"Emma," she said, her voice husky. "The subtext may rapidly become text if you keep spilling what's on your mind."

"Again, it doesn't give a lot of direction."

"Concede," she mumbled.

"No way."

"Concede," she repeated, smoothly turning me onto my side so that her hand curled beneath my shirt and rested against the skin of my back. My body was pulled much closer so that we could feel each other's breaths. "Concede."

She kissed me, and the world fell away. It was slow and soft, comforting in ways that words would never be. Her fingers slowly trailed their way down my back until they slipped out. Her thumb then caressed my cheek for a moment before she returned her hand to my spine, running her fingers down it and pulling me closer until there was no space left between us. I could feel the beating of her heart against my chest.

The scent of roses swirled around us, even as she removed her lips from mine so that they were apart.

Opening my eyes, I said, "Wow."

She rested her forehead against mine. "Now that you've conceded, and I've won the courtship, it's over."

I blinked. "What does that mean?"

"We're officially together."

"Cool."

"Quite."

FIFTEEN

Waking up, covers wrapped tightly around my body with Vivian's arm flung around my waist and our legs intertwined, could there be a more perfect morning? When her warmth slipped away, leaving me in only a bundle of covers, a lost and numb sensation flooded my system. I wanted to burrow my head back into her warmth and never leave. She tumbled back beneath the duvet and sat on my stomach with a satisfied hum. A thinly veiled tingling sensation moved across my chin, making my eyelashes flutter slightly. Then it moved up my cheek and onto my eyelids, and finally onto my nose. Vivian wore a mildly serious expression of concentration, lips pursed and eyebrows furrowed. It was such a simple moment that for a split second, I forced my eyes to close, fearing the stinging sensation that made its way through them.

"What are you doing?"

"Upgrading your face, Emma," she informed me briskly.

"Upgrading my . . ." She gave me a second to investigate before she pulled away and continued her doodling. "You're using the glitter. On my face. Glittering my face."

Another flick, glide, and splat.

"Emma, Emma, Emma, this is all part of the sleepover experience," she said. "We skipped the movie, and I felt terrible about it. Just dreadful. I had to ensure that your first sleepover was one to remember."

"You," I said, prodding her chest, "stole my idea."

"Your idea?" She stopped her glittering for a moment, eyes gliding across my face. She reached for the cap of the glitter bottle and screwed it back on. She slipped out of the bed. "You know, Emma, I believe I courted you enough, having over fifty points and all, but you, you may not have. You need to leave."

"Oh. Right. Okay." I got up and got my clothes from where she now stood by the desk, bundling the pile in my hands.

"We're going to the lake today," she said as she sat in the chair and began brushing her hair while considering herself in the mirror. "I'm not exactly sure what I'll have you do when we get there, but at least there's an outline for the day. Maybe I'll leave you to entertain yourselves for once. What do you think?"

"Sure," I replied.

She brushed a particularly hard tangle. "Not that I want you to leave, Emma. Everyone will be up soon. They can't see you leave here."

"This is going to be complicated, isn't it?"

She nodded her head sagely. "Even our most simple conversations are complicated, Emma."

"Interesting though."

"Always interesting," she agreed. "Go on, get dressed."

Vivian placed one hand over her eyes and parted her fingers to peek through. I snatched a cushion from her bed and threw it at her. Unfortunately, it didn't prompt a pillow fight. She was right. I had to leave before everyone—especially Lauren—woke up.

"Your phone," Vivian said, spinning around in the chair with it between her fingers. "I could have put it back in the shed after confiscating it from Lauren. I'd give it back to you, but that would be playing favorites. Though knowing you, you'd accidentally get yourself kicked out of camp. Unless you purposely would?"

"No, not now," I confirmed.

"I'm glad." She took my hand in hers. "You can admire your cat when you're in here. Sadly, you'll have to go about your day without seeing his precious face."

"Oh, the horror," I joked, backing out of the cabin. "Okay, I'll leave you to it."

✦

Like Vivian had mentioned that morning, we went to the lake. And unlike every other time we did anything related to water, because we wouldn't be traveling far from the land, we didn't have to wear bathing suits, and unfortunately for others, there was no option but to wear a life jacket. There was no point in the campers debating with Vivian whether they were strong swimmers. When signing up for camp, everyone ticked the boxes indicating whether they could swim or not.

We walked along the wooden ramp that led into the lake and jumped onto the portable, inflatable trampoline, which was strapped down so that it couldn't completely drift away from the walkway. Vivian stayed on the ramp, and she brought my phone rather than hers to play with. I hung back with Vivian for a few minutes, despite Gwen's pleas to race and jump into the water.

"Smile, Emma," Vivian whispered.

"You're using my own phone to take pictures of me? Why not use your own?"

"It's dead," she explained. Then directed, "Come here."

"Don't you see me walking?"

"Faster."

"Oh my God." I stood in front of her, superpose displayed by placing my hands on my hips and tilting my chin upward in a self-righteous way.

"All you need is a cape," she murmured, taking more pictures.

"No capes."

"Sorry?"

"Haven't you seen *The Incredibles*?"

"No."

"We're *so* watching that. There are so many life lessons in there."

Vivian spun around and hiked the phone up so that she could take a picture of both of us. I was caught off guard, which a superhero was never supposed to have happen to them. I charged forward and snatched the phone, making sure to keep my back to the campers.

"There are so many pictures," I commented.

"They're beautiful, aren't they?"

"Hundreds of your selfies . . ."

"Your point?"

"Enough to entertain yourself while I go shove Gwen off the trampoline."

The thing about nine people on a trampoline was the constant movement. Even if you didn't want to participate, the bouncing bodies made enough movement that your body couldn't stay still. Miserably, I crossed my arms as my body was forced up and away from the black, elastic fabric below, the only barrier between me and the clear water.

Daydreaming on a trampoline was dangerous. A body knocked against my shoulder and sent me flying into the lake. The submersion under a quick flash of colder-than-expected water killed any rational thought, kicking in rapid survival instincts. I tried opening my eyes while I was under the water and ended up seeing a white blur. My capability to think fast in high-pressure situations was obviously not that great. I rose to the surface by kicking my legs as hard as I could then gasped, inhaling too much air to feel comfortable.

"Sorry, Emma, you zoned out, and this isn't the place to zone out," Gwen chirped from her position at the edge of the trampoline. I'd failed. She'd pushed me off first. "It could get you hurt. Besides, your face is sparkly! I thought a quick dip in the water might help."

"It could get me hurt. It *could*? I think you stole my breath away, and not even in the good way."

"I'm not my sister, Emmykins."

"Gwen," I hissed, hiding beneath the water.

"I feel powerful up here with you down there." Gwen's eyebrows furrowed as Jessie knocked against her. In a split second, she slid off the trampoline and gracefully splashed into the water next to me. She rose to the surface and offered a wry grin. "I probably wouldn't wield that power well, huh?"

"Probably not."

"Your faith in me is remarkable."

"I know," I said, pushing now-wet hair away from my face. "So, what's up?"

Gwen made small ripples with her arm movements and hummed innocently. "I heard from a little birdie that you snuck out of your room last night. Okay, the bird was me. I was the bird and was hungry and . . . you weren't in the cabin."

I swam over to the edge of the trampoline to hold on to something. "And you know that how?"

She floated on her back. "I might have lookedthroughthehole."

"What was that?"

"Not important," Gwen mumbled, letting herself face-plant into the water, sinking and then popping up right in front of my face. "What is important, Emma, is the way you zone out. Your face when you do it. It's not so bland and ugh. No blah. It's more like sunshine and rainbows. Not the gay rainbows. Just, that pureness. Okay, so maybe some gay rainbows."

"Next thing you'll tell me is that you're writing fan fiction about us?"

"Maybe I am a little?"

I shoved her. "Gwen."

She shoved me back. "Emma. I'm kidding. Maybe. Mostly."

It turned into a water fight. How else could we battle in the lake? For such a small and frail-looking girl, she sure created some gigantic waves that ended up with me spewing water out of my mouth most of the time.

I ended up removing myself from above the surface and swimming beneath the water. The camp T-shirt clung to my skin, like an outer layer. There was something about moving with eyes closed firmly that was soothing, like the heaviness that weighed me down floated away as the serenity of the water carried its burden. When I came up for air, I was near the shallow edge of the lake.

Standing up, the water came to my waist. Gwen was back on the trampoline, jumping a little too high. As soon as she spotted me, she shot me two thumbs-up and a not-so-subtle wink. If I looked hard enough, I could see specks of glitter sparkling from the side of my nose. I spun around as people from the trampoline jumped, facing my direction, pointing and whispering about the wonder that was my face. Yeah. That was enough of the trampoline for that day.

✦

That night after dinner, Vivian and I went to the back of the counselors' cabins near the picnic tables and swing sets. We sat on the swings and enjoyed the setting sun as it shone down on our faces, swinging our legs back and forth to gain momentum. Not too long after we took our positions, it turned into a competition for who could go the highest.

Vivian dared to go higher than me. I tucked the secret of me fearing heights into my pocket for that moment because the out-of-character fist pump she shot into the air when she beat me was too adorable.

Idly swinging, Vivian reached for her bag with the tip of her shoe and managed to scoop it up onto her leg, where she easily had access. She tucked something that glittered and hurt my eyes in her hand.

"That's chocolate, isn't it?" I asked, gaining a hum. "Give me a piece, and I'll follow through on a promise. I'll tell you a story."

The moment it clicked what I was talking about, she threw me a piece. "You don't have to, Emma. I wanted to trade stories to get to know you better. Gwen mentioned those letters were deeply personal."

"I want to trade stories with you too." I popped the chocolate into my mouth, humming in appreciation. "As you know, before coming here I had no friends. People avoided me like the plague. They didn't even conjure up the effort to bully me or anything. It's kind of like what the Beavers are doing to Gwen—the isolation."

"You have friends now. Even if they are my siblings. You have me."

"I know." The entire Black family had welcomed me with open arms since day one. "The letters were a way to vent. That's how Jessie and I kept in contact. It was like sending my problems off to a familiar stranger."

"Do you still want to keep a journal?"

"Sure, but that will have to start up again after camp when I have the chance to get one."

Vivian came to a stop at the same time as me. She got up from the swing, grabbed her backpack, and planted it on my leg. She took out a smooth, jet-black journal and came to stand between my legs. "If you want, you can keep it in my room so there's no chance of anyone having a peek." She wrapped her fingers at the back of my neck and heaved a content sigh. "And if writing doesn't work, I'm here for you. Even if we swing here for hours in silence or if you want to vent."

"Here come the waterworks," I complained. "I'm here for you too. Now it's your turn—tell me something that would make both of us cry."

"I do have a secret. Promise not to get mad?"

I hooked our smallest fingers together and mocked her from when I told her about my fear of camping. "I promise to conceal my anger."

"I deliberately kept you at camp."

"There was no debate about that."

"But I never told you why," she said, and avoided making eye contact, which was hard because she was standing between my legs. "Sometimes we get campers who need a little more help than others. You were so angry at the world. Isolated. Shutting yourself off from everyone. I didn't know at first that you were afraid of camping . . . but it's my duty as a counselor to help people and you, Emma, it seemed like you needed help. If I had known about your fears originally maybe I wouldn't have tried so hard to keep you here, but I think, at the end of the day, being here helps you. The closer you got to people, Gwen, me . . . it seems worth it. You're quiet. Are you angry with me?"

"I thought you hated me," I said, trying to process her big speech. "Thanks for telling me that. You're right. It has been a good thing—something I wouldn't have chosen for myself, but it *has* been worth it."

✦

Later that night back in the cabin, with an exhausted Lauren already snoring because her additional duties made her so tired, I wrote about how my days kept getting better and better. They were mostly stress-free, besides the anxiety that came with camping, but even then, that was improving. I wrote about Vivian and our intimate conversations, about Mrs. Black's lessons in the kitchen—not once mentioning that I wanted to get kicked out of camp. For the first time, maybe in my life, I felt positive, like a normal teenager.

SIXTEEN

The next morning I had gone to breakfast and instead of joining the rest of the Beavers in the arts and crafts center, Julie had requested my help in the kitchen. It wasn't like she needed my help, but she had set out lesson plans that she'd do with me all throughout camp. Today's lesson? Homemade burgers. There were at least ten bowls sitting there containing a meat mixture ready to be turned into burger patties. I was hesitant to put my hand inside, and that seemed to delight Julie.

"Think of it as a way to prepare for college life," she told me, tapping the bowl with a wooden spoon.

"Isn't that the time when you discover applications on your phone that deliver food to your house?" I asked. "Or steal from your roommate?"

"Surely you're not that ill-equipped when confronted with meals, Emma," she said, leaning her hip against the counter beside me, urging me with her hands to start taking out pieces of meat. So I did.

"From what I've seen, you've got quite the knack for it." She took the offered, rolled-up patty from my hand and plopped it onto a wooden board. "Roll this for me."

I started using the rolling pin, not missing how we'd swapped roles. "You make cooking easy. Following your instructions is chill, sure. Coming up with the recipes? Now, Mrs. Black, that's the real deal."

She rolled some more meat between her hands until it was smooth and round. "You don't give yourself enough credit, Emma."

"Leave me in here for a day without you and the whole camp will burn down. That's not a risk you want to take, seriously," I warned, seeing the glint in her eye.

"There is the annual campfire party, involving everyone—all the campers, staff, counselors—with activities like singing, making s'mores, dancing. I heard it's fun. I believe I'm due prep time off." She clapped her hands. "I'm sure one of my children might consider keeping you company. Besides, I'll be there to help you serve. We could trade off."

"They're more likely to distract and taunt me. I'm up for the challenge."

Julie turned on the griddle, and while that heated up, she showed me the right amount of seasoning to add, because there was nothing worse than bland food. She was in charge of her half of the station, and I occupied the other half, pressing a spatula on one side of the patties for three minutes. We flipped them at the same time we, reduced the heat, and placed a lovely, orange cheddar cheese on top. They were gooey and mouthwatering in a few minutes.

Three solid knocks sounded against the entrance door. Julie quickly ran the tap and rubbed her hands beneath the water before wiping them down the front of her apron.

She opened the door, and it quickly turned into a mush-fest with Mr. Black—their whispers too low for me to hear, the whole romantic shebang. I gave them as much privacy as possible, turning back around and buttering the burger buns on each side before tossing them on the griddle to crisp them up a little. There was nothing better than a crispy bun and gooey cheese with a burger.

They shuffled into the room, wearing delighted expressions until Mr. Black pointed at me and spoke quietly to his wife. The sheer joy of the room sobered into something quite depressing, like all the air had been sucked out of it.

"Emma," Julie called, leaning into the touch of her husband. "Your mother is on the phone for you."

"Mom?" I repeated in surprise, dropping the spatula on the counter and blinking rapidly.

Mr. Black led me into his office, where his desk telephone laid on the table.

The first thing I heard was my mother's breathing, and the second was the delighted laughter huffing from her lips as she spoke quietly to someone, muffled as though the device on her end was pressed against something.

"Emma! Sweetie, how are you?" she asked, sounding excited. "I tried ringing you, but of course, your phone was taken at the entrance, wasn't it? It was only after the tenth call that I remembered! I can see why they have that rule in place. They hold you back from talking to people, you know that. I hope you're not angry about that anymore."

She was lying about the calling-me thing. There were no such notifications on my phone. "I'm good."

"Good? That's all I get? Please don't tell me you're still angry about the change of plans, Emma."

I pulled the phone away from my ear and stared at it in disbelief. Putting it back against my ear, I snapped, "Tell me, if I locked you in a room with a bunch of knives sticking out from the ground and walls, would you be a happy camper, Mom?"

"That's different. You know that."

"How is it, though? Phobias, fears, they create the same feeling. Where it originates doesn't matter."

"Emma—look, I didn't call to fight with you." She released a quiet sigh. "I called because Ethan has offered to take us both to Rome for the rest of summer, after our trip to Spain. You'll be out of there in no time. Hopefully you won't be leaving any boyfriends behind."

"You mean, Ethan as in your husband? The husband I never met until the day you dropped me off here?"

"Please, Emma, don't start." She cleared her throat. "Your dad is seeing someone. Did you know that?"

"I did."

"You never complained to me about it. Honey, that's not . . . have you thought about how you reacted to my news? Why you reacted that way? Why haven't you reacted that way to your dad's new relationship?"

"He didn't keep me in the dark about the relationship and introduce his wife at the same time he was ditching me at a camp for two months. A place where I told you for years I didn't want to go to, a place where—"

"I can't talk to you when you're like this." She interrupted me.

"Why can you never listen?"

"Two weeks, Emma, be ready."

She hung up the phone.

Mr. Black knocked on his own office door and stuck his head inside. I had no reason to stay in there anymore. It had been a subconscious decision to put life outside of camp into a little box at the back of my mind and keep it closed. Now it burst open, and like a circus, all sorts of activities played out, nothing singularly stood out, making the chaos even more frantic.

I zoned out without realizing and began walking aimlessly. When my vision was no longer blurry, low and behold, there I was, somehow in front of the same waterfall where Vivian and I had kissed for the first time. I lay back precisely how I had the first time on the boulder and then understood why Jessie needed a while to herself to stare up at the sky the night she got drunk and lost in the woods. Today was brighter, and the clouds moved with the wind. They weren't stationary like the stars. And for some reason, I wanted them to just . . . stop. I wanted a stopwatch that could freeze time, preventing the inevitability of me leaving camp and Vivian and Gwen and the entire Black family earlier than anticipated.

Leaves rustled a little and I sat up, elbows behind my back. Vivian pushed her way through a stubborn branch. "I brought chocolate," she announced in greeting. She sat on the boulder and scooted close so that our sides touched. She broke off a piece and held out the chocolate in her palm. "My mother mentioned something about you cooking for us all."

"If she's willing to take that risk."

Vivian held the chocolate up close to my mouth, stopping half an inch away. "She wants me to help you."

I inched closer toward the chocolate. "Well, you are my counselor."

The chocolate grazed my lips. "She's fond of you."

Just as I was about to clamp my teeth down, she brought the chocolate away and popped it into her own mouth, eyes closed and moaning in appreciation.

We linked our smallest fingers together. She placed a piece of chocolate on my closed lips and leaned her head against my shoulder. We lay there, stretched out for a good twenty minutes in mostly silence, gorging on the most pleasant chocolate. Usually, I didn't like silence because my thoughts would run freely, wildly. It was like she knew that I needed the time to sort myself out, to pinpoint my emotions and what reactions were suitable for it.

The unpredictability of my mother held me back from telling Vivian about the phone call. Maybe Mom would change her mind and not pick me up. Having a conversation about it would make it real, and I wasn't ready to entertain the thought of leaving Vivian behind when all I wanted to do was spend all my time with her.

"Your mom's cool," I muttered after reaching for more chocolate but finding none.

"And what about your mom? Mom mentioned she called," she insisted, voice oh-so-casual.

"Do you always talk about your camper's personal lives with your mom?"

"I'm beginning to think she's trying to set me up," Vivian said.

"Your family is obsessed with your love life," I grumbled, scrunching up my nose.

"With you, you idiot," she clarified.

"And how I welcome that obsession."

"She's always the one to bring you up in conversation." Vivian crumpled the chocolate wrapper. "Somehow, you charmed her so that she thinks that me spending more time with you is a good thing and not against protocol."

"Shut up and kiss me?"

"See? You can be charming."

Vivian was the embodiment of sensuality, not because of the way her jacket looked cool even when laid on the boulder or the way her hips moved. It wasn't even because of the way her neck stretched and invited kisses along its smooth skin. It was in her eyes. Those damn brown and sweet eyes. It was the deep, magnetic look when they met mine—the way she said nothing but everything with only a look made me breathless.

Our traveling hands slipped between our bodies and caused my T-shirt to bunch up below my ribs. Nails lightly raked over my abdomen. My breath shook as I exhaled, our kiss coming to an end so I could whisper Vivian's name against her mouth instead. She had me right where she wanted me, all flustered and scatterbrained. If she asked me to jump off a cliff or to climb that stupid rock wall, I'd do it in a heartbeat. It shouldn't have come as a surprise what she asked me next.

"Tell me about your mother," she requested, brushing a strand of hair out of my face.

"She's a different woman at different times, so you need to be specific," I told her.

"How about now?"

"Absent."

"Before?"

"I don't know what you want me to tell you. She's my mom. Not like yours. She never taught me to cook, and she's not as warm. Not after the divorce. But every mother is different. Maybe even before the divorce she changed. I bet your family held the charade of Santa until you were old enough to be made fun of by other kids," I said. "I found out on Christmas Eve. There were harsh footsteps up in the attic. It made sense that Santa would be up there. Our chimney was blocked. Maybe he went through the window? There was whispering when I climbed the stairs, and do you want to know what I saw when I peeked? Presents, ripped wrappings, my parents arguing, red in the faces. It wasn't bickering. There was hatred. Christmas morning, no one spoke."

"How old were you?"

"We had moved to Boston. Probably seven."

"I'm sorry, Emma."

"I told my parents that I was gay before coming to camp for the first time, you know. Dad was great. Mom was silent. It was the start of the silence, really. When I came back from camp, they were getting a divorce, but it wasn't until I was fifteen that Mom moved out. First I lived with Mom and moved back to York. It was awful, then Dad saved me and brought me back to Boston. Thank God."

Vivian cupped my cheek. "It wasn't your fault. You know that, right? None of it was your fault."

"I know. Their relationship was hell anyway, but I think I was the last trigger."

"What did your mom say to you earlier?"

"Nothing important," I lied. It wasn't like she chose to start spending time with me on my birthday or anything. Oh wait. She did. "I think she might remember my birthday this year. That's something, right? Maybe it'll be the start of something decent between us."

"Maybe," Vivian said.

I didn't notice that I'd cried until she wiped away my tears and held me close to her, my face searching for comfort in her neck. She rubbed my back as the tears refused to fall from my eyes. The anger that I'd felt toward my mom all summer suddenly shattered, and all I was left with was disappointment and a deep sadness. I'd finally found people to share myself with, and my mom decided now was the perfect time to swan in and take me somewhere else. Nothing about this was fair.

The only reason I didn't break down completely was because Vivian was there, holding me steady as I cried.

SEVENTEEN

A week flew by, and with it nearing the end of the month, and only five more days until Mom's promise to get me out of camp, I found myself staring at things, people, everything, for much longer than I usually would. I didn't want to admit to myself that I savored every inch of the place, but I did, and that sucked.

Fridays were set aside so that we could do whatever the hell we wanted, and Gwen didn't hesitate to take the opportunity to show me Jenga, one of her favorite games. I couldn't find it within myself to derail her excitement at sharing this with me. It'd be like kicking a puppy. The sun that day was unbearably hot. This activity required movement on a big mat placed across the grass. My shoulders rolled, hyping me up to get into the mindset to play but also have fun.

"I can't believe you've never played this before. Me, Walter, and Vivian used to play for hours and hours when we were younger," Gwen told me, standing back with her hands on her hips to admire the setup. "When it was Walter and me playing, Vivian would stroll along and whack the entire thing down, like Godzilla. You ever wish you had siblings?"

"All the time," I said truthfully.

"I'm going to be as forward as to say, you got some now." She placed her hands on my shoulders. "I approve of your relationship with my sister. You're my first real friend outside of my family. My best friend. I'm your first proper friend too. I can tell. We're both figuring this out together, and we have so much fun doing it. What I'm trying to say is, you make me happy. You make Vivian happy too."

"I guess a cloud decided to rain over my head and no one else's," I grumbled.

Gwen wiped away my tear. "Feel the emotion, Emma. It can be good for you sometimes."

"Let's get this Jenga game on!"

The tower reached Gwen's waist, and when we plucked a piece from the structure, we had to place it on top to make the structure higher, but not so high so that Gwen couldn't reach the top. Gwen was somewhat of a master at Jenga. She poked and prodded middle pieces, determining whether they were worth her time before she pushed one through and placed it on top. Just to spite her, I nudged it into a perfect position.

It was my turn, and I decided to copy her technique. Instead of going with the center piece, I pushed a finger against the lowest three pieces and, with effort, took one on the side, making the entire formation wobble.

"You're one of those players, huh," Gwen mumbled, walking around the tower, stroking her chin. "You play dirty, Em. The aim is to make the structure safe and sound for as long as possible. You removed a vital piece."

"It's *strategic*."

"That's what Vivian says too," she muttered. "You're very much alike in certain things and opposites in others. It's fascinating."

It shouldn't have come as a surprise when Vivian walked right on by me with her arm stretched out. It collided with the entire Jenga set, destroying the structure in under a second.

Gwen knelt down, surrounded by all the pieces. She crumpled into the smallest ball, bringing her knees up to her chest, signifying her betrayal by petting one of the blocks. She flopped dramatically on her back, threw a hand over her forehead, and whispered, "Is she showing a hint of remorse?"

Vivian simply walked away from us and toward the lunchroom.

"Not one bit, you can drop the act now," I said, offering a wave when Vivian paused by the door before heading inside.

"Wow," Gwen murmured, sounding pleased.

"Surprised you're not in hysterics over this mess."

"Trust me, I am, on the inside."

"Then . . . ?"

"You're smitten." Gwen touched my leg, concerned. "What's going on in that brain of yours, Emma?"

"I got a call from my mom last week. She's a little homophobic."

"How can you be a little homophobic? Either you are or you aren't. I don't know what to say, other than I'm sorry she's so awful." Gwen climbed over a block so that she sat opposite me with her legs crossed. "Is that what's up? Thinking about your mom? Did she say something to you?"

"The usual. Hinted at me having a nonexistent boyfriend."

"That's not it, is it? It's not what's bothering you."

I knelt beside her. "If I tell you, will you promise to be chill about it?"

Gwen thought about it for a moment. "Promise."

"She's taking me out of camp. She wants to go on vacation to Rome. With Ethan, her new husband."

Gwen quickly rose to her feet, making me panic and stumble over myself to catch up to her. Instead of running off to do God knew what, as I expected, she balled her little fists and kicked a block as hard as she could.

"To Rome? Why Rome? Who's Ethan? When next week? Have you told Vivian?" she fired off. "You never mentioned Ethan."

"I'm sure I did once. I don't even know him, other than his name."

"Let's not get into that right now," she said, coming to a standstill. "When?"

"I assume my birthday. Wednesday."

"It's your birthday next week?" A new wave of panic coursed through the small girl, forcing her legs to move again at a much quicker pace. "Oh my God, Emma! So many problems, so little time to combat them. Why are you only telling me now? Last week. You spoke to your mom last week. Have you told Vivian?"

"No."

"Why did you tell me?!" Gwen shouted.

I began to panic a little too. "You said friends share secrets!"

"Yeah, I know!"

"Why are you mad at me for sharing a secret?"

"I don't know!" she yelled back. "I haven't been put in a position like this before, okay? But it's in all the romantic comedies, Emma. I learned everything I know from Netflix. You tell your partner important stuff before the best friend! Right? We need to write down some friend rules because we suck at this. You're telling Vivian. Because you're not that stupid to keep it away from her. But stupid enough to tell me first."

"You said best friends . . . you're always on about sharing secrets and secret observations. I thought this fell into that sort of stuff," I said.

"I know, but you're also best friends with her." Gwen slowed down again and fell to the ground in a fit of sadness. "Dammit, Emma. Why do you have to become my best friend and move away to Rome? Not even in the country! But to Italy! I bet their pizza isn't even all that good. Don't even get me started on their pasta."

"I'm not *moving* to Rome. But I don't think I can take a vacation from camp and come back for the last week of camp. Damn, I'll be missing two weeks of camp. Crap. Besides, your mom and I made pizza this morning. They can't beat that."

"Let's go eat that significantly better pizza than anyone else can offer."

The emotional outburst in response to my confession left me helpless. I wasn't sure of the reasoning behind sharing that secret, but it needed to be done, and that was all I was sure of. Navigating a field of friends was difficult, and responses were hard to predict. Now, settling in at a random table that soon was occupied by the Black siblings wasn't anything surprising. Lately, we sat together, and it didn't come across as strange because they were siblings, and I was friends with Gwen.

What did nearly make me choke on a slice of pizza was the fact that Vivian didn't sit across from me as she usually did in the lunchroom. She sat right next to me, pressed against me with her hand on my thigh like it was the most natural thing in the world. It was, but the environment tampered with that feeling. In a canteen full of around fifty teenagers, some in line to get their food and others at tables that faced our direction, there was no privacy to be had at the counselors' table, and by rights, I shouldn't have been able to sit there anyway.

The siblings knew each other, so when Gwen was quiet and timid, Vivian and Walter shared a look, and Vivian nudged me for an answer. I shoved nearly an entire slice of pizza in my mouth to avoid speaking.

"You okay there, squirt?" Walter asked, nudging Gwen's shoulder.

Gwen looked up from her hands, clasped on the table, and looked directly into Vivian's eyes and said, "It's Emma's birthday next week."

Walter accidentally flung his pizza slice across the room.

Vivian held up a hand with a menacing glare on her face. "If anyone even thinks to declare a food fight, I will annihilate them."

People who'd stood up with a mixed array of foods in their hands quietly sat back down.

That menacing glare turned to me. "Emma's birthday, you say? And when is this birthday of hers?"

"Emma was rather vague about that detail," Gwen lied.

"The first of August. Wednesday."

Vivian turned to face me and crossed her legs for better access. "In five days? You always find a way to surprise me, Emma Lane."

"Remember that being a good thing?"

"It's a distant memory."

Suddenly she left the table, even stealing the last slice of pizza from my plate.

"Oh come on!" I called after her. "Don't take it out on my pizza!"

"Too late."

Walter, Gwen, and I remained seated and shared the rest of our pizza. Gwen had made valid points about Rome. Not that I'd move there or anything, but if I stayed at camp instead of going off on the vacation, I'd have more time to spend with them. It would've been way different if we were all heading into senior year and knew there would be another summer to band together like this or if I lived with my mom in Maine. But the fact was we were all going to be in different places after summer ended. The three of them were family, and I wasn't so lucky; I didn't have those same ties. The same refrain of it all not being fair echoed in my mind, over and over.

EIGHTEEN

There were four days left at camp, and sitting outside at a campfire, in the woods instead of near the main building, would've had me reeling a couple of weeks ago. The idea didn't faze me when we sat down on the logs. I didn't focus on the roughness of the log under my fingertips or the fluttering leaves on the trees. The sputtering and snapping blaze was overbearing with its whooshing flames. I wasn't forced to be out there by any means because it was after hours, which was time that we got to ourselves. The Beavers decided to listen to the stories under the shadow of trees. Gwen wanted to go, and with my time at camp now on a countdown, where she went, I went.

The odor of sweat and dirt contributed to the sinking feeling in my stomach. It was mostly down to the fact that I couldn't sit beside Vivian. Being near her made me forget that I was in the woods these days. She had opted out to have some alone time. But another contributor to my nerves was Lauren, who grabbed a flashlight and held it beneath her chin, illuminating her face. I couldn't quite trick my eyes into seeing green skin or gnarly teeth. She wasn't a monster. She was a teenage girl with an ambition to become a Mapplewood counselor next summer but who went about it in all the wrong ways.

After I rejected her, she hadn't so much as said one word to me. She never retaliated. Sharing the same cabin as Lauren wasn't as bad as it could've been, but the fact that I snuck out most nights and stayed with Vivian helped out a lot. But if I were in Lauren's shoes and she turned me down, I wouldn't have been long looking to see if I could change cabins.

"Have you turned anyone down before?" I murmured to Gwen, leaning close to her.

"Once. I'm *almost* sure. Don't roll your eyes. There was this foreign exchange student in junior year. Sean. He was handsome. Beautiful, really. His eyes, Emma? A stormy grey. He was the one person who sat with me at lunch. There was only *one* problem. I couldn't understand a word he said. For all I know, he *could've* asked me out."

"Where was Sean from?"

"Ireland."

"Gwen. They speak English."

"Yeah, but he had a *really* thick accent."

"So, you came to the conclusion that before he swanned back to Ireland, he *could've* asked you out?"

"Yep! Because otherwise, no, Emma, I haven't turned anyone down before. So your subtle way of asking for advice when it comes to Lauren? I'm useless. You and me need to sit in front of a TV at some point to figure this stuff out together."

"Should I change cabins? You know, to be nice? Considerate?"

Gwen knocked her shoulder against mine, smothering a laugh. "You're leaving in less than a week, remember? Speaking of which, have you told Vivian yet?"

"I'm getting around to it! Building up the nerve. Telling you was hard enough. Let's stop talking about me. Have you got any scary stories to tell?" I asked. I prodded her shoulder. "You'd be a good storyteller. *Stormy grey eyes.*"

We stopped our whispering because Lauren directed the flashlight's yellow beam in our direction.

"You got to go out and take what is yours. That's what Laurel thought." Lauren focused the flashlight back on herself. "Do everything possible to achieve your dream. Was it worth chipping away the things that made her who she was to get what she wanted? Maybe. She failed to seduce one sister into offering her an opportunity at a . . . company . . . and failed to make the other so miserable that she wouldn't take the opportunity for herself. What was there left to do but admit defeat and cut her losses? Apologize?"

"Is this . . . is this an apology?" Gwen muttered.

"No idea," I replied.

Mike let out a huge yawn. "Boring."

Offense washed over Lauren's face. "It's a prologue."

"A boring prologue." He took the flashlight from her hands. Then he wiggled his eyebrows. "So, anyway, Abby, scary story—go."

"Going back to my cabin every night," Abby said without a second of hesitation. "And waking up in the cabin every morning."

"Snap," he said, whacking the flashlight with the palm of his hand since the light flickered. "Lauren. Emma. Responses?"

"In my defense, I haven't made a mess in there in *ages*, if that's what you're referring to," I said.

"Was it really that bad?" Mike asked.

"I sat down on the toilet seat one morning and suddenly there was *ketchup* on the back of my legs. Emma planted ketchup packets under the toilet seat."

"My bad. You won't have to put up with me much longer."

"What?" Abby asked. "I didn't say that so you'd change cabins. I might still have nightmares about the ketchup, but it was funny . . . eventually."

"Abort conversation," Gwen whispered, reminding me that I hadn't told her sister yet and telling everyone but Vivian was a no-go.

"I'm kidding. I'm in that cabin for the long haul." I lied. "Speaking of the *scary* cabin, I'm heading to bed."

Going back to the cabin was a bad idea; I knew this, yet my feet trekked through the little patch of woodland back to the open spaces and went inside. My phone wasn't at arm's length. Not that I blamed Vivian for keeping it in her cabin. All I had to do was ask and it was mine for the taking.

I sat on my bed, legs swinging back and forth, discomfort swirling in the pit of my stomach. This cabin didn't offer any semblance of comfort. From day one, all I'd wanted to do was escape this space. Everything I did to get out of camp affected my cabinmates in some shape or form. Lauren's apology hit too close to home; when doing little tricks like placing a ketchup packet beneath the toilet seat or whipping toilet paper all around the cabin, *all* I saw was my end goal. A bad case of tunnel vision. At the time, it didn't matter how it affected others as long as it bettered my chances of getting out of there.

I owed them an apology. A huge one.

The door to my cabin opened, and I was ready to fling myself beneath the covers to avoid talking to my cabinmates. I wasn't mentally prepared to soothe my guilt and apologize sincerely, but Vivian lingered halfway through the door. Hesitance shadowed her features. I inclined my head, so she knew to come in.

"Tired?" she asked, coming up to the bunk bed.

"Drained," I answered honestly. "And missing my dad."

"Later on, come back to my cabin, and we'll call him?" Vivian took my hand and held it close to her face. "Is something else bothering you?"

Thinking about Lauren's story and the huge-ass change of attitude she had thrown my way, I frowned. "Yeah, but we don't have to talk about it right now."

Vivian climbed up onto the bed and kneeled in the center. My arm automatically reached out because we were high up, and it was strange not worrying about my own potential falling but concentrating on someone else's. "Do you have to sit like that?"

"Is that your way of asking me to cuddle with you?" I asked.

"No." As she said that, she moved behind my back and laid down flat on the mattress, cheek pressed against the pillow. "You can stay there. I don't think the cabin floor will survive the impact of your body, but that's just my opinion."

I drew my legs back from the side. "Why are you in a camper's cabin so late at night?"

"The ghost stories. All fake, of course, but I came to make sure you weren't scared."

I flopped back onto the mattress and turned my head so that we were face to face. "You know what combats being a scaredy-cat? Physical contact."

"Seems like someone's clingy."

"Says the one who came by my cabin."

Vivian was about to respond but was cut off with a, "*Psst*, guys!"

The abrupt voice made me spin sideways, only to hang off the bed instead of sprawling across the floor because Vivian was quick to grab me around the waist and keep me dangling from the side of the bunk bed. We were swift to gather ourselves together, and both peered down from the top of the bed.

"Lauren's coming!"

"Gwen?" Vivian called, eyes zeroed in on her sister almost immediately.

"No time for thank yous."

Vivian jumped from the bed, practically rolling on the floor so that her body slid beneath Lauren's bed and seemed to be sucked up into another dimension. What the hell? Gwen dragged her sister quickly into the *tunnel* that was apparently below the floorboard as the cabin door burst open. Suddenly, Vivian was outside the window directly above Lauren's bed.

Lauren strolled in and then sat down, with her hands clasped and her lips open like she wanted to say something. I didn't give her the chance and hopped down from the bed and kind of sprinted out of the room, which was particularly immature of me. No apologies happening tonight.

As soon as I was out of there, I glanced around for any sight of the Black siblings but was left standing awkwardly between Gwen's cabin and my own, not quite sure where the hole began and ended. Instead of going back inside, I ventured toward Vivian's cabin and found her sitting on the steps. She stood as soon as she saw me and left the door open after she walked inside.

As I followed her, I said, "I knew there was a hole, but I didn't know it was a freaking tunnel."

Almost immediately, I got pulled onto the bed and back into our comfortable position, facing each other. "Do you want to talk to your dad?"

My eyebrows furrowed. "You were not surprised. You made it?"

"I happened to be in the same situation as you are right now, sharing a cabin with Lauren, as you know. Walter helped me make it after Dad refused to let me change cabins, to build something that I apparently lacked."

"Patience?" I guessed.

"Yes." Vivian sat up and retrieved my phone from her bedside locker and left it on my stomach. "Talk to your dad."

"'Kay."

I got comfortable on my back and let my eyes close. His gruff voice came through the phone, sounding both warm and surprised. My stomach fluttered; it was both a combination of Dad and the way Vivian trailed a finger down my wrist. For a few minutes, the world seemed perfect. Vivian's featherlight touch, which if I thought about it more, was an attempt to tickle me. It was nice to hear his deep voice again. It wrapped me up in a warm, protective bubble. Damn, had it really been a month? We were never the biggest texters. We spent every day with each other face to face, so we never needed to. Every time I spoke to my mom over the phone or after we hadn't spoken in a while was awkward, but with Dad? It was the complete opposite.

"How's Thomas?" I asked.

"Not going to ask about your uncle?"

"You're only going to complain about something stupid he did."

"You're right," Dad admitted. "Tommy boy, well, he's warmed up to me, Em. Big time. He's my little buddy now. He might like me more than you!"

"Oh yeah? Hasn't run away from you?"

"He sits still like a statue and stares at me from a distance," he said proudly.

"No way! Does he blink slowly?"

"Sometimes?"

"He loves you; it's confirmed." Man, I missed that cat.

"He's a bit chubbier now. Natural old age, I guess."

"Dad. He's five. Cats live up to twenty."

"Twenty?!"

"Yeah . . . so slow down on the feeding, Dad."

When Vivian turned her attention to brushing her lips against my neck, I pulled in a sharp breath and opened my eyes.

"You okay, kiddo?" Dad asked.

"Yeah. It's nice to hear your voice."

"I don't want to pry but . . ."

"Yes, I'm taking my anti-anxiety meds when I need to. Don't be afraid to ask. I'm having an off day, but it's been a good while since anything major," I told him honestly, feeling Vivian's lips pause for a second before she bit down. "I got this new journal that I've been writing in. It's supercute. You know how I thought those breathing exercises were a load of crap? Well, they worked. Who knew changing up something you need to do every day could be a good thing?"

"That's good. I'm proud of you. And, uh, how's your mom?"

At that question, I sat up and realized that he had no clue I was at camp.

My mouth dropped at my forgetfulness. Even I surprised myself by this oversight.

Vivian sat up, mouthing, Are you okay?

I made a face and put the phone on loudspeaker. "I'm not exactly staying with Mom? I'm at Camp Mapplewood, you know . . . still in York, and she's kind of on a cruise with her new husband? Well, no, the cruise is over. She's in Spain right now."

There was another stretched silence. "Husband? Cruise . . . camp . . . why didn't you call me?" he asked, breathing a little heavier. "You're at camp?"

"It's okay, now. It's hard, but I might've managed to make a friend or two, and maybe have a girlfriend."

Vivian cocked her head to the side and mouthed "Girlfriend?"

"You don't want me to come and get you?"

Trying to cover my rising blush, I placed a pillow between my face and Vivian's. "I'm good, Dad. Thank you."

"Em? I love you." He sighed and then said playfully, "So, a girlfriend, huh?"

Vivian tickled me as I scrambled to get the phone. "Love you too. Bye, Dad." I turned to her. "Why are you looking at me like that?"

"Girlfriend?" Vivian said.

"Nah, you can't tease me about that. You were the one who made us official. How embarrassing for you."

One eyebrow cocked up. "Yes. How embarrassing for me."

NINETEEN

In the past month I'd probably felt more carefree than I ever had in my entire life, a miracle, considering I was at a camp and all. At school, I sat in a library and spent my time reading. And as much fun as it was, jumping into a character's adventure for a couple of hours every day wasn't something that I found complete and utter joy in. Thanks to the help of Julie, I found out that I had a passion, and that passion was cooking.

When Julie decided to take the afternoon off, which was the food-prep time for the annual all-Mapplewood campfire party, my first reaction wasn't panic, it was hesitation, but it didn't immediately put me into a bad headspace of second guessing my own capabilities. She did promise to be by my side when we served the food. A nervous thrill was set into my body. The idea of spending a couple of hours in the kitchen throughout last week was probably my saving grace. Without that to look forward to, I would've cracked under the knowledge that it was my last week. Julie gave me permission to skip the exercise activity that afternoon.

It was nearing two o'clock, and I wrapped an apron around my waist, ready to make a tester batch of plain cheese pizza just in case they didn't turn out so well. At least then I could rectify the recipe if I needed to. I was about to get the ingredients out of their respective places when a noise came behind the door, a jangling of keys. The intruder came inside. Once they did, my face transformed into a dopey smile, which was met with the dangling of keys from a finger.

"What was the point in my mother giving you keys if you break in at any and all hours?" Vivian asked, dropping the keys pointedly on the nearest countertop to the door. "You look—"

"Cute?" I suggested, cutting her off. I ran a hand over the apron with a panda face on it and jiggled my hips, to emphasize its features. "Your mom got it for me."

"She adores you," she said, her tone one of complaint. "She always wanted someone to cook with. Sadly, her kids aren't quite cut out for that line of work."

"I probably have a better relationship with your mom than my own," I muttered, shaking my head at the thought.

"You won't talk about that phone call, but you do keep bringing your mother up." She tangled her fingers between the strings of the apron and pulled them loose. "It's been a week. Whatever she said, whatever you talked about, is still bothering you. Will you let us try to figure it out together? I can be good at listening, at times. Offer spectacular advice too."

"Okay."

She tugged me along by the apron strings to the table where Gwen usually sat. "Let it all out."

"Do you remember the night I heroically cleared your cabin of a dangerous spider?" I sat down as she nodded. "I know I normally wander around at night, but I did actually plan on sleeping that night." She reached across the table and held my hand. "Lauren wanted to clarify our situation. She likes me. When I let her down, she hopped onto thinking that I'm seeing someone at night. Getting a midnight snack never even crossed her mind."

"Has she said anything since? Your body language suggests that you're holding something back."

"She tried to prevent me from leaving the cabin," I said. "Her behavior may be described as *slightly* aggressive. But then she left me alone. Heck, she even publicly apologized yesterday at the campfire. Maybe. It seemed genuine. I feel a little guilty because I made it hard for her and Abby at the start of camp and I never really owned up to it. Now I feel even more guilty because I don't want to stay there and *feel* that guilt. I don't know. I've got too much emotion these days. Dealing with people is hard. Even worse, considering their feelings. What a ride."

Vivian took in that information and, in doing so, slipped her hand away from my fingers. Like a panther stalking its prey, she made her way to the exit and escaped the room before I could even think of something to say. I couldn't follow her to make sure she didn't do anything rash. Vivian had the patience of a saint—dealing with rowdy campers during the summer months needed a person like that. She'd be fine. Right? Plus, she had to deal with the exercise activity for the next three hours.

I did what I was there to do, and that was cook. Pretty soon, the first batch of pizza was done, and they turned out perfectly. So well, in fact, I sat down and ate it all, leaving only a dirty napkin behind. For the next few hours, I pushed through the sleepy haze that came from a full stomach and managed to power through making enough pizza for everyone.

My back ached, and the pads of my feet hurt like a bitch, but the victorious feeling of seeing the pizzas lined up and ready left a warm feeling that spread through my body. It was a power surge. Nothing could defeat me in that moment of pure bliss.

I left the kitchen a few minutes after five thirty to take a break.

Julie, as promised, served the campers who came in to get dinner to bring outside to the campfire. I headed out to change my clothes into something less sweaty and pizza smelling. Serving campers while looking like a hot mess? No thank you.

Campers ran wild around the place, free of the leash often held by their counselors. There was one massive fire set in the center of camp, where we were gathered the first day. The taste of s'mores flashed through my mouth—the campfire reminded me of when my friendship with Gwen was officially branded an unstoppable force. Associating certain aspects of camp with happy memories helped with the tension in my body and mind when strolling around the grounds.

I flung open my cabin door and stepped inside, only to stop dead in my tracks because what I saw was plain weird.

Vivian sat with her feet dangling off my bunk. She offered no greeting, but the twisted expression on her face told me all that I needed to know. On the single bed was Lauren, who wore a similar expression to Vivian's, prompting me to ask, "Do I even want to know what's going on here?"

"Surveying the room for your stuff. You're moving cabins. We've taken into account your interaction with the local environment and see it as imperative to give you the best chance at sleep." Vivian slipped off the bed and inclined her head toward my suitcase. "Shall we get the move done now?"

I sighed. "Where to, exactly?"

She grabbed one bag and offered me a smaller one. "Under the advisement of my mother, we're preparing a spare cabin nearest to the main building. Its isolation was pointed out, so Gwen will be joining you."

Lauren was clenching her jaw, making me want to hurry. "Yeah, let's get out of here."

Vivian knew what was mine to pack. If I left anything behind, it could stay there. With so much in our hands, she was forced to kick the door shut. It slammed behind us. As soon as it shut, a rather long exhale escaped my lips. How was I supposed to act in this situation? On the one hand, I was glad that I didn't have to wake up and see Lauren's face every morning. On the other hand, Vivian had promised to just listen.

We came up to the new cabin, coincidently near the counselors' cabins, and ventured inside. It was a spare counselor cabin. I could tell right away by the furniture. The only difference between Vivian's room and this was the two single beds and the lack of a television. We dropped the bags to the ground and I let myself flop back onto a bed, too exhausted to even think, never mind shower.

"I'm a good listener, Emma. I offer fantastic advice. Communication is the key, Emma." I stretched out my legs and let out a groan.

"I also offer quick and efficient solutions. I'm sorry." The bed sank under her weight. I felt a graze across my forearm. "The original plan was to . . . there was no plan. I got in there and saw your things. They made me realize the impact my actions could have. So I improvised."

"Your mother suggested—"

Vivian interrupted. "She did. I didn't make that up. She wanted Gwen to have someone with her."

My clothes started to annoy me. "You do realize that this doesn't really solve any of my problems, don't you? I still want to apologize to both of them."

"Having your own space might help with your anxiety. Besides, Lauren's acting suspiciously, and I wanted to get in front of it."

"I think the time she spent on cleanup duty and away from everyone gave her time to think." I sat up and looked at Vivian. "I know her dad gives the camp a chunk of money, but if you're worried about her this much, why didn't you report her for stealing the phone? Take the opportunity to get rid of her?"

She shifted guiltily. "I may have had underlying intentions by keeping that a secret."

Oh boy. "And that was?"

"If you had the opportunity to make someone's life a little harder than need be, after a year of harassment and general annoyance, would you take it?" she asked, eyes wide enough to make it seem like a genuine question. "I know how this girl operates, and she becomes obsessed. There's only one way to combat that type of behavior."

"She employed an isolating tactic on Gwen. How did she get to you?"

"She wouldn't take no for an answer. Sometimes I wondered if she *actually* had a crush on me. The idea of becoming a camp counselor wouldn't let her give up, though. Besides, the whole point when Dad set this camp up was for teens to find themselves and to have something to do during the summer in a safe environment. Maybe help a lost kid here and there. If she wants to be a counselor so bad or have a position of power, especially one that involves taking care of kids, she needs to see how it's done *properly*. People who act out like she does, there's always a reason, and maybe being here at camp can help. She might have a second chance here, but that doesn't mean I want you stuck there with her."

"That's a very mature outlook," I commented.

"She's quiet, and offering apologies. That's all well and good, but don't under any circumstances let her know about *us*. If she gets the idea that you're getting any special treatment, she will backtrack on her apologies, mark my words."

"She really didn't want Gwen to be a counselor over her. I can't imagine what she'd do if she found out about us. We're continuing the supersecret affair. Gotcha." I wiggled my eyebrows. "How did you get her off your back, though?"

"I do owe you this story. Lauren refused to take no as an answer, as you know, so I had to be creative. I told her to get elaborate, and she did. She made a banner and declared her love for me in the canteen, and I turned her down. I thought that was the end of that feud until I came to learn about her treatment of Gwen."

"Huh."

"What?"

"Nothing. Just reveling in the love I feel for you, I guess."

"What?"

"What?!" I echoed.

My heartbeat kicked up a couple of notches. I stared at my hands in horror, processing what I'd said. In the simplest of terms, I confessed my love for the girl sitting on the bed, who owned the hand still on my forearm. Not even a single twitch. Not that I could blame her. Apparently, my subconscious liked to headbutt me to make it something that I could access easily. And it was easy, loving her.

But dear God, why did I have to blurt it out like that?

It was like Vivian said, my emotions were easy to read, but what she didn't mention was the embarrassment that came from a trait that I never knew I even had. Now that it made itself known, I wanted to physically slam my head against a wall and never wake up. Denial of the situation was welcomed like an old friend. Denial had always been there for me. Dad telling me Mom wanted me down in Maine for the summer? Denial held my hand until we landed on her doorstep. The fact that my mother got married and didn't invite me to the ceremony? Mom not being around helped denial whisper in my ear that the situation didn't happen. Yet trying to deny those words I said to Vivian? Denial abandoned me.

"Did you just . . ." She paused. "Emma. What did you say to me?"

"I'm reveling in the lovely day I'm having?" I slid off the bed to cut the contact between us. Black spots invaded my vision. Lie. *Say something*. "Lauren did mention saving some pizza for me . . ."

Vivian let her legs hang over the bed. "You're suddenly craving pizza."

I took a step backward, facing her. "Have you tasted my pizza? You'd crave it too . . . okay. Bye."

As soon as the door shut, I shot out of there like the place was on fire. I wasn't brave. Cowards ran, and that was what I did; who I was. At camp, the most secure place that I always thought to go to was the kitchen. By the time I got back there, it was in full swing, with Julie and a bunch of other people handing out the pizza I'd made to the campers.

I threw my hair up into the messiest bun ever, one that was a little like a ponytail with strings of curls and frizziness from how badly my hands shook. The hair managed to fit into the net hat with a little bit of shoving and poking. My brain went silent as I took up the spare space beside Julie and started mindlessly giving out pizza slices.

"You seem to be in possession of my daughter's jacket." She fixed my collar. "You hold something else of my daughter's, don't you? Her heart."

"Oh sweet baby Jesus."

"Now, Emma, I'm quite fond of you," she told me, beckoning me to follow her back into the actual kitchen. She untied her apron and sat down at the table her daughters or son usually occupied and patted the seat opposite her. "Come sit."

I reluctantly sat down and fidgeted with my hands beneath the table. "I'm fond of you too."

The motherly vibe rolled off her in waves as she tilted her head to the side. "Relax, Emma. You're not in trouble. I am curious, what are your intentions with my daughter?"

"Friendship."

"My other daughter," she was quick to respond.

"Er . . ." I looked around, as though I'd find a suitable answer there.

"Emma, believe me when I say you're not in trouble."

Julie got up from the table and stood in front of the sink. She turned on the tap, waiting for me to take the silent hint to grab a tea towel to dry the dirty dishes after she washed them. The silence was suffocating. I dried a plate and set it aside and thought about the situation a little bit deeper. Julie Black was doing her motherly duty and interrogating her child's love interest. She was a woman of gold, loving her children to the end of the earth. The fact that her daughter liked a girl? Nothing pivotal. Just life.

Why couldn't my mom be as open-minded as Julie? It strained my chest just thinking about it. Julie wanted her kids at camp with her day in and day out. My mother, on the other hand, didn't want me with my father or herself. Pinpricks stabbed little parts of my body. So, with that, I thought about something that never failed to put a smile on my face and ease the burden of my intrusive thoughts.

"I love your daughter," I blurted out, breaking the silence.

"Yes," she said, without an ounce of doubt. "What are your plans after the summer? You mentioned something about stealing from your roommate's stash of food, but dear, where will that be? Back home in Boston? At a college? I know it's a four-hour car journey from here to the University of Maine, but it would be an extra hour from Boston?"

"It's too late to apply anywhere, I'll probably be back home. But at least I know what I want to do now. I have you to thank for that. Maybe a culinary school? I need to speak to my dad about it. He knew I'd find something that really interested me, and I didn't believe him."

"I know there's a course at Eastern Maine Community College. It's down the road from Vivian's college."

"Maybe I'll apply there next year."

"And in the meantime? Long-distance relationships, especially a new relationship after you spent such a short amount of time together . . . it will be hard. Who will feed my child?"

"Momma Black, have you been preparing me to be a suitable girlfriend?"

"You're perfectly suitable as you are, Emma." She stopped cleaning and rested her hip on the counter. "You're a natural cook. You, Emma, wanted to learn as much as I wanted to teach. Now, I'm glad you want to feed my child. A friend of mine could train you in your year off, if you're interested? Get some real experience before going to college?"

"Really? That would be cool. You'd speak to them for me? I'll miss cooking with you, though," I said.

"Me too, dear." She patted my back and waved her hand toward the exit. "Now go join the party."

I accepted Mrs. Black's order and left. The campfire was gigantic and so full of life. The sparks and shadows created imagery that could've been something out of a storybook, it was that credible. I sat on a log beside the fire and took the offered marshmallow, deciding this time there wasn't a need to impale it on a stick and heat it up. The sweetness and fluffiness by themselves were enough.

✦

Eating marshmallows and watching people dance took my mind off of the craziness that was my camp life. Lauren sat down beside me, placing a plate of pizza on my lap. "Here's some pizza."

"Not hungry, but thank you," I said, placing it on the ground by the log. "Since you're here, I wanted to apologize to you. We might not have got on, even at the beginning of camp, but that doesn't mean I should've made the space for winding down and sleeping one of chaos. Our cabin should have been neutral territory. I'm sorry."

"Oh. I figured because you moved cabins that you still hated me." She sighed. "Can we talk? Somewhere private? We don't share a cabin now, and with your cooking and my cleaning, we don't see each other much during the day anymore."

"Lead the way."

I stood up and accidentally stood on the pizza. The squelch made me pause. For good measure, I twisted and flicked the piece off my shoe before following Lauren. Walking for less than ten seconds made me realize that I had no particular destination in mind, and so my footsteps slowed down. Almost instantly, my arm was gripped, and I was pushed into the toolshed quite harshly. I spun around and accidentally knocked against Lauren's shoulder.

The little grunt sobered me up. The last time Lauren invited me somewhere to spend time with her alone was when we were twelve years old, but at least this time around, instead of climbing up trees, we were cooped up inside the shed. Forgiving Lauren? I could do that. Forgetting what she had done? That was a whole other story. My shoulders hunched, waiting for her to speak.

"I've nothing else to say, but you go ahead," I offered.

"I'm sorry, but I can't spend next summer with my parents. You . . ." She laughed bitterly. "You getting buddy-buddy with the Blacks so easily? How? You managed to do what I tried to do for two years, in less than a month."

"I mean, Lauren, you did *bully* Gwen."

"Ever since I told you about that counselor job, you've been sucking up big time. Cooking with their mom. Even going as far as to get into a relationship with Vivian. Yeah, I know about that. You realize we shared that tent, right? I wasn't sure until she moved you from our cabin and placed you close to herself—easier to sneak out at night. Fair enough if it was Gwen who got the job. They're family. But if you're in a relationship with Vivian, it's obvious that you won't spend next summer apart. If you can persuade her to change cabins to be closer to her, you can persuade her to do anything. Where does that leave me? I'll be too old to be a camper. Not close enough to the Blacks to get the job. It's my only chance to get out of my parents' house for the summer. You understand, don't you? I have to do this."

"Why can't you leave the town?"

"Because they won't pay for my college if I do and the only way I'll spend time in this town is by having a job where I can live somewhere else. I have to do this."

"Have to do what?"

One second she stood there, twiddling her thumbs, and the next she brought me into a hug and somehow managed to shove my head near her neck. It lasted for less than two seconds before she took a step back and raised her hands as if to tell me she didn't mean me any harm despite her preemptive apology.

"A hug? That wasn't anything bad. I'm missing something, right?"

She grabbed a phone off the shelf and pressed her thumb against the screen. "You can go now."

"You recorded that? What's your plan here exactly?"

"You can't get special treatment from Vivian or her family if you're not together."

Swiping her phone from her hand, I dodged past her flailing limbs and shot out of the shed, eyes wide and body shaking from the extra adrenaline.

A hand gripped my forearm, almost making me swing again. Almost.

"Emma?"

"You were right, Vivian. I'm completely gone by you. Like, tragically. Wait, no. Bad choice of words. Totally in love. With you. Yup. Wow."

"I'm glad you could admit that to yourself."

I grinned. "I'm proud of me too."

Vivian squeezed my hand. "We can come back to that. Now, can you explain why you have *another* phone?"

As she took it from my grasp, I explained, "I might've stolen it from Lauren."

She froze in response. "Can you repeat that? I didn't hear you right."

"She tried framing me? To try and make you think that I cheated on you? You were right about that. What the hell?"

"Where is she?" she asked calmly.

"In the toolshed. You know, that's a great place. I met you there. Confessed my love for you there, officially in front of it. Good times, good times."

"One of those instances literally happened two seconds ago." She thumbed toward the shed. "I'm going to deal with . . . that." Vivian slowly released my hand and put her hand on the shed's door handle. "And Emma?"

I rocked back and forth on my heels. "Yeah?"

"You can add a third instance to that list."

"Oh?"

"Are you going to make me say it."

"I'm afraid implying it isn't enough."

"Fine. I love you," she muttered quickly.

"See? Was that so hard? Good luck in that compact space with Lauren."

✦

Once again, Lauren and I were brought into the office in front of Mr. Black to resolve the issues between us. The last time he made it quite clear that there were no more chances if we were to do anything to disrupt anyone's time at camp, including our own. I waited outside the office, sitting on a plastic chair as he spoke to Lauren first.

Vivian sat beside me, loving me. Probably a little angry that I'd gotten mixed up in this mess even after she moved me to another cabin.

"You'll have to stop grinning like a fool once you go inside," she told me, not sounding all that mad.

I couldn't help it. We *loved* each other. But speaking to Vivian's dad was a whole other ball game to speaking to her mom. "I'm screwed, aren't I?"

"No." She brought my hand up to her lips and kissed it chastely. For a moment she seemed horrified at her own actions before kissing it again. "Once you tell your side of the story and maybe have some witnesses back you up, it will be over. She might not open up to him about why she's so intent to stay at camp, but she can't stay at camp. It's not a healthy environment for her, but Dad will be able to help her."

Bringing my hand down to her lap from her lips, I mindlessly played with her fingers. "I've got to know something." I glanced back at the door, making sure it was shut, before leaning in close so that no one else could hear. "Does your dad know about us?"

"No."

"Well, your mom does for sure."

Vivian began to smile, one of those secretive smiles. "Interesting that you'd have a heart to heart with my mother after you ran away from me. What else did you two speak about?"

"I'm expected to feed you after camp."

The door swung open and Lauren sauntered out far too confidently for my liking. Vivian let my hand go, but I didn't stand up straight away. It was only when Vivian nudged my knee that I moved.

Mr. Black's office wasn't comfortable like Julie's kitchen. All that laid there were consequences of my actions and talks with my mother, both coincidently moving toward my end of time at camp. One or the other was going to happen sooner or later. Whether it was today or on my birthday, my time at camp was limited.

I took the seat opposite Mr. Black, not even thinking to ask for permission to sit down. He scribbled on a notepad, too engrossed in it to greet me. It was for the best; it gave me the opportunity to wipe my sweaty hands off on my shorts and steady my breathing.

"Can you start from the beginning?" he said.

"Okay . . . Lauren was isolating Gwen. Lauren constantly mocked her, maybe not to her face. She made sure Gwen wasn't included in anything. I'm friends with Gwen, sir, and Lauren didn't like that. That's why the food fight started in the canteen." I released a sigh, knowing I had to tell the whole truth. "Lauren since then told me of her feelings for me, which I rejected. She was . . . aggressive in our cabin."

"Aggressive?" Mr. Black frowned. "Did she—"

"Nothing physical happened, but it's been stressful in that cabin, and that's why I haven't been sleeping there much."

"Why were you in the toolshed? Why did you have Lauren's phone?"

"She wanted to talk privately. She'd already kind of apologized to me, so I thought it would be okay. I probably shouldn't say this, but she has a hard time at home. You should try and talk to her about it. Help her."

"Anything else?"

From the way he asked that question, I had to assume that Lauren, to improve her chances of work placement, might've mentioned the fact that I was with his daughter. Perhaps Lauren was wrong about the intentions of our relationship, but the fact that she implied any ties at all held some truth to it.

His wife knew of our relationship. Making assumptions in interrogation was hard since the environment was filled with pressure. To believe he and his wife told each other everything because of the blatant love they shared was a risk. Keeping the information from him if he already knew from a reliable source, well, my narrative wouldn't be trustworthy.

The longer the silence dragged out, and the longer I prolonged it, my credible account grew dimmer and dimmer. I knew this, but spewing out everything without at least contemplating it would've been a stupid move too.

"I'm seeing your daughter, Vivian." I continued to stare at the wall, but eventually, I needed to know what he thought. "Lauren found out. Made some hasty accusations, and that's the reason for our conflict in the shed. She thought I'd get a job working here over her next summer. It's kind of her dream job. I think that's everything, sir."

He nodded slowly. "I'll have to consider this for a while. Get other accounts of your behavior that isn't biased, so to speak. Thank you for your time. You may leave."

Shaking off the uneasiness that I felt, I made my way out of the building. The fresh air was soothing in comparison to the stuffy feeling within the office. Taking steps up to my cabin, I heard voices. Loud voices. Neither of which belonged to my roommate. I hesitated halfway up the steps. Eventually, my feet took me up until I stood in front of the door. The argument sounded heated. Private. I almost knocked because of that. I shook my head at myself because it was my room.

Seeing who was inside my room, well, it left me releasing a huge sigh. Lauren, and Vivian, who stood too still by my desk. "You okay?"

Vivian barely moved. "I'm perfectly fine."

I frowned at the chilly response. Lauren needed to leave. "Mr. Black wants to speak with you again," I lied.

She slowly stood up, as if savoring the fact that she was on my bed and Vivian wasn't. She chuckled as she walked by Vivian, who was utterly stiff, jaw and fists clenched tightly.

Right before Lauren left, she turned her attention back to Vivian. "If you don't believe me, why don't you ask her?"

Vivian's expression was too smooth. "You're nothing of relevance. Leave."

I snorted, which apparently wasn't an appreciated response. Vivian moved to the door and shut it, much less forcefully than I would've predicted, considering the storm brimming right beneath her skin. Instead of acknowledging my staring, she moved toward the bed and smoothed the creases left behind. Once she was happy that the bed was newly made, she sat down and crossed her legs.

Then I felt her stare. It was my turn to avoid eye contact. It was long and agonizing, so much so that I found myself sitting on Gwen's bed opposite her, crossing my arms and waiting—waiting for what she was about to come out with. It was endless interrogations from the Blacks that day.

"Okay, what do you have to ask me about?" I eventually broke the silence, knowing she was stubborn enough to keep quiet for ages.

"That phone call with your mother . . ."

Dread pooled into my stomach. "I have a feeling I know what you're going to say."

She maintained eye contact. "Is it true?"

Suddenly my hands were far more interesting than her eyes. "I really don't know how Lauren knows about that. Mom's not going to pay for the rest of camp. She's taking me to Rome."

The affirmation that Lauren had told the truth, well, I could only imagine what ran through Vivian's head. The facts were laid out on the table. I was selfish, keeping it from her for this long. I knew that. What made it worse was the fact that I wanted an immediate response. Something. Anything. She didn't give it to me. Instead of reacting, she walked straight out of the cabin. I guess that was a reaction in itself.

I didn't know how long I sat there on the bed, staring into space and running everyone's actions through my head, over and over again. By the time the door opened again, and my head spun around, it was dark and disappointing. It wasn't who I wanted to see.

Gwen's response was immediate. She wrapped an arm around my waist and let me lean my head against her shoulder. She told me about her day, words low enough that it was background noise.

✦

At some point, I fell asleep. That was apparent once I woke up in my own bed, with Gwen sitting at the bottom of my mattress, back pressed against the wall.

"You're awake," she noted quietly. "You look like hell."

"Not surprised. I've spent most of the day there."

"Lauren got kicked out of camp. Dad's talking to Mom about helping her out, though. And you're not even in the least happy about that, are you?" she asked, but she didn't need me to answer. She knew what had happened. Maybe not every detail, but she had the gist. "Emma . . ."

I rubbed my eyes harshly. "I know. I should've told her. I was going to. But it's too late now. Everything's just . . . ruined now."

"Get. Yourself. Together," she said, standing up and pointing toward the door. "You're wallowing. I hate that look on you. Go to my sister, sort it out. Now."

"But—"

"Now!"

The time it took to get to Vivian's cabin was longer than necessary. I paced. A lot. Back and forth between the cabins, indecision dictating my direction. I ended up sitting on the steps outside of Vivian's cabin and grumpily resting my chin on top of my knee.

Maybe twenty minutes later, the cabin door opened. She sat down beside me, leaning against the opposite rail and mimicking my body's position. It felt more natural to breathe with her right next to me. I almost scoffed at the thought because I didn't deserve any reprieve.

"Am I the last to know?" she asked but didn't give me enough time to answer. "It feels like it. It's petty, this sense of jealousy. Lauren knew before me. I'm sure Gwen did too. I shouldn't feel this insecurity that you didn't tell me first. But it's not really about that. Is it? That's all and well, not knowing. You knew you weren't staying, and you continued to make things so hard."

"I was going to tell you."

"When?"

"I don't know."

"That's not good enough, Emma."

"I know." I breathed out slowly. "I know. I was scared and stupid . . .

so stupid. It wasn't real. It wasn't going to happen if I didn't tell you. That's what I was thinking. It's all real now. I'm in love with you. No, that's not me saying that to fix this. I'm in love with you, and I'm leaving? With a woman I barely know with a husband she probably barely knows? We'll be thousands of miles apart. The unknown of what happens next? Your reaction? It was scary, and I'm sorry. You deserved to know."

"I did."

"You did. I'm sorry."

"It's going to be okay," she said, pressing her forehead against mine. "This is new to us, but we have to learn to communicate without *fearing* each other. Otherwise, what's the point?"

"You're right," I agreed. "I promise to do better."

"I do too."

Words ultimately meant nothing unless they were followed with action, and that's what I had to do to make it up to her, to show her how committed I was to our promise. The only question was, how?

TWENTY

That morning before breakfast, Gwen and I were strolling through camp and may have been a little nosy when we noticed that Lauren's dad stood outside my old cabin, luggage piled beside him, talking to Mr. Black. Lauren was leaving camp. Her eyes were red from crying. Jessie embraced her, whispering something in her ear, and then Lauren followed her father into his car and left. While everyone ate breakfast, Mr. Black took the opportunity to hold a small assembly for the campers to explain why Lauren had to go, and to reiterate that bullying, blackmail, and other deplorable behavior wasn't the Camp Mapplewood way. He also stressed that he and the counselors at camp always had their doors open if anyone needed to talk.

The buildup of stress over the last week, concerning my guilt over my behavior with my cabinmates, Lauren quickly changing her tune back to doing anything possible to be the camp counselor next summer, keeping the secret that I was leaving camp nearly two weeks earlier than anticipated, and then having Vivian find out in the worst way possible?

We deserved a day-long break from the drama that followed me around. The punches wouldn't stop until my mother came to camp, but we had a short amount of time to breathe again and I didn't plan on doing that while Vivian acted as my counselor during day-to-day activities.

During breakfast—my usual apple and a backpack full of food I'd taken from the canteen with permission from Mrs. Black—I caught Walter downing a juice box outside while staring sleepily into space.

"G'morning," he said. "I thought you'd still be asleep."

"I normally would be, but I want to ask you for a huge favor. I want to saddle you with the rest of the Beavers while I take your sister on a date."

He sipped his juice box. "What do I get out of it?"

"The knowledge that your sister is having a great day?" I offered. Not enticing enough. "Fine. And a sandwich assistant at your beck and call until I leave."

"You're leaving in two days."

"Think of how many sandwiches you can have!"

"You have yourself a deal."

✦

A warm breeze circulated around the campground, making the stuffy and overheated shed much worse. Breaking into the shed had become such a habit—from the very first day to my panic attack to shuffling in there with Lauren—that I chanced my arm during the day. On my last scavenge around the small, enclosed room, I had noticed a rather large object occupying such a significant amount of space that it was hard to ignore. That's why I ended up in there again after dragging Vivian from the canteen to join me on this date. I pulled a large white sheet from the large picnic basket and admired it. It was a cute place to store the food I'd gotten from the canteen. This was how I'd make it up to Vivian for not telling her that I was leaving camp early.

I brought the basket outside with some steady pulling, and quickly reveled in the expression Vivian wore as I placed it on the ground, gesturing to the other side for her to help carry the thing. Her look was a mixture of disbelief, mild shock, and a knowing glint, as if she should've expected something like this from me. Success.

"What exactly is the plan here?" she asked.

"I'm taking you on a day-long date—just me and you. No drama! No secret touching. No campers around to catch us sneaking looks at each other."

"What about . . ."

"Walter has the Beavers trailing after him today," I answered.

"Well, aren't you going to help me out?"

She asked, "Why didn't you set this up before dragging me outside?"

"You were the one who said I needed to up my courting game," I pointed out. "Here I am. Upping and awaying, and my feelings are quite hurt. That picnic basket could have been discovered while I went and got you. Discovered by animals. Rodents. Even worse, the Beavers. No, wait. I thought of something even worse. Walter. You know what? I'll even grant you, like, ten points for helping me carry this thing."

"The courtship is over," she reminded me, pressing her hand against my chest, making my knees wobble a little. "We've already established that I won."

"Is a courtship between us really ever over?"

"Never."

Reluctance clung to her as she finally got on board with my idea. She grabbed the other handle with an exaggerated huff, letting the basket sink to the ground a little. I blew her a kiss and off we went across the grounds, crunching pebbles below our feet, hair wildly blowing in the wind and cheeks flushed from the sun, the breeze, and the exercise. A sign that said CAMP MAPPLEWOOD welcomed us before we stepped onto the footpath and down through the towering trees.

I heard a sigh from behind me, making me slow down and ask, "What's up now?"

She sighed again, this time more dramatically. "I can't believe you persuaded Walter to take my campers."

"Sometimes, I'm even impressed with myself."

Vivian sighed louder and repeated, "I'm abandoning my duties to carry an obscenely heavy basket. With you not pulling your weight."

"Hold up. I'm pushing my shocked heart to the limit."

"And I'm not allowed to touch the delightful-smelling food at all."

"Patience, Vivian."

With my slightly labored breathing, strained calf muscles, and rising heat to every portion of my body, I could admit to not preparing or giving much forethought to this exercise routine. It was much easier when I was younger, hopping on a bike, never being scared, and racing off around the house countless times or down the street, never breaking a sweat. It was a whole other ball game at the age of nearly eighteen to be so out of breath within the woods. What if I needed to run to safety for some reason? I had already wasted so much energy.

Vivian was there. It was okay. When we arrived at the spot where the scavenger hunt began, the place where our relationship officially started, the sudden drop of the basket beside the tree we'd leaned against as we'd awkwardly discussed our feelings for each other made me release a wondrous sigh of relief.

The area was as I remembered. Only this time, instead of worrying about campers looking in our direction, we were in the clear. There was no one around looking for stuffed animals or people lost and drunk in the woods.

My body fell to the ground and my head tilted backward. Through awkward, upside-down vision, I saw Vivian remove the lid from the basket.

"I suppose you were right. This date is special. Whatever you do, do not think about the fact that we have to travel back to camp later," she reminded, bopping my nose and subsequently setting a horrified expression on my face. "Do not think about that at all."

"Whatever." I groaned.

After taking a blanket out of the basket and placing it on the ground, we sat side by side against the tree trunk, me immediately toppling over myself to get into a position where the bark didn't dig into my back, and Vivian started plating up our food, taking a few moments to inspect each item that came out of the basket. She pushed a chocolate milk shake toward me and brought the straw from her own strawberry one up to her lips and sipped.

I pinched my straw and swirled the liquid around. "Would you look at this, we're perfectly capable of normal dates."

"If by normal, you mean acting like a ten-year-old child. Did you make these milk shakes?"

"Yeah, they're good, right?"

Vivian stayed silent, slurping the milk shake greedily, giving me my answer. I slumped back into the trunk. It was just the two of us, sitting side by side on a blanket and nibbling some sandwiches. There was no fear of being caught. It wasn't even about her parents anymore. It was the campers. They'd think of it as preferential treatment. And maybe it was.

I had never been on a proper date before, so I had to rely on all the heterosexual movies and what their first dates entailed. What did they do? Ask each other questions? It was different because we had already known each other for a month and a bit. How was a date supposed to be different from being around each other every day? How were we supposed to act now that others weren't around?

Start simple. Ask a question. See how it went.

"Vivian. Tell me something about yourself. Something that nobody else knows."

"How cliché," she commented, tapping her fingers on the basket. "I'm pansexual?"

"Cool. I'm gay. So, now do you want to tell me something that I don't actually know?"

"Fine, fine," she said, complying. She took a few minutes but eventually came up with something. "Do you know how you were scared of the future?"

"Were? Bitch, I still am."

At that, she slapped my arm lightly and admitted, "I'm also scared of a few things. There's a certain way I act in York, and there's a way I act at college. A distinction so deep that I'm afraid that perhaps you won't—"

"Vivian, let me ask you a question," I interrupted. "Are you yourself when you're around me?"

"Yes."

"Are you afraid of being with me while being at college?"

"No."

"You mentioned that camp was something predictable for you. College isn't. I'm guessing you're free there without the judgment of people in this small town. If anything, Vivian, we'll be happy there."

Her eyebrows furrowed. "We? You're going to my college?"

I coughed. "Er—there's a culinary school near there. Your mom has a chef friend she said she'd talk to about training me up. I was thinking of going to college next year."

"I'm significantly less . . . terrified. Thank you, Emma."

"You'll have your chef nearby, don't worry."

My knee bopped back and forth, a fact that I didn't realize until a hand trapped my knee in its snare and refused to let go. Eventually, Vivian leaned forward, keeping my leg trapped, and slid her other hand on top of mine. "What's making you do all that?"

"You mean the upside-down frown?"

"Yes, your upside-down frown. What prompted that? Are you—"

she paused, studying me. Then, after coming to some sort of conclusion by herself, she grabbed my free hand, ignoring my pout as I was denied access to my milk shake. "Are you shy, Em-ma?"

"Hell no."

"Why are you still smiling like that?" Still looking at me like I was cute or some shit, she let go of my hands, released my trapped leg, and pushed her milk shake to my side of the blanket, instantly slapping my hand away once I attempted to grab the milk shake. She brought her knee up and circled her hands around her leg. Vivian rested her cheek against her palm and said, "Tell me."

I mimicked her position and closed my eyes. "I heart you, that's all."

Warm, strawberry-tasting lips pressed against my own, melting on my tongue like sugar. Then they were gone, leaving a warm feeling in my chest. "So, that's what the heart eyes were for?"

My nose scrunched up. "You ruined the moment."

"The moment where we expressed our love for each other?" she asked, trailing a thumb across my chin. "Well, I heart you too."

I leaned in and kissed her on the cheek. I sucked on my milk shake and leaned my head against Vivian's shoulder, and was content to sit there in silence. A little rustling caught my attention. It was an owl but not just any owl; it looked nothing short of illustrated. It was a cute little thing with its low hooting and ear-tufts. They looked like they belonged to a small teddy bear because its head was round. The most intriguing thing about this owl was its eyes. As sunlight swept across the trees, its brown eyes grew more prominent, dark rings circling them. The owl matched the color of my key chain exactly with its grey-brown feathers and its yellow beak, the only difference being this owl had two eyes instead of one.

I gripped Vivian's thigh and silently pointed the owl out for her to see. She was in the middle of taking a bite out of a brownie, so she shooed me away at first. As soon as she caught sight of him, the owl let out more hoots and opened its wings out wide and mighty before it soared into the air and was carried off by the breeze, landing in another tree.

"That's beautiful," I murmured.

"Have you seen an owl before?"

"No. The only time I came close was making that key chain," I admitted. "It's fitting, don't you think? Seeing one right now? You here with me, seeing this owl, is like a commitment to each other. You kissed me for the first time and had that owl key chain. Now? We don't know what the future holds—I'll be gone for the rest of camp, then you'll be at college. Who knows where I'll be? I could be back in Boston. Maybe your mom will hook me up with that job. The point is, we don't know, and yet here we are together, watching this owl, and it feels so right. Here and now and hopefully in the future too."

"It's the symbol of our relationship."

"No matter what happens, owls will always be our thing." As I stood up, the owl flew away entirely. I grabbed Vivian's hand anyway and hauled her to her feet. As we packed the trash into the basket, I said, "This date is not over, m' lady."

"That's the unfortunate truth about nightmares—the ability to end said nightmare doesn't exist."

"Consider my feelings hurt," I joked. "Let's go."

"I'll consider moving if you tell me what we're doing," she demanded.

I walked away without a single backward glance or an ounce of hesitation. "You'll follow, Vivian, because I know in my heart that you won't be able to escape the curiosity that is me."

For a moment I thought my bluff was called, but then I heard footsteps trailing behind me—well, she stomped through the grass and huffed until she walked by my side, and even then, she kicked rocks. It was the most adorable tantrum.

Now that the contents of the basket were devoured, it was much lighter. I swung it back and forth like it weighed nothing. I tilted my head back and through the gaps of the leaves the clouds were fluffy and white in the sky. The leaves rustled under the strain of the breeze, but when it came to making contact with my skin, it seemed averse, circulating around my body like it was afraid that I might reach out and strangle it. Vivian's hair mimicked the leaves; the breeze loved to run through her strands and against her skin. She was perfect, and then there was me—hot cheeked and dying, yet she was the one to complain about the exertion. It literally made no sense.

"I've never been this side of the lake before," I said and trotted up to a bridge, jumping onto the first step before pivoting and facing Vivian.

"You might not live to see anything else if you don't watch where you're going," Vivian warned and grabbed me by the arm as I was about to topple back onto my ass.

I waved a hand and hopped backward up a step without somehow falling and breaking my leg. "Death is scared of me, don't worry. The number of times I should have tripped and fallen to my death is so high that I've lost count."

"That is slightly worrisome," Vivian muttered as she trailed a hand over the edge of the bridge and a huge chunk came off and landed in front of her foot. "Correction. This bridge is worrisome. Hurry up."

I purposely stopped walking backward and picked up the chunk of wood and tossed it into the basket. "No wonder Gwen calls you grumpy all the time."

"Is there a reason why you stashed away the rotten piece of wood?"

"A memento for your bitchiness today."

"Maybe a reminder that we made it across the bridge alive," she muttered in response as she turned me around using one hand and shoved slightly.

"Never change, Grumpy." When she flicked my ear I gasped dramatically. "I mean, a reformed Vivian Black, no longer Grumpy, but what other dwarfs are there? Happy?"

"That must make you Sleepy."

"I can accept that."

"Or Dopey."

"No way."

"Look at you, strolling in front of me, hands in pockets, you're even whistling." She hopped off the final step of the bridge and hooked her arm in mine before she said, "You're annoying me today. It's your sunny disposition. You remind me of Gwen."

Instead of thinking about the way she compared me to the literal boundless energy that was Gwen, I reached into her back pocket and took out her phone. "Smile, Viv."

"One of these days your heart will combust."

"Just because you know the effect you have on me doesn't mean you have to point it out."

"That's the very reason why I have to." Vivian took my hand, spun me around, and leaned me up against a tree trunk. Her face grew closer and closer to mine until her lips grazed mine. "I love it."

"Yeah?" I said before swinging under her arm and out of her personal space.

"Running, Emma?"

"Would you chase me?" I stretched my arms above my head and twirled my ankle as she took in my every movement, calculating what I was up to. When she didn't respond, I casually pointed in a direction and said, "We're going that way."

"Into more trees," she said glumly.

"What's beyond the trees, Vivian? Think on that."

She didn't have time to figure out what I was about to do because I took off running. I knew Vivian couldn't resist the temptation to put me in my place and lord herself as the winner of whatever sort of competition this was—because in no way did I mention rules or regulations. I ran, plain and simple.

"Emma!?"

Fallen leaves swirled in the wind in my wake. It had sounded like a fun idea in my head, getting Vivian to chase me. It seemed romantic even. But the reality was, I wasn't used to running or even moving quickly in general. I wasn't coordinated enough to turn my neck and see where Vivian was, but I thought running backward was a brilliant idea. I shifted and turned, spinning around in a circle, and a growl emerged from Vivian's chest, making me laugh. The tree seemed to doubt my commitment and refused to move out the way, so I skidded to the side of it to avoid crashing into the trunk and knocking myself out. Kicking up a cloud of dirt with a mumbled "Excuse me" and continuing on around the bend.

A sharp pain entered my gut, and it had me hopping up and down as I ran to slow my movement until I leaned over and gasped and flung my hand over the spot, as if my guts were going to emerge from my stomach if I didn't hold them in. The lake and the rowing boats didn't even register. I heaved in the air—and suddenly the air that I had been sucking so desperately was knocked out of me in a grunt.

I was tackled to the ground. I put my hand on Vivian's shoulder to push myself up. Whipping her hair back out of her face, I gave a loud cough.

"Are you all right?" she asked quickly and scanned my entire body as if she couldn't believe what she'd done. "I tackled you."

"I'm glad I'm not the only one having a what-the-hell moment," I said with a laugh. "But as usual, you took my breath away, so instead of going on the canoe, like I had planned"—I heaved out a huge breath and lay flat on my back beside her and left my head in her lap—"we can chill here."

"You have a stitch, don't you?" Vivian ran her fingers through my hair, and the smugness she gave off didn't even bother me. It faded slowly until she wore a serious expression. "You were right. That owl is a symbol of our commitment, but it extends *further* than today. Wherever and whatever you decide to do, if you're in Boston, if you're in York, if you're ten minutes away from me at college, it doesn't matter. I'm in this for the long haul, Emma. That's my promise to you."

"First date and we're practically U-Hauling it."

"Stop," she said, tugging on my hair. "Be serious."

"I'm in, Vivian. I'm *so* in. You *tackling* me to the ground answered quite literally that you'd chase me no matter what."

TWENTY-ONE

A day later, I woke up to agitated whispers buzzing right next to my ears, whizzing around in an unstoppable storm. The harshness of the voices forced me to pull the covers up and over my head to avoid direct sunlight, making the orange-tinted shade across my closed eyelids disappear. It wasn't long until there were footsteps on either side of my bed in the form of both stomps and featherlight contact with the floor of the cabin. My body prepared for disaster by gripping the covers, clinging to them like they could save me from danger.

As I was about to fall back asleep, three small knocks rapped the side of my head. My hand swung around and managed to slap away the annoyance. I knew at that point there'd be no return to my rather beautiful dream, so I violently flung the covers off my body and sat up.

I rubbed my eyes as the voices continued. The sound of the people only registered once I glanced up.

"Happy birthday, dear Emma, happy birthday to you!"

"No," I said.

"You can't reject birthday wishes," Vivian said, with an eyebrow cocked.

"Hate to tell you guys, but my birthday isn't until tomorrow."

"We know," Gwen chirped, sounding overly pleased with me pointing out the obvious.

"We're not that terrible of friends," Walter said, pouting.

Gwen laughed at him mockingly and said, "Well, I'm not."

Vivian rolled her eyes. "If you're implying I'm a terrible friend, that's possibly true. We blind the friendship barrier every time our lips meet."

The impish expression fell away from Gwen's face. "Ew. No. I'm not implying anything. I'm stating a fact that you're a terrible girl-friend. I secured the information regarding Emma's birthday. Not you."

"True," I agreed, then receiving a scathing glare in response.

"Gwen, go away." Walter put his hand on her face and pushed her away. He turned back to me. "Today is unofficially your birthday because tomorrow we'll be too sad to celebrate anything." He placed a single cupcake with a candle on my lap. He lit it with a lighter. "Selfishly, we brought it forward a day."

"I told them letting you sleep in would be a fabulous birthday present, but alas, I was outvoted," Vivian grumbled.

I reached up blindly and grabbed Vivian's hand, heart swelling a little at the sound of her voice. "That would've been the best birthday ever."

"Alas, I can't give you too much special treatment. Blow out the candle."

I blew it out without hesitation.

"Emma," Gwen whined, awkwardly handling my phone. "We need to do that again. I didn't catch it on video."

"She's not reenacting anything." Vivian moved toward the cabin door and essentially kicked a camper out of her own cabin, silently motioning for her brother to follow. She ignored the pouting and protests and slammed the door shut behind them. "Now, get up, get dressed, and let's get out of here."

After doing what I was told, we left the confines of the cabin during breakfast and joined the land of the living. The onslaught of birthday wishes once we traveled across camp was a foreign feeling, to say the least. I had a group of people in my life who cared enough to celebrate a day people deemed essential to remember. Each time someone said it, I'd take in an extra-deep breath, unable to respond because of the surprise.

Throughout my life, my birthdays became less and less important to my mom, especially after she and my dad officially split up. The day went by without a thought from her, only to be recalled a week after the monumental day with a phone call and the promise that a birthday card was in the mail. Living with my dad? He was different. He remembered every single year—even when I lived in York with my mom when I was fifteen. Even though I didn't want to leave camp, it was a big deal that she was turning up on my birthday. At least this time she remembered. She was making some sort of effort, even if it was an effort that didn't coincide with my wants.

My emotions were scattered and uncontrollable. Seeing a picnic set up on the camp grounds during lunch, with sandwiches and people wearing near-identical dimpled smiles, well, let's say if it wasn't for the hand pulling me along toward them, I would've run away from the overly positive, emotional response taking over my body.

"Emma," Gwen sang, pulling me down onto the blanket, "because it's your birthday, and you're legally an adult, we have supplied some presents! Wrapped and cute and with bows on top!"

"I'm surrounded by a bunch of nerds," I muttered, secretly amazed.

"Nerds who have brought you presents," Walter said, tossing a wrapped parcel onto my lap. A second went by before Gwen tossed a somewhat similar-looking package onto my lap. They both turned to Vivian with expectant expressions on their faces, only for them to be tarnished when she threw them a huffy glare.

Everything was a competition to them.

Without prompting, my fingers untangled the ribbons from the top of a package, tantalizingly slowly only because Walter and Gwen vibrating in their positions on the blanket was amusing. It didn't come as a surprise to see them both lean forward as I took out the first present. I pointedly looked at the name tag, *Walter*, before turning my gaze to the gift itself. It was something that I had forgotten entirely about in my haste to not disturb Vivian after she kissed me for the first time, then I got caught up in the whole courting thing. I brought the stuffed bunny up to the side of my face.

"Mine's the best," Walter boasted smugly.

"She hasn't seen mine yet," Gwen retorted, impatiently bobbing up and down.

"It's not a competition." I rolled my eyes when they both shared a hum of disagreement. "I'll like them equally."

Walter proudly smacked a fist against his chest. "If she'll like them both equally when she sees yours, that means she'll have liked mine best for a time. And because she saw yours second, she can't favor that one because she'll like them both equally."

I blinked slowly in an attempt to follow his logic. "That sounds—"

Gwen huffed. "Barbaric."

My eyebrows rose. "Actually, it makes sense. Kind of?"

Vivian patted Gwen's gift in my lap. "Open it before she has an aneurysm."

Hesitation only had power over me for a moment. It seemed like the edges of Gwen's lips were about to cut into her cheeks with how much strain she was forcing them upward. Boy, was she impatient. This time I ripped the wrapping off, not being careful in the least because their impatience had settled into my system. They were quiet as the object slid from one of my hands to the other in my contemplation. Delicately, it was placed right next to Walter's bunny, so they sat on the blanket together.

We all admired the two presents, leaning back so our hands were on the ground behind our backs, legs stretched outward, mine and Vivian's interlocked. Admittedly, drowsiness still consumed my thoughts and bodily function. A certain warmth came from sleepiness and being surrounded by those who wouldn't judge you for the black shadow beneath your eyes or the mess that was bed head.

My fingers reached out to play with Gwen's present. "Best friends forever, huh?"

Gwen jabbed her finger in the present's direction. "Now that's what a capybara actually looks like. You've upgraded from the second-best rodent to the best!"

Walter huffed. "The story behind my bunny is all we need to bind our friendship, Emma."

"What? Me asking you to get it during that scavenger hunt?"

"Yes and no."

"This will be interesting," Vivian commented, tone dry.

"After I left you two to sort your awkwardness out," he began, bringing the bunny into his lap, "I went on to search for this bunny for my best friend. I fended off countless campers. They surrounded me, nails sharp, muscles bulging—nothing compared to mine—but they bulged, dude. I fought my way through the masses, bunny safe in my hand, and . . ."

" . . . lost a camper," Gwen muttered.

"That has nothing to do with my heroics."

"Yeah, your lack of heroics," she mumbled.

Vivian gathered a bunch of sandwiches and the presents in her arms and stood up. "Want to leave these two to squabble?"

I stood up, taking the capybara from her hands. "Want to go make out?"

"And scare the masses with our affection?" she teased.

"Yes?"

"It's your last day tomorrow." Vivian offered a wonderful smile. "Inflicting our happiness on everyone? Sounds delightful."

"If only we could actually do that . . ."

"After summer," she promised. "No more secrets."

"After summer," I agreed.

We walked away from the two on the blanket, leaving them with nothing. They didn't even notice. They were too busy taking jabs at each other to realize we had stolen the food too.

TWENTY-TWO

It was a strange feeling, feeling connected to the walls of a cabin that hosted one of the most complex people that I'd ever met. It was the same cabin Vivian had destroyed, creating the iconic hole beneath the floorboard. It was the same hole that Gwen used to sneak in during the night to pester me to make sandwiches. In the beginning, I was forced to attend Camp Mapplewood by my mother. Now, on my last day, I couldn't find it within myself to find the things that I may have left behind in my haste to move to a new cabin.

I allowed myself to bask a little as I scanned the single bare bed. It was a small comfort that Lauren left the camp before I did. After all the schemes—me trying to get kicked out and Lauren trying to stay in for another year as a counselor—it was funny how, in the end, we both got the opposite of what we wanted.

My throat hurt, and not because I bawled my eyes out or anything. It hurt because I forced myself to remain without tears. Seeing my mother properly for the first time in a month and a bit and before that a full year, well, I didn't want the destruction of my life to be bared in front of her or her new husband. I didn't want to let her know how much influence she had on me because that was power I didn't wish for her to wield, and yet she did. She was my mom and she was here for my birthday. She actually remembered. That had to count for something.

Someone knocked on the door, snapping me out of my thoughts. Vivian stood there, leaning against the wall. She avoided eye contact, and I couldn't blame her. What was there to say but goodbye? That wasn't something we wanted.

"Vivian," I said, standing up. "This is about to get mushy, isn't it? Go on, I'm ready, hit me with it."

"You asked for it. Whatever you do, wherever you go," she whispered, moving toward me until she could place her hands on my hips. She breathed out slowly and closed her eyes. "Please, Emma, don't let me become a memory that is waiting to be forgotten. Because I won't forget you." She hooked her hands behind my neck and nuzzled her face into my throat, breathing and holding me like a physical manifestation of love. "Never in my wildest imagination did I ever predict that I would have to force a smile while having to say such a cruel word: goodbye. I'll miss you."

"This goodbye means nothing. Dork." I felt her freeze in my arms, making me sigh. "It's a prelude to the awesome hello I'll say to you soon."

"When is this soon you speak of?"

"Hopefully tomorrow morning." I breathed out shakily. "On the phone."

"Happy birthday, Emma," she said, moving back enough to see my face.

"I do not cry on my birthday. That's why we rocked yesterday."

"Close your eyes," she said.

I let her slip out of my arms. It felt wrong. My breathing felt more sharp and painful now that she wasn't pressed up against me. The smell of roses invaded my space, making me tilt my head to the side. Hands slowly slid up my arms, making me shiver, and a cool breath brushed against my lips. There was a chuckle before fingers slipped into the front pocket of my T-shirt, pushing aside the jacket, her own jacket.

Before I opened my eyes, she grazed a finger across my upper cheek. I couldn't believe it. I felt the sting, the happiness as it over-took my system.

"This isn't fair. I gave you a deformed ostrich."

"A misunderstood owl, Emma." Vivian rattled the keys in her pocket, smiling.

"Yet here you are, trusting me with your beaver."

"He'll guide you along your way."

"He'll stalk me? You totally hid a camera in here, didn't you?" I joked, bringing the little beaver puppet up to my face and flicking my stare between the little thing and her. "I'm afraid the only thing this little guy will see is the fabric above my—"

"Heart," she cut me off.

"I thought I was the one obsessed with your heart? Not you with mine?"

"I may have picked up certain habits from you," she admitted.

"The ugliness of Mike will keep creeps away."

"A hero," she deadpanned, lips quirked up.

"I'm not saying you took away my phobia," I told her, placing the beaver back into my pocket and kicking my heels back and forth. "But you did help me manage it. I don't do this, I don't connect well with people, but we did it. Don't you know how exciting that is? Do you feel it too?"

Vivian sucked in a sharp breath. "I do, I love you."

Ignoring the stupid tear going down my cheek, I said, "Let Gwen steal your phone once in a while."

She scoffed. "Walter's already tried to get your phone number."

"You haven't given it to him?"

"Don't look at me like that," she said. "This isn't jealousy or some warped way of disliking your odd friendship. He wants to ask you to send care packages—more specifically, sandwiches. He'll only grow more obsessed with you."

"I'm kind of obsessed with the lot of you. Congenial way for him. Best-friendie way for Gwen."

"And my heart."

"You and your heart."

We made it out of my old cabin only to have to walk over to hers. Over the past couple of weeks, the stuff I left there grew and grew until it looked like it was *our* room. I had to swallow back hard-core tears once everything was in my bags. The only thing that could settle me was holding her hand, and that's precisely what we did.

It was an achievement, walking across the camp without a bruised face or injured body. The day I arrived, I thought my only escape route would be in a hearse. I didn't even notice that campers stared at our joined hands until I made eye contact with Jessie, who wore a half-sad, half-happy expression. In the end, I offered her a wavy thumbs-up. Sometimes friendships weren't supposed to be rekindled, and that was okay.

We dropped my bags by the exit and leaned against the barrier separating us from camp and the real world. A car drove up and everything in my system, my every instinct, was to cling harder to Vivian's hand. She had too much of a similar reaction.

The gates opened, and a couple of seconds later, in came my mom and my stepfather.

"Emma," Mom said warmly, bringing me into a hug.

"Mom." I did smile, a little.

"It's nice to see you again," Ethan said, offering a hand.

I looked at it, at his face, at Mom's face, and finally settled on looking at the spectacular face of my girlfriend and holding on to her hand, because that could never go wrong. Apparently, it was the wrong choice, but that wasn't my perspective.

"Emma," Mom hissed and wrapped an arm around Ethan's waist. "I know you're still surprised and confused about Ethan, but you'll understand once you get yourself a boyfriend that sometimes relationships are placing that trust in a person . . ."

"You never listen to a word I say," I mumbled.

"What was that?"

"Emma!" a deep, childlike voice screamed. "You're going to go without saying goodbye?"

"We already said goodbye, Walter. We ate all those sandwiches?"

"Your birthday sandwiches don't count." He brought me in for a hug anyway, forcing me to release Vivian's hand.

Mom gasped. "Oh, sweetie, you're eighteen! My baby girl, an adult. I see you've finally got yourself a boyfriend. Look at him and those dimples. You chose well. You're all grown up."

Walter adopted a confused expression. "Emma's . . ." Clearly thinking he was about to out me, he continued, "I mean, she's not my girlfriend. We're friends, and she's a girl. There are no bumping uglies, I promise you, Mrs. Lane."

"Mrs. Hank," she corrected.

I facepalmed as he repeated the exact sentence he used in explanation to his dad, then said, "You know, I was kind of stupid for believing I'd only have to come out once. You've got to do it with different people all the time. But what I didn't anticipate was doing it repeatedly with the same person and having the same reaction each and every single time. For the final and last time, Mom, I'm *gay*."

"Emma, please, I gave you all summer to think about what we talked about."

"This hand I'm holding?" I grabbed and held up Vivian's hand. "It belongs to my girlfriend."

"I would say it's a pleasure to meet you, Mrs. Lane, but it's quite the opposite," Vivian insisted.

"How dare you?" My mom gaped.

"Mom, come on, let's not make a scene," I said.

She breathed out through her nose. "I'm not the one making a scene, Emma. Look around you, it's not me they're staring at. Your rubbing this . . . this nonsense in their faces. You don't need to rebel any more honey, I'm here now."

"I believe the one garnering the attention is the one spewing hatred, Mrs. Lane," Vivian said.

"For the last time, it's Mrs. Hank. How do you even like this girl, Emma? She can't respect my wishes to be called by my name."

"I wonder where we see a parallel?" Vivian released a scoff and stepped closer to me, as I frowned at my boots, not knowing what to say. Throughout the years, I'd said all I could. "Like you won't respect your daughter for who she is?"

"I don't need to explain myself to you."

I took a step away from everyone, avoiding their eyes, and plopped myself on the ground beside the suitcases. Vivian handled herself fine. If I couldn't get my own mother to listen and accept what I told her, how could I get her to respect my girlfriend?

Everyone started bickering. Gwen and her parents turned up at a certain point, but my zoning out had gotten the better of me for roughly five minutes.

I looked at the cases and at my mom and Ethan, and felt the little beaver within my front pocket and came to a realization. Something that both scared the hell out of me and offered a solution at the same time.

"I'm eighteen."

"Emma, come on, we've got to catch our flight. We'll get your dad to send your stuff over if we need it."

"I'm eighteen, Mom," I repeated, grinning like a fool from the ground.

"Yes, sorry, I forgot about your birthday. We can do something like shopping over the weekend?"

Julie unhooked herself from her husband. "I believe what your daughter is trying to say is, she's an adult and doesn't need to go anywhere with you," Julie told her, as she placed her hand on my shoulder. "Emma, I'm afraid I'd be at a loss without you in my kitchen."

"Emma can't cook," Mom scoffed, releasing a little chuckle afterward.

"Emma is, in fact, a popular cook here at Camp Mapplewood, so much so that we'd like to offer employment, effective immediately," Julie said.

Mom turned red in the face. "This is ridiculous. Come on, Emma, we have to go."

"I can't do that. What happened to us, Mom? Is it silly to hope that you'll wake up one day and miss me and how we used to be?" I asked. "Because I miss you. I've missed you since I was twelve and I came out to you, when you disappeared completely, even when we lived in the same house. When Dad told me I was going to York this summer do you know what I thought? This summer would change everything between us, but you ditched me! Now you want me to shift my life around again at your whim? I don't understand, Mom. Help me understand."

"Emma . . ."

"You need to make up your mind. Make the commitment. Or don't."

"I'm here to get you. You'll have me for a month. We can . . . I miss you too. I do. I really do. Your dad called me. He made me realize that I've wasted the years. You're my daughter, Emma. Rome could be good for us. All of us."

"I can't go while you still don't accept me for who I am. I can't do that to myself."

"I'm trying here, Emma. I am."

"You know what? Reach out to me when you're ready to accept me fully. When you're ready to be a *mom* to me. But for now, I think it's best that you figure that out by yourself. Alone."

I grabbed the suitcases despite the many protests and hauled a bag onto my back. I began whistling as I turned my back on my mom and made my way back to the camping grounds. There was a moment of silence behind me before various footsteps against gravel followed me.

A rather large hand belonging to Walter took a suitcase from me and carried it. With my newly free arm, Gwen offered a scrapbook containing all the photos everyone had taken on my phone. And Vivian's arm looped itself around my waist.

Our journey at Camp Mapplewood continued.

EPILOGUE

The *Beaver* title hadn't applied to me for almost two weeks now. What I didn't know about the counselors before now was the fact that they sometimes snuck out and wandered the grounds at night, ensuring that no one was out of bed after hours. After all my nighttime activities and not coming across any counselors other than Vivian, when she attempted to herd a spider out of her cabin, I found the idea not all that plausible.

Despite my camper title being stripped away from me and replaced with a work placement as a cook, I found myself hauled out of my snug cabin in the early hours before we were to go back to Boston with my dad, and joined Vivian as she patrolled the camping grounds at five o'clock in the morning. All she'd had to do was linger by the door of my cabin and tell me about her plans for the night and she had me hooked.

There was a notable lack of patrolling, and more of having my back pressed up against a tree and being kissed, like if we didn't forge this connection, the sun wouldn't continue to rise. I clung to her, hands mindlessly roaming her back, having slipped them under her jacket. It was as if she replicated my movements, hands gripped at the back of my neck, trailing her fingers beneath my hairline and tugging my lips with her teeth, creating a vortex of pleasure.

Before Vivian, my experience in, well, anything physical, was nonexistent. My worries over not knowing what to do were thrown out of the window because when it came to Vivian, when it came to the way she made me feel, it was natural; the way we moved, the way we communicated with and without words was a bond that couldn't be destroyed.

When we stopped, breathing hard and pressing our foreheads together, small kisses were planted on my chin, my cheeks, and the tip of my nose before she pulled back and admired her work. "There's lipstick all over my face, isn't there?" I asked, already knowing the answer, wrinkling my nose because, of course, there was.

"Did you expect anything else?" she returned.

"To be patrolling the campground, but look, we're in the woods, macking the life out of each other."

"If you're complaining . . ." she said slowly, backing up a little.

"No, put your hands back around me."

"We're patrolling this portion of the woods, Emma. Have you noticed anything about your thoughts?" Vivian slid her hands from my neck and all the way down my back. "Or something lacking from them, perhaps? Look around you, Emma. Look where you are. You've associated the woods . . . with?"

I opened my mouth to answer, but then realized what she was getting at. Vivian had somehow manipulated it. When it came to my fear of the woods, she managed to make it so that when I thought about entering them, it correlated to kissing or spending time with her, and anything connected to Vivian couldn't be bad.

The way she just knew made me want to kiss her and hug her, to have her as close to me as possible. I ended up kissing her cheek in my haste to bring her into a hug, clasping my hands behind her back and sinking into her embrace. It was a small detail to rectify, but in the long run, it would make my life easier.

"You know what?" I mumbled, snuggling into her.

"What?" she asked quietly.

"My dad is just going to love you. Are you nervous about meeting him?"

"No," she lied.

"Only a few more hours until we see him," I sang.

"Excited?"

"Hell yes!"

This time I was prepared to leave camp, especially with Vivian spending a couple of days in Boston with us.

✦

At seven o'clock Dad texted saying he was outside the camp and ready to get us. We stumbled in our journey through the woods back to the main campground. It wasn't all down to me. Vines and rocks didn't need to be sticking up in a way that wrapped around my ankles or stubbed my toes. Eventually, we were only connected through our hands, clasped together tight enough to prevent the other from falling, but also loose enough not to drag each other down. Who was I kidding? Me, I'd be the one dragging, she'd be the one pulling me up.

We swung our hands back and forth and Vivian was quiet. She was nervous, and it was *adorable*. It reminded me of the first time we held hands.

Seeing Dad's van again after six weeks was quite a sight to behold. Tears sprang to my eyes as it pulled up to the wall outside of the camping grounds, leaving one side of the van parked on the footpath and the other on the narrow road. It was tilted ever so slightly, as was my luggage, the same baggage that was meant to be onboard a cruise ship all summer long.

One hand was occupied by Vivian's, loosely laced in a warm embrace. It was one of those times when being around the girl wasn't making my heartbeat go crazy but beat evenly, almost calmly. The comfort her presence offered was something that I'd always imagined impossible. Yet there she stayed, by my side, eyes all knowing.

Dad got out of the van and ran a hand through his spiky and untamed hair, standing there, shuffling his feet. One squeeze of my hand reminded me to greet my father, but my feet actually had to move in order to make that possible. When he caught my eye, there was that awkward smile that burst through my memories. It was probably the only time when I didn't mind getting all warm and fuzzy from being submerged in a great, big hug.

"Emma," he sighed. "I had no idea about your mother's plans. If I had, you would've come up to Uncle Pat's house with me. But you had fun, and that's all that counts in the end. Look at your face. It's glowing! No more dark circles, hey?" He thumbed back outside and wrinkled his nose at the pile of luggage beside our feet. "Girls, huh? Always packing heaps of stuff. Never experienced that with you, Em, mind—"

"Yeah, so, the owner of these bags is Vivian. This is Vivian."

"Vivian Black," he finished, offering his hand. "Great to put a face to the name. Although, Emma's rather adept at describing said face—"

"Dad," I hissed, breaking their handshaking forcibly.

"What? You even mentioned the exact length of her hair."

Vivian personified smugness. "Suddenly a wordsmith, are we?"

Dad nodded. "Oh yeah."

My girlfriend's body inched closer. "Do tell."

My eyes rolled heavily. "Dad, here's your chance to interrogate her while I get the bags into the van."

"Nice try, kiddo." He grunted, clearly displeased about the size of the bags and pulled the largest one onto his back. "Well, maybe the summer has been good to you. Finally got yourself a girlfriend and all that."

"Yeah," I agreed quietly. "And Mom thought this place would avoid all that."

"Well, that's your brand of normal. Don't hold back. Now, Vivian, has my daughter been treating you well?" he asked.

"Hmm . . ." she hummed.

"Just get in the van, already," I mumbled.

"Did she show you pictures of Tommy?"

"She did." Vivian opened the door for me as Dad rounded the other side of the van, and she confirmed, "They were the only pictures on her phone."

Before we drove off, Dad pulled out his own phone and showed her his own album dedicated to Thomas. A story accompanied each picture, and Vivian sat there, head against my shoulder as I held Dad's phone up so that they could both see. Dad swiped from one picture to the next, captivating Vivian with his simple tales on the daily life of Thomas. Then, for some reason, he had a whole album dedicated to me and all the various places that I had napped in.

Suffice to say, chucking the phone beneath my thighs and hearing a slight crack was hidden behind the laughter of the two other people in the car. Seeing them smiling at each other, sharing jokes at my expense, just talking, I could see why Vivian always commented on my relationship with her family. It left my stomach feeling all warm and fluttery.

It was a couple of hours later that we arrived at our house, and the first thing we saw was Tommy, rubbing himself against the patio door. As soon as the door to the van opened, Vivian made her way toward the cat, who stared up at the divine creature with his back arched.

I waved her off. "It's cool. I'll bring in our bags. Not like they're heavy or anything."

Dad ruffled my hair. "Like you'd offer to bring them in if she wasn't here."

"I'm offended you'd think I'm capable of that rudeness."

"Emma, when I dropped you off at your mother's, you slammed the door in my face."

He got me there and he knew it. He left me and carried some bags to the front door.

There Vivian was, sitting on the steps of the patio at the side of the house, letting Thomas sniff her hand. I wandered over and collapsed onto the ground beside her, gaining the cat's attention, who promptly planted himself in my lap and rubbed his cheeks against any portion of my body.

I wiggled a finger beneath this chin. "He's re-marking me as home territory."

Vivian stared even harder after that explanation. "Cats don't wiggle around like that."

"Do you have a cat?"

"No," she admitted reluctantly.

"I'll even show you something, something also normal for a cat." I bent down so that the cat and I were eye level. I blinked very slowly and he, in turn, did the same. Vivian scoffed at my behavior, making me sit back up. "They blink slowly when they trust you and love you. They're not like dogs. They like their affection in other ways."

"What is another way other than blinking like a fool at them?"

"I'll show you," I said.

I allowed the cat to headbutt my face.

"Of course," she muttered.

"Don't you ever want to rub your cheeks against something?"

She didn't dignify that with a response.

We went inside where Dad sat at the kitchen table, panting a little from bringing in the bags. He read his newspaper, content to ignore us as we shuffled into the room. Vivian was occupied by the creature close at my heels, meowing away, and not for attention, oh no, because he already had that, and not only did he know it but also was about to take advantage of that very fact. We went to his cupboard and I allowed Vivian to fetch a cup of his favorite fish-shaped food and place it in his bowl on top of the counter. Thomas quickly leapt up to his bowl and started nibbling away at his food.

As I took a seat opposite my father, he slung his arm over the chair behind his back and eyed the house phone. We both knew what that meant, and for once in my life, I was wholly against the idea.

"No takeout," I stated firmly.

"No takeout?" he mumbled, turning to face me. "No . . . takeout. Did you mean, yes takeout?"

"Nope."

"Emma turned into quite the cook," Vivian explained, still by the countertop near the feasting cat.

"I thought Em was playing a prank on me? You can cook?" my dad asked incredulously.

"I can cook," I confirmed.

When my face showed how offended I was, he threw his hands up and left the room, shooting Vivian a look that kind of looked like he couldn't believe that he was about to be fed by his daughter. And so the time had come to prove my cooking skills to my father. It hadn't started as well as I'd had hoped.

Since Dad had left the kitchen, I wrapped my hands around the lid of a jar and struggled to pry it off. Vivian placed herself in the best position to watch me struggle, with open amusement. My struggle took my body as I walked around the small space of the kitchen as if pacing would help my predicament.

"Do you miss camp?" she asked.

I huffed, closing the fridge with a little too much force. "You and I both know you're ecstatic to get out of there. I'll miss your mom doing stuff like this." I waved the jar around. "I'll miss your family.

Cooking there. Other than that, nope." With an absolute lack of grace, I crashed into the seat opposite Vivian and propped up my chin with my fists. "I might miss the days kicking it back with my bully."

Vivian's eyes narrowed. "You'll miss Lauren?"

I cleared my throat, holding back a laugh. "I forgot about her existence entirely. I was talking about you."

"Pardon? I am not a bully."

"You've locked me in toolsheds, stolen my phone from me, made me get rid of that spider, made me climb shit so I threw up, made me share a tent with Lauren, woke me up at ungodly hours, stole my pizza—I mean, I could go on."

With a hum, Vivian dipped her fingers into the cup in front of her and flicked water in my face. "I am suing you for slander."

"Face it, you're a meanie."

"Hmm, like that jar?"

"Damn right!" I shot out of the chair and snatched the offending object off the counter. "Why is cooking so hard?"

I flipped off the lid. It smashed against the tiled wall. With inspection, I came to the conclusion that the big crack in the wall was already there. Fumbling around, I started the curry sauce on the stove and idly mixed it with a wooden spoon.

"You can be my personal cook when the semester starts if you like. More practice at the mundane."

"No," I said, staring a little too intently at the sauce.

"You promised my mother," she reminded me.

I threw a casual glance over my shoulder before turning my attention back to the bubbling sauce. "I said I'd keep you alive." I went for another jar, and Vivian came up behind me and opened the jar in less than two seconds. "Personal space," I grumbled, dumping the contents into the pot. My actions contradicted my words, leaning back against the girl.

Vivian wrapped her left arm around my waist with a hum. She

pushed aside some of my hair so she could nuzzle my neck. "I am there."

"The hair. Your hair. Hair is everywhere. If your hair gets curry in it, I don't want to see you cry about it. Don't get your hair in my food," I rambled, using one hand to stir and the other to keep a bunch of her hair from pooling in my damn pot. "Bad hair."

Vivian pressed a soft kiss to my neck and started to purr. "I trust you."

My heart thrummed. "Trust means the job of holding your hair? I'm making food, Viv. Creating a masterpiece."

She straightened and gave me a light squeeze. "So make it."

"Well, I got to gather ingredients. That means moving."

Vivian rested her cheek against my hair. "All these excuses to get rid of me. Quite frankly, my feelings are hurt."

"What I'm trying to do is hurry this up so there will be food when Dad comes back and we're on my bed . . . food already eaten."

Vivian sat back down in the blink of an eye.

After we had eaten, we went up to my bedroom. Have you ever imagined a perfect date? Something imaginary, something you assumed would always be a daydream because it was almost too embarrassing to ever admit out loud? This was that. Something simple. Something perfect. Something that made my eyes sting and got me all tongue-tied so that I was a useless gay, standing there beside my not-so-useless girlfriend.

My hand covered my mouth, shocked. Vivian stood still, almost apprehensive as I wandered around, surveying the area, taking in the smallest of details. Beanbags. Blankets. Cushions. A projector.

Gesturing wildly, I asked, "What the hell!?"

"I gather you . . . approve?" she said pensively.

I flopped back onto one of the beanbags with a big hefty laugh. "Not only do I approve, I love."

At that, she let out a long sigh. "Good."

"*The Incredibles*, Vivian? *The Incredibles?!*"

"No capes?" she said, incredibly unsure.

"No capes. Come here," I murmured, with what I was sure were big heart eyes, and pulled her down so that she sat on the beanbag beside me. "It's kind of like the toolshed. Somewhere . . . compact. I can't believe you've done this. Well, I can, I really can, but I also can't? You got Dad to set this up. Have you been speaking to my dad behind my back?"

"How articulate of you. And maybe."

Half an hour into the movie, we were perched strangely on our respective beanbags. My legs were thrown over the side and Vivian's hands roamed them with no specific intention, not sexual, not to make me giggle from tickling—just the warmth of my skin beneath her hand, a constant reassurance that I was there.

There was no pressure to speak, to fill the silence. We were both enraptured by the movie and each other's presence. If I had to choose a word to describe that moment, it would be familial; the same sort of comfort that came with hanging out with my dad, a silence that wasn't noticed. A silence that didn't matter, that communicated all we needed.

When it came to the montage, when the Edna character showed why capes weren't a feasible costume choice for heroes, Vivian sat forward on her beanbag, elbows placed on her knees. Her chin was propped up on one hand and the other gripped my leg so it didn't hang off the front awkwardly. She stared intently at the screen like it was an important lecture.

When a dude got sucked into an airplane engine, the small widening of eyes and the glance in my direction was so darn cute.

"No capes," she finally said, not questioning, not unsure, but definite.

"No capes," I agreed, holding back from teasing.

"Why did you say your father would love me?"

At the seemingly random but serious question, I sat up, removing my legs from her lap, and tapped my fingers against my thigh. "You're there for me. Even since the beginning of camp you knew how to make me feel safe."

Vivian nodded. "I'm glad."

I said, "Dad is always unsure of how to handle me when I go through those bad months of depression. There's nothing anyone can do. Not really. Isolation . . . it's my go-to response. It's a reaction, not a thought process. I don't really decide, but I do. I have no energy, Vivian. No motivation sometimes. But walking around, it's nice. Having time to myself and sharing a space with you, not needing to entertain or accommodate . . . Dad will love you. Not how I love you, but I guess love in any form, it's just as genuine. And another thing? You'll be the best social worker, I promise."

"You have a beautiful mind, Emma Lane."

She wasn't smiling or forcing some sort of expression on her face. It was natural and content to look me in the eyes, like how I sank back comfortably in the beanbag and threw my legs onto her lap again.

"Are you only going to slowly blink up at me?" she asked.

"Well, I'm telling you that I love you."

"I will smash my head against yours. How is that for showing affection?"

"It'd be nice to know that you're totally in love with me too."

"You're clingy," she complained, touching my cheek.

"And now you want to rub your cheek against mine. Admit it."

"We're not cats, Emma."

I turned my head to the side.

That's when I felt a pair of soft lips press against my cheek.

I could accept that.

"Speaking of not-cat things," I mumbled, reaching for my bag and pulling it on top of the bed. I unzipped it and grabbed the parchment banded together by lousy stapling and tossed it onto her lap.

"The letters."

"Yeah."

"Why would you hand those to me?"

"I want you to know me. All of me."

THE END

ACKNOWLEDGMENTS

I want to thank everyone who originally read *Camp Mapplewood* on Wattpad and supported the book as I updated it daily for an entire month back in 2018! It had been a fun project I wrote for NaNoWriMo, and it was the support for that book and the comments resonating with Emma's journey that made me realize how important it was to write stories that reflect who we are, without our characters being killed off or categorized as secondary and nonimportant. It's an amazing feeling to have characters that represent you. You guys urged me to continue writing and I thank you sincerely.

I'd also like to thank Kortney Morrow, Monica Pacheco, Deanna McFadden, Jenny Bullough, and Rebecca Mills—the people of Wattpad HQ who were there to hear my shock and speechlessness on the phone when they presented the opportunity to help me craft the book into what it is today. It's been an amazing journey and an invaluable learning curve. And of course, a huge thanks to Jenn Kitagawa who created the very cute cover of the book!

And then there are my family and friends, who spoiled me with endless cups of tea and Malteasers. They cheered for me during my journey with this book and helped me juggle college responsibilities at the same time! You kept me on track and were amazing cheerleaders. Thank you so much.

ABOUT THE AUTHOR

Rebecca Sullivan is a twenty-two-year-old student at the National University of Ireland, studying English Literature and Geography. She is obsessed with fluffy socks and anything to do with owls, particularly in the form of candles and other odd trinkets. Even when sleeping there's no escape from writing for Rebecca as she plans story arcs by inducing a lucid dreaming state.

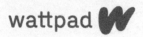

Where stories live.

Discover millions of stories created by diverse writers from around the globe.

Download the app or visit www.wattpad.com today.

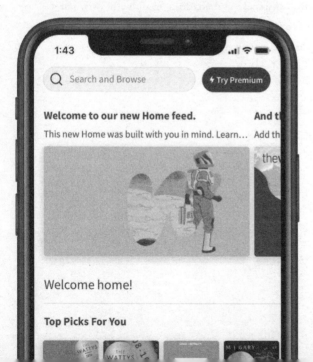

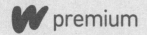

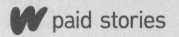